First published in Great Britain in 2020

ISBN 979-8-65882-225-9

Cover design and photography by Cally Higginbottom

FOUL

Arton James

CHAPTER 1

The clip-clop of football boot studs on concrete echoed through the tunnel over the hum of distant crowd noise. A drenched team of players wearing black kits with gold trim plodded towards their dressing room. Not a word was uttered amongst them. All eyes were down except for one pair. Gunnar Magnusson, the number four – a six foot four stubbled Man of Steel lookalike – glared at the back of the number seven, Casemiro 'Cas' Velasquez – five six, tipping nine and a half stone with a solid meal in his stomach. Cas scraped his wet, mousey hair out of his eyes. He kept facing forward but his gaze involuntarily flickered in Gunnar's direction. He felt the glare almost burning through his jersey.

As the team and some of the coaching staff filed into the dressing room, Cas made his way towards his locker area. Even in this gargantuan old stadium, the dressing room was somewhat modernised. 'Lockers' were now more like shallow, doorless wardrobes. As Cas was just about to reach his portion of the bench, a teammate's crumpled shirt zipped past his feet. Its golden Spartan badge faced upwards. He did not look around to see who had hurled it.

Cas sat and slumped his head into his hands. He felt the bench to his right give. A moment later, he was jolted out of his personal darkness as something soft hit his hand, immediately followed by a jingle. A towel rested against his right hand and a set of Range Rover keys had dropped to the floor below. A large pair of feet wearing Copas stood by them. He scooped the keys up and, without looking to his right, set them back on the towel. Then he swivelled to his left and unlaced one of his boots. Beside him, the shirtless Gunnar picked up his towel and started scrubbing his hair dry, disgust etched deep into his face.

A yell came from a player having his knee examined by a physio on a treatment table in the middle of the room. 'How many times have I fucking told you? I'm sick of you fannying around with your daft gadgets and your exercises. You don't look like you've done a rep in your life and you keep telling me it's gonna work. It fucking hasn't. I want the real shit,' said Krugg, loud enough for everyone to hear.

'It is the real shit if you listen and do as I say,' replied the physio, nudging his thick-lensed glasses back up his nose.

'You do realise you work for us, don't you?'

The physio nodded, resigned. 'What, so the customer's always right?'

'There we go. You get it, Goggles,' said Krugg, a smirk spread over his face.

The physio rubbed his smooth scalp for a moment as he thought, then reached into his treatment back and pulled out a vial and a syringe.

Krugg laid back, hands clasped behind his head, victorious. 'There's a good boy.'

Gunnar's booming voice suddenly filled the room. 'You call yourself a man, turning your back on me . . . on us . . . and pretending nothing's happened? Say something, you little prick.' He rose to his feet, towering over Cas, who had now turned away, frantically stuffing his clothes into his holdall. Something jingled as he forced the last items in.

'This is on *you*, you spineless cunt.'

Wascoe, the number three, shouted over from across the room. 'Gunnar! Tonight's been bad enough. Leave it.'

'For when?'

Wascoe clammed up.

Gunnar walked to the centre of the floor and addressed the team. 'We'd be champions right now if he'd done his job . . . fucking *Little Sculptor* . . . he's infected this team. He's turned a pack of winners lame, and *you* stick up for him? Fuck that.'

Cas, still in his full kit, now with trainers on and his boots in one hand, threw his holdall over his shoulder and scuttled towards the door. Gunnar, seeing this escape attempt, lunged towards Cas, grabbing the back of his collar and giving it a vicious yank. The second tug ripped the front open, exposing Cas's skeletal chest. Gunnar spun the startled Cas around, deftly stepped his leg behind one of Cas's and – with another pull of the shirt, which was now twisted around Cas's neck – tossed him to the floor with a thud.

Wincing, and nursing his right rear ribs, Cas squinted. Rattled from the impact and flushed with adrenaline, his ears rang. Everything seemed at half-speed. Gunnar, almost foaming at the mouth, loomed large and was moving in to do some damage. Cas planted his feet and hands against the cold, hard floor and slid himself away. It was like a nightmare he could not wake himself from; as fast as he moved, he could see it was not fast enough as his attacker got closer still. He watched Gunnar shape up, like he had countless times before to smash a crossfield pass. The irony was that all he could do was ball up to protect himself. Yet after what seemed like an eternity, still no boot came. Like a sea turtle checking if a nearby shark was still lurking, Cas poked his head out of his hands. Wascoe and six other teammates were restraining the rabid Gunnar, who was trying to break through them with everything he had.

Glassy-eyed, Cas snapped out of his stupor, scrambled to his feet, clasped his bag and ran for the door.

'You don't deserve that shirt, you cocksucking bottlejob! I'll make sure you never wear it again!' bellowed Gunnar, still tussling with his other teammates.

Cas flung the door open. In front of him stood the team's manager, Cedric Johnstone. Mister Johnstone, as Cas called him, was a portly man, hardened from decades in the game. It was as if his face wore a wrinkle for every dropped point.

'Where d'you think you're going, son?'

Cas sheepishly broke eye contact with him, brushed past him and sped away down the tunnel.

'—Cas?!'

Cas darted along the tunnel, ignoring the shout, and nipped through a side door. His footsteps reverberated down a metal staircase before he navigated his way into a winding dark corridor lit only by red fire alarm LEDs. He fished for something out of the top of his bag. As he reached the stadium's subterranean players' carpark, he pulled out a set of keys.

He hurried towards a white Range Rover, paused, and glanced over each shoulder. Coast clear. He unlocked the car and checked again for good measure. Dropping the keys and boots, he took his holdall from over his shoulder, gripping it by its long strap with both hands.

Like a track-and-field hammer thrower, he swung the bag away and back then arced it up above his head and rotated it over and down – *crruunncchh* – smashing it down onto the bonnet of the car.

He dragged it off, revealing a hefty dent, and swung again. *Crrruunncchhh.* What he lacked in size he made up for with fury. He thrashed his bag down over and over until the bonnet barely hung on. Eventually, he dropped his bag. Exhausted, he bent forward, put his hands on his knees and sucked in some deep breaths. After a guttural sigh, he picked up a boot then stepped around the side of the car. *Chsssshhhhh!* He smacked the studs of the boot against the rear passenger window. It chipped but held. He wanted more. He thwacked his boot against it, harder each time, until at the fourth attempt it shattered, glass spraying all over. Eyes wide with the adrenaline, he dropped the boot and surveyed the damage. After gently pressing his lips closed, he inhaled slowly and deeply, held the breath for a few seconds and exhaled a sigh even louder than before.

Cas gathered up the boots and keys, opened the car and walked around to the driver's door. He climbed in and threw his gear onto the back seat and started the engine. Beyond the battered bonnet, Cas sat expressionless. With his anger beaten out, or at least beaten down, he slowly pulled the car out of its space past a nearby black Range Rover with the license plate 'GUNN4R 1'.

CHAPTER 2

Three and a half years later

His pristine bonnet gleamed in the moonlight as he rolled along the empty country road. He fiddled with the polo neck of his beige jumper – the cashmere made him itch – as he sang along in his thick Spanish accent to Curtis Mayfield's 'Move On Up' on the radio. As he slowed to turn right, he noticed his lights reflect off something metallic amongst the trees ahead. Craning his neck but unable to make it out, he switched his attention to turning in. After pausing for a moment at the gates, they allowed him into the empty car park.

The training ground looked like a small leisure centre but behind it, surrounded by high netting, grass pitches stretched as far as the eye could see. Frosted into the glass of the double doors was a circular badge containing a lattice-like pattern, around the outside of which was the name 'Weavers FC'.

With a jangle of his keys Cas let himself, shutting out the bitter cold behind him. He flicked on the lights and marched along the white and sky blue corridor, waking the building up with more lights before stepping into an office. Here, he turned no lights on – just a projector. As it fired up, he made himself a milky latte then loaded up some game footage on his computer, streaming it to the projector. He grabbed a notepad full of pencil scrawlings from the desk and meandered to the other end of the room. The game transfixed him. All that moved were his eyes across the screen and his pencil across the page.

The sky was cloudless and bright by the time other cars surrounded Cas's. A group of twenty or so fans in white and sky blue stood by the gate as more cars filtered in past them.

A towering, wiry player – Ian Finney – heaved himself up out of his Ferrari with a groan. As he ran a hand through the grey fleck in the front of his hair, he saw one of his teammates hurrying towards the training complex entrance. 'Dimmy!'

The hurrier stopped in his tracks and looked over. Dmitriy Lebedev, age twenty-three, looked like a Hollister model with his casually perfect golden waves and strong, symmetrical bone structure.

'Over here, mate,' said Finney. 'There's a decent few out there waiting.'

Dmitriy looked back to the entrance and then at the backpack in his hand.

'No rush. We're well early,' said Finney.

Dmitriy thought on it for a moment then headed over to Finney, who could sense his reluctance.

'You ever meet any of your heroes when you were a lad?'

Dmitriy searched his mind, nodded, and smiled fondly.

'Who'd you meet?'

'Well, I meet the captain of my local club the day they sign me but you know who else I meet?' His smile widened. 'Drago.'

'Like from *Rocky*?'

'Yes. *Rocky* number four. Dolph Lundgren. I grow up watching his films.'

'So did I but I'm nearly old enough to be your dad. You boys are a bit behind the times over there, aren't you?'

Dmitriy shrugged.

'You know he's not Russian?'

Dmitriy nodded.

'And he didn't portray you guys in the best light?'

'So?'

'Ha. Anyway, you get my point. Let's do our bit and enjoy it. They won't be asking forever.'

The pair carried on over to the gate, where they exchanged pleasantries with a few of the fans through the railings and posed for some selfies.

A timid blonde boy, no older than eight, in a market-bought replica shirt, waved for Dmitriy's attention and held out an autograph book through the railings. Dmitriy smiled at the boy and took the book and pen. As he signed, the boy jiggled with excitement and his father beside him lit up.

'Thank you so much, Mr Lebedev,' he said in an Eastern European accent, maybe Czech. 'Show him, son.'

The boy turned to show Dmitriy's surname, Lebedev, on the back of his shirt.

'Seeing somebody like us in the league makes him feel like he can fit too: in school, maybe in the football when he's older.'

Dmitriy warmed further as he passed the book and pen back. 'Thank you for supporting us.'

The father embarrassedly whispered, 'I'm sorry it's not the real shirt.'

Dmitriy shook his head, indicating there was nothing to apologise for, then unzipped his backpack and pulled out a sky blue training top with his initials on it. 'Now you have real one too. It's little bit big but only me and you have it,' he said as he passed it to the boy, whose eyes welled up.

'Thank you so much,' said the father, heartily shaking Dmitriy's hand as he cupped his son's head, trying to shield his tears from view. The father and son stepped away to gather themselves.

The rev of a sports car whipped the heads of the other fans around. A metallic gold-wrapped Lamborghini sped towards the gate before slamming on its brakes, stopping a foot shy of the railings. Its plate read V01 EZY. The fans buzzed, all of them momentarily forgetting about Dmitriy and Finney except for another boy, a few years older than the first, who turned back towards them and offered Finney a foiled cardboard cutout of a trophy and a marker pen.

'Bit early for that, little man. How about I sign your shirt instead?'

'Yes please, Mr Machine,' said the boy as he turned to present his back for the autograph. The golden car pulled up and rolled its driver's window down next to the boy.

'Yo. Pass it here, little man,' whispered the driver, Victor – a twenty-one-year-old British Nigerian with a fresh fade – as he gestured at the cardboard trophy. 'Just don't tell Birdseye.'

The boy confusedly looked back at Finney, moving away just enough for Finney's marker not to reach his shirt. He then looked back to Victor, trying to gauge what was meant as he hadn't said a word and Finney had clearly heard Victor.

'Cataracts, youngblood.'

With even less of a clue than before, the boy stepped forward and gave Victor the trophy to sign. Dmitriy chuckled under his breath seeing Finney try to hide his irritation as the rest of the fans swarmed to Victor. Two other cars were pulling up behind the golden Lambo.

'This is why we drive in *then* come back to sign, Easy,' said Finney as he tried to direct Victor's attention to the queue building behind him.

His fingers shaped like a V and an E as a fan snapped a selfie with him, Victor was oblivious to the complaint and the cars.

The passenger-side door of the second car behind Victor's opened. Out climbed Bryan Lawler – twenty-two, pit bull-esque, skinheaded. Having started towards the gate, the car gave him a little toot. The female driver tapped on the inside of the tinted windscreen and beckoned him. He walked around to the driver's side and the window rolled down. He and the driver leaned towards each other, swapped a flirtatious exchange of words then kissed lustily, tongues splaying out and around for a short eternity.

Finney noticed Dmitriy watching on with mild disgust.

'Not your style, a sloppy P.D.A.?' said Finney.

'P.D.A.?' asked Dmitriy in his coarse Russian accent.

'Public display of affection. Some people reckon you should keep it behind closed doors, get a room, you know?'

'Yes, probably. Maybe a kiss of the cheek, holding the hands but this is too much. For sure when is not your wife.'

Finney strained his eyes to look through the windshield. 'For fuck sake,' he muttered. After a quick mental calculation, he shouted over to the crowd gathered at Victor's window, 'Any last pics before we go get changed, gang?'

The crowd turned towards them. Judging by their lack of reactions, Finney did not think anybody had seen the tonsil hockey. The boy came back to him.

'You sure I'm cool enough to sign now?' said Finney, feigning offence. 'You ran off pretty quickly there and I don't have a shiny car or those gang sign thingies.'

The boy laughed. 'Yes please, Mr Birdseye.'

Fluorescent yellow flashed around the sky blue and white circle. Lawler and Victor, yellow bibs in hand, dashed about inside the ring of seven players, trying to win possession of the ball. It bounced between teammates with all the speed of a pinball but none of the randomness.

The piggies in the middle moved as fast as they could to get a touch on the ball, but as the pass count grew Lawler was becoming more reckless in his efforts. As the ball zipped towards Dmitriy, Lawler launched himself into a meaty slide tackle. Dmitriy beat him to the ball, dinked a pass over him and hurdled his challenge, avoiding contact. A couple of players jeered Lawler as the ball circulated between a few more. As he regained his feet, the ball came back towards Dmitriy. Scowling, Lawler charged in for another bite at the cherry. Aware of the incomer, Dmitriy took the ball out of his feet and away from Lawler, almost turning his back on him. Determined not to let him get away, Lawler lunged forward to reach a leg around Dmitriy. The next thing he knew, Dmitriy and the ball were gone and the group let out a collective howl.

Dmitriy had rolled the ball back through Lawler's legs and spun away to the other side, ghosting what had looked like a certain clattering. The circle had disintegrated, a few players falling about laughing.

Lawler was jolted out of his rising humiliation by a whopping slap across his arse.

'Wooooooo! I'll give Dimmy some KY next time you spread 'em like dat!' taunted Victor before he peeled away to give Dmitriy a celebratory backslap.

Lawler pushed a smile out through his clenched jaw. Everyone else was having too much fun to notice.

The odd one out in front of the cluster of uniformed coaches, Cas was still in his casual tan winter jacket and polo neck jumper, with his club-badged hat, gloves and training bottoms. He walked out to a space thirty-five yards from goal. The players were stood in their positions in one half of the pitch, their eyes and ears on him.

'To play fast, we must play with the harmony; and for that, we must trust.' He darted a few metres into a new space. 'I trust in my mate to make a quality pass when he sees me in the space. I must trust in my touch however the ball comes.' He gestured to a nearby player with a ball to fizz it in hard to him. He took the sting out of the sharp pass instantly with one of his sleek, blacked-out boots, perfectly set it out of his feet, and passed it back.

'If teammates trust in my touch and my awareness, they start to move for me before I even received the ball. They know I'll control it and find them. Their running will be rewarded.'

Cas waved to a player on the wide left. 'Get to the byline fast,' he ordered him. The player started sprinting. Cas gestured for the ball back from the player he had just exchanged passes with. With his receiving touch, he flicked the ball up, pivoted and skimmed a volley with the outside of his foot over to the sprinting player, who received it without breaking stride. The players nodded and looked at one another, impressed.

Victor nudged Dmitriy and Finney either side of him and whispered, 'Stone cold baller. Best hope boss man doesn't lace back up or one of you fools is a bench bitch.'

Lawler, in front of them, looked over his shoulder, fired Victor a piercing glance and looked back at Cas. Victor furrowed his brow and shot Dmitriy and Finney some satirical scowls of his own. 'Bench bitch,' he silently mouthed at the back of Lawler's head as Cas continued.

'A moment too long, a bad touch, a bad pass, if he slows or stops, nothing works. Nothing. You hesitate, you doubt in yourself or your team, it kills us all.'

Cas scanned around the group, trying to look as many of them in the eyes as possible. 'Be honest about what you must improve; work with it and you will trust in yourself more. That trust, it will spread. It raises us all higher.' He paused for a few moments as he processed a new thought. 'Guys . . . anybody can win. Teams cheat and win. Teams play ugly and win. Nobody remembers them. I want more. I want us to give the fans the football they'll remember forever. I want that we play so well that they are going to make their grandchildren bored talking about us one day.'

The players chuckled.

'Good. Now, let's restart at Dmitriy.'

After the session, as a few players stretched off and most of the others strolled towards the training complex, Dmitriy was the sole man on the pitch. He stood twenty yards from a goal that had a target-training net stretched over it, which left only the top and bottom corners of the goalmouth penetrable. He rolled one of the cluster of balls by his feet a few yards away from him and slammed it into the top right corner. He returned to the cluster, rolled another ball out of it, and bent it for the other top corner. It pinged off the post and in.

As he carried on, Cas and his assistant Steve Frank – a six foot three, still-athletic fifty-year-old; his nose broken from countless heading duels – stood off to the side with Finney and Lawler.

'I want you in position, ready to pass to that half-space. They don't cover it fast enough when their attacks break down,' explained Cas. The two players nodded.

'OK chief, but where do I need to be before that to break their attacks down in the first place?' asked Lawler in his strong Scouse accent.

'You'll know, Bryan. Trust in your instincts.'

'Ta but you know better than me. Where do they go through most?'

'Watch. You will learn for yourself where to break their passes. Just be patient and trust in your qualities.'

Lawler looked short-changed by Cas's answer. Noticing this, Finney wrapped a long arm around Lawler's neck and playfully grated his knuckles against his understudy's scalp.

'The only patients he knows are the ones he puts in hospital, aren't they kid?'

Lawler violently shook Finney off. Short-changed was now fucked off.

Recognising the sudden animosity in the air, Cas grinned, awkwardly angled himself away and let the moment go by. 'Come on. Let's go in,' he eventually said.

Steve hung back as Cas and the players set off. 'Bry. Come here a minute,' he called after them. Lawler wandered back. Steve waited for the others to get out of earshot. 'You've gotta be patient, Bry. I know you want solid answers but trust his methods. Do you know how good you'll be if you learn to think for yourself instead of relying on us barking orders at you?'

Lawler stood there like a child being told off, averting his eyes from Steve.

'The squad's settled till summer. Ian's a nose ahead of you. A nose. Keep grafting, making it a harder choice for the guv and your time'll come.'

Lawler received the message with a tiny, reluctant nod. Steve patted him on the shoulder and the pair began towards the training ground complex.

Ping-pong, nine-ball, darts. The common room was a hive of gaming and shit-talking. One player slapped a fifty-pound note onto Victor's palm. Victor smirked at him and swaggered over to the area behind the games, full of players lounging around watching sports news on the TV. He sat with Dmitriy; Charlie Allen, the team's right back; and Finney.

The OmniSports news anchor talked away, '. . . as we head into the penultimate day of the transfer window, let's see what's going on across the Alpha League.'

'What you reckon, lads?' said Finney, raising an eyebrow. 'Anyone gonna try to mix it with the big boys?'

'Warriors been spending a bit. New owner looks like he means business,' said Charlie.

'If business means fighting for a Mickey Mouse Euro spot.'

Victor chimed in. 'Nah man. They splashed, you know. Brought in some ballers. They're sniffin' around some African don in France. Man's no Easy but who is?'

'The world can't handle another shit-talker of your proportions,' said Finney.

'If you don't wanna hear the truth, just turn your hearing aid down, Birdseye. All I'm sayin' is another one or two and they'll be a force fo' real.'

'If we're lucky, they'll come buy you. Do us all a favour, *innit?*' said Finney with a side of imitation. The wider group around them chuckled.

Charlie closed his eyes and raised his hands in joke prayer. 'Maybe Chuka can put a word in.'

Victor rolled his eyes. 'Why you praying to fresh air when you've got a real live king right in front of you, fam?'

'Don't listen to him, Charlie,' said Finney. 'He's just trying to get you to kneel and kiss the ring.'

Victor sucked his teeth in disgust as the others snickered. Eventually, their attention returned to the news anchor on TV.

' . . . So what do you make of the Weavers' window so far?'

Pete Gossamere, OmniSports' main pundit, answered. 'It's sensible. They're flying – seven points clear, undefeated and Victor Ezemonye's on fire – so why rock the boat just before the deadline?'

'BOOM! That's what I'm sayin'!' yelled Victor at the screen, raising a few smiles from his teammates.

'And what are your thoughts on those demanding defensive reinforcements, Pete?'

'Well, nobody's really able to get at them given how well they keep the ball; but for me, when teams do, they're still suspect. The quality of their midfielders just about makes up for their overly open style of play. They need to pray they stay fit. Also, they're profiting from the weakest league in years. Town are the walking wounded, the Surgeons haven't recovered from their slow start and the Warriors are still rebuilding. Defensively weak as they are –'

Victor pointed mockingly at Charlie and a few of the others around the games tables.

'– that still gives them the clearest run at the league they'll ever have. My money's on them to do it. It'll be a remarkable achievement for them and Velasquez. They weren't even in this league eighteen months ago. But next season, when the big boys are back at it, they'll have to shore up if they want to stay competitive.'

'And is that down to the players or the manager?' asked the anchor.

'Well, given that it's a systemic issue, I think Velasquez has got to take respons—'

The TV channel changed to a foreign match. Confused, the players looked amongst themselves before checking behind them to spot the culprit. With a remote from another TV, it had been Cas.

'Did you see this last night, guys? Watch how Sporting overload the left again and again. Beautiful,' said Cas. He admired the game for a few seconds before wandering off with the remote.

As the players shared a moment of collective bemusement, Dmitriy grabbed a bottle of water off the table and stood. 'Time for me too. I see you tomorrow, guys.' Before he had even finished his sentence, he was off.

'Whoa. Where's Clark Kent dashing off to today? Haemorrhoid cream advert?' said Finney.

'Advert, yes. New Russian whiskey called *Khrabryy*,' replied Dmitriy as he slowed.

'Never heard of Ruski whiskey. I thought your boys only drank that potato piss?'

'You never hear because it's real alcohol for real men, not you *suki*,' said Dmitriy as he set off again.

'Bring us back some bottles, Dim,' shouted Finney to no response. He turned to Victor and Charlie. 'Quite interested in a go of that, off-season of course. They make their shit strong for those winters.'

'You'll be waitin' till off-season for him to bring you shit. Man's too busy for us. Fingers in all the pies. What you got, Machine?'

'Got my hands too full babysitting you clowns to be worried about any of that shit. Someone's gotta make sure you're sitting still with your legs crossed and arms folded *actually* listening to some of the gaffer's gems.'

'Nah, man. You got time. Still got bare commercial opportunities in you. I can see 'em now. Just For Men sponsorship. Viagra ads for all the other grandem who're absolutely battin'.'

Finney shot daggers at Victor, who piped down sharpish.

CHAPTER 3

A tiny blonde girl sized up a football a few yards in front of her on the immaculate lawn. Her pink jacket, dress and the layers they covered were caked in mud.

She ran up and pinged the ball, only for it to bounce off Lawler's leg. They both chased the rebound, her squealing as Lawler beat her to it. She launched herself into a slide tackle and Lawler hurdled it, laughing. Before she climbed to her feet, he grabbed her by her ankles and started swinging her around. She let the centripetal force straighten her dangling arms and shrieked, 'FASTER, DADDY! FASSSTEERRR!'

As he spun faster, a Hummer drove onto the mansion's drive, continuing onto the lawn near them before stopping. Lawler slowed the spin, flipped Polly right-side up and eyeballed the car as she steadied herself.

Out of it jumped a diminutive, round man in a suit and mirrored shades. Lawler's agent, Arnold – more like his namesake's brother in *Twins* – tottered over to them, leaving the door open.

'Who are you?' said Polly as she folded her arms.

In a poorly imitated Austrian accent, Arnold answered, 'I'm the party pooper.'

'This silly man is Arnold, darling. How silly does a man have to be to drive onto our garden?' Although light in tone for his daughter, Lawler was clearly irritated.

'Very, very silly! Hi, Silly Arnold.'

'Hello, Silly Polly. Your papa's told me all about you but we don't have time for chit-chat.' He outstretched a hand towards Lawler. Persevering with his painful Austrian accent, he waved Lawler towards him. 'Come with me if you want to live.'

'You what?'

'No respect for the classics,' muttered Arnold to himself, defaulting to his native East London accent. 'Just come on. It's Judgement Day.'

Lawler gawked at Arnold, confused and further irritated.

Arnold lifted his shades. 'Bry – it's *Judgement Day.*'

Realisation washed over Lawler. After a few seconds processing the gravity of the situation, he spoke. 'Now? It doesn't make sense now.'

'Trust me, kid, it makes sense. *Plenty* of sense.'

Lawler cynically looked at his agent.

'C'mon, kid. Give me a little more credit than that. Obviously, yes, it always makes sense for me; but I mean for you. You literally won't believe it. I'll fill you in on the way. We have to go right now.'

Lawler still wasn't sure.

'The future is not set, kid. There's no fate but what we make for ourselves. Right now, you have a chance to get in this car and set a course that'll make Silly Polly proud.'

Lawler looked down at his muddied, smiling daughter.

'Are we going somewhere, Daddy?'

Lawler started to nod and went to speak, only to be cut off by Arnold.

'*We* are,' said Arnold to Polly, pointing to himself and Lawler, 'but you're not. You're staying with Momma Bear. Where's wifey, Bry?'

'Suze is at her ma's for a few days.'

Arnold shook his head, looked Polly up and down and turned his gaze past Lawler across the garden. 'She'll fit in there, won't she?'

Lawler looked over his shoulder to see what Arnold was referring to. It was the dog kennel.

'So would you.' He stared at Arnold.

'Looks like you're rolling with us then, Silly Polly!' chirped Arnold.

Polly tugged her dad's hand. 'Can I sit in the front next to Silly Arnold, daddy?'

'That's a place no girl should ever sit, darling. We'll sit in the back.'

'Ha. Rich from you,' said Arnold as he ushered Lawler and Polly towards the Hummer. Lawler scooped Polly up over his shoulder and playfully jiggled her around as he jogged car-wards. As Arnold scuttled after them, he bellowed out the Terminator theme tune, going heavy on the percussion.

The timber of the cabin glowed golden brown in the unnaturally bright sunshine. Dmitriy, dressed in a checked scarlet flannel shirt with its sleeves rolled up and a pair of threadbare light denim jeans, smashed an axe down through a log on a hefty stump. He took a breather, wiping the shine from his forehead. As he reached for another log, a voluptuous woman in a skimpy polka dot summer dress walked up behind him.

Hearing her approach, he looked over his shoulder and grinned. In her hand was a whiskey on the rocks to reward him for his graft. He laid his axe down. She ran her hand along his shoulder, up his neck and into his hair as she handed him the drink. The light glistened off the tumbler as he raised it to savour a taste. She kissed his neck, looking thirstier for him than the whiskey. Dmitriy locked his eyes dead ahead and in a bassy register said the words, 'Play by your own rules.' He held his gaze . . . and held it . . . and held it.

'CUT! Beautiful, people. That's a wrap.'

Cheers passed around the set at the sound of the director's words as he walked onto the fabricated dirt ground and over to Dmitriy and his co-star.

'My God. You'll have to see how divine that looks in black and white on the monitors before you go. Thank you so much, both of you. We've got exactly what we need and in quicktime. Dmitriy, after football, you have a calling for acting – you're a natural. And Emily, your accent was sublime, wasn't it Dmitriy?'

Dmitriy warmly smiled and flipped into Russian. '*Ideal'no.*' After letting Emily have a moment with the compliment, he continued, 'Thanks for all today, both of you, the crew for making easy for amateur like me. I need to change the clothes and go for next appointment. Sorry I rush but thank you again.'

'My pleasure, Dmitriy.' The director shook his hand and headed off, leaving him with Emily. He turned to her and opened an arm out to invite a goodbye kiss on the cheek.

'Lovely meeting you,' he said.

'You too, babe.'

'Maybe we see each other on another shoot.'

Emily kissed his cheek and stayed close. In a low voice, close enough for him to feel her breath, she purred, 'You don't have to leave me just yet, do you? I can at least help you out of those clo—'

'DMITRIY. We must make a move sharpish.'

Emily looked past Dmitriy to see who had interrupted them in the well-spoken European accent. Andriy – mid-twenties, wearing a fitted black suit, shirt and tie combo, and sporting a tightly shapen chinstrap goatee – marched over, beckoning Dmitriy with his hand.

'Perfect timing like always,' Dmitriy said quietly to Emily as he rolled his eyes. Raising his volume so that Andriy could hear clearly, he continued, 'He never lets me have any fun. Another time, maybe.' He peeled off her and began to turn away.

She gently stopped him with one hand while conjuring a business card from her bosom with the other. 'Another time,' she said with a kittenish smile as she pressed it into his palm.

'Chop chop,' said Andriy.

Dmitriy smiled back at Emily, stashing the card in his pocket as Andriy put a hand on his shoulder and guided him away.

As they got a few yards from earshot, the interrupter grinned. 'She certainly looked . . . affectionate. She'd make a ravishing Barbie to your He-Man.'

Dmitriy smiled wryly. 'Andriy. You'll always be my Skeletor.'

Andriy chuckled as they paced off set.

Cas shut out the nippy afternoon with a sigh. He tossed his jacket for the hook and kicked off his shoes towards the rack before noticing a crooked photo on the wall. In it, with one knee down on dusty yellow earth, he held out a ring to a beautiful copper-haired woman with a glowing smile on her face. It had been taken in that sublime hour before sunset when the light is at its most magical. A mosaiced balcony separated them from the city below, off in the distance. Cas polished the glass using his sleeve, then straightening the frame before walking into the open-plan living area, beginning to hum Lionel Richie's 'Hello'. Flooded with daylight, matt light woods and sprigs of burgundy, the house was classy yet modest for a top-flight manager.

He picked up a couple of remote controls, eased himself into an armchair and began scrolling through recordings on the TV menu. They were almost exclusively football matches. He began to play one and picked up an electronic tablet from against the side of the chair, opening a drawing app on it. A frenzy of concentrated activity followed.

Fast forward. Pause. Make notes. Press play. Slow motion. Pause. Get up and mimic the body position of a player on the screen. Make a few variations of it to feel what is better. Make a note. Slow motion. Pause. Scribble a tactical drawing on his screen.

As Cas deliberated over where to draw a line on his tablet screen, the bang of a closing door took him out of his productive trance. He noticed the daylight was gone. The clock read 8:20. The sound of a bag being set down and shoes being kicked off was followed by that of sprinting footsteps thudding closer until *whhooomp* – the copper-haired woman from the photo landed in Cas's lap, nearly sending his tablet flying. This was Amber, Cas's wife. Bright-eyed and with what looked like a permanent smile on her face, she wore a red team polo shirt. The badge on it featured a snake wrapped around a scalpel.

'Whatcha watching?' she asked, smacking a kiss on his cheek.

'Just a game from the other night. We play them soon.'

She nodded over to the sofa as she got up off him. 'Come sit over there so we can be close?'

Cas thought on it for a moment. 'OK.' He gathered the tablet and remotes and lumbered over after her, sitting at the other end of the sofa from her and placing the remotes beside him. After realising the gap, she scooched over towards him, popped the remotes onto the floor and tried to snuggle into him. After a few seconds of her uncomfortably resting against his unaccommodating frame, he eventually changed his shape so they could meld into each other. As he tried to continue watching, she fidgeted and let out a tiny groan as she repositioned herself. A little irritated that he could not focus on his viewing, he moved them both out of their comfortable positions, reached for the remote from the floor and hit pause.

'*Y al masajista ¿quien le da masaje?* Come on,' he said. She grinned his way. The two shuffled around into bobsled formation: his back against one end of the sofa and her sat between his legs, both of them facing the same way. He began kneading her shoulders. She instantly melted.

'Did you book El Palauet yet?' she asked.

'Not yet.'

'Do you want me to?'

'No, no. I will. Give me a bit longer so I can see more what the summer will be like at the club.'

She nodded, too relaxed to get further into it.

'How are the girls?' he said.

'Coming on, ta. Lizzie's getting stronger. She could be back a week or two early. Ruth's hamstring needs loads of manual. I need thumbs of bloody steel.'

Cas reached for one of her hands and massaged that instead. 'Did you talk to your parents?'

'Yes. He's feeling better than a few days ago but she's still mithering.'

'That's good news. Your mama will never change, bless her.'

'Hard to stop hoping though!'

He nodded.

With her free hand, she caressed his massaging mitts, bringing them to a halt. I need to wash the day off me and unwind. Wanna come help?' She kissed his hand sensually.

'Ummm, maybe soon. I should finish this part. Fifteen minutes maybe.'

'Oh . . . OK. I'll take my time.' She recovered her full smile as she bounced up off the sofa and strolled towards the stairs. 'Don't be too long!'

Cas tiptoed into the dark bedroom, lit only by the flicker of a few ornate candles. Amber was fast asleep on the far side of the bed, her grape purple lingerie poking out from under the sheets. He looked at the candles, decided to leave them to burn, and then peeled off his clothes, trying not to make the faintest sound. Pulling back the minimum amount of duvet necessary to get under, he slid onto the mattress, trying not to disturb her.

The clock on her bedside table only read 22:10. Cas lay as far from her as possible, turned away and closed his eyes. A few moments later, she opened hers. She had felt him climb in. She silently sighed and pressed them back closed.

She climbed her dad like a yoga-pose-shaped tree. Finney tried not to laugh too hard, knowing he needed to keep his tension to stay balanced in his lunge-like stance. Swiftly, he grabbed her and drew his back leg into a regular standing position. Chuckling as he tried to regain his breath, he hugged her.

'I think this stuff's meant to keep Daddy healthy, not break me!' he said as he gingerly walked over a yoga mat next to his, shaking out his groin.

'You need to be strong enough to carry me though,' said Lulu.

Finney laughed out loud. 'This is true,' he said as he carried her across his state-of-the-art home-gym to the only old thing in there – the water cooler. He sat her down on the table next to a line of supplement bottles.

'One of the droitins,' she said, fishing a capsule out of a bottle and placing it on Finney's palm, 'two of the ashwas, and a little fishy,' she said as she plopped a few more into his hand.

'Cheers, Little Princess,' he said, ruffling her hair a little. Next, he reached for a protein shaker that already had a scoop of powder in it and went to fill it with water. The cooler gave him nothing. He cursed under his breath.

'Can't miss the anabolly window, Daddy.'

'I know. We'll phone Mammy then I'll sort it. I don't think a few minutes will do too much harm.'

'You've only got about nineteen.'

He chuckled to himself again. 'But you've only got like two till bed so you'll just have to trust that I get the job done.'

He slipped his T-shirt off, used it to towel his face and sat on the table with his daughter before dialling a video call to Nova. As the line rang for longer, he grew restless and combed his hair with his free hand. The call rang out. 'Maybe tomorrow,' he said as he stroked Lulu's hair.

He put the phone on the cooler and tried in vain for another glass of water. RING-RING. Scrambling to grab the phone, he only accepted the call after sitting back down, puffing his chest out and pulling the skin under his eyes taut.

Nova appeared on his screen in what appeared to be a dressing room. She looked the best part of ten years younger than him and was made up to the nines with facial gems in intricate patterns around her eyes and forehead.

'Princess! Glad I got you. Just finished some Machine maintenance with the help of our Little Princess. How was tonight?' he said in an uncharacteristically sing-song manner.

'Sweet pea! How's my treasure?' she gushed to Lulu.

'Good, Mummy. I helped Daddy with his yoga and pose-workout.'

'Did you now?' she said with a little chuckle. 'Is he as good as your mama?'

'Noooooo. His legs don't go very wide and he's very sweaty.'

'Oy you!' Finney flopped some of her hair over her face. 'You need to get your cheeky bum to bed.'

'Noooooo.'

'Yeeeees,' Nova chimed in. 'I think it's way past your bedtime, sweet pea.'

Finney caressed his daughter's head. 'Blow Mammy a kiss goodnight.'

Lulu pulled the screen towards her and blew a kiss through the screen.

'Sleep well, little love,' said Nova.

Lulu waved, jumped off the table and sprinted for the door.

'I'll be through in a bit. Brush your teeth,' he called after her before returning his attention to the call. 'And here we are. So, how was the show tonight?'

'A-ma-zing. The energy was ridiculous!' she replied.

'Class! Where you at tomorrow?'

'I've lost track.'

From out of frame, a young guy shouted something that Finney couldn't make out. His face screwed up a touch. 'Who's that?' he asked. The video of her stalled and the audio muffled for a few seconds. Finney scraped his hand through his fleck, checking it on the tiny video of himself that still ran in the bottom corner of the screen. The video of Nova clarified.

'How was Lulu's piano tonight?' she asked.

'She's good, she's good. The teacher said she's coming on leaps and bounds. She'll be on the road with you soon. Tell Loridana to watch out.'

'Ha. Lori hasn't been here for months.'

'Yeh? Bloody hell. I lose track. I was thinking maybe next week I can come to see . . .'

'Hey, I've got to go. We're off to some after-party . . . the label are introducing me to someone to chat about a fresh collab. Kiss Lulu goodnight from me.'

'OK, Princess. Have a good one!'

'Cheers, ma—' The call cut off before her word ended.

He tightened his jaw as he stared at his empty screen then laid his phone back on top of the cooler. He tried for water again. Nothing. 'Useless.' His eyes wandered over to the two mats, side by side, empty.

A pair of swans bathed in the light of a full moon, floating on the middle of the lake's vast, glassy surface. Water babbled five metres under the old stone bridge the guys stood on. The night air was bitterly cold, but cosy to them in a way; Dmitriy especially. From the north west of Russia, the winter night air was the closest he ever felt to being back home.

Dmitriy zipped up his black cagoule, rubbed his hands together and clasped them.

He looked over at Andriy, who unwedged his hands from his designer overcoat pockets, pulled his scarf up tight over his face then quickly wedged them back in.

'Next time, how about we foil-wrap you?' said Dmitriy in his mother tongue. Here, he was so much more at ease; like a different person. 'Now you've gone soft, maybe you should buy yourself a jacket that's suited to more than just a catwalk.'

Andriy chuckled sarcastically underneath his scarf then replied in Russian. 'Down jackets. Parkas. They're all so shapeless on me. I'll survive.'

'Suit yourself.'

'You, on the other hand, can't afford to get sick. You need something warmer. Maybe something nice and warm in the same red as that shirt earlier. Seems the ladies like you in that. Play the tough man all you want but you're bloody shivering.'

Dmitriy laughed off his comment. 'I'll survive.'

Andriy wandered over to the bridge's edge and panned around the lake and surrounding woodland. All this was on Dmitriy's doorstep, gated off from the rest of the world. His modern house, much of it floor-to-ceiling with two-way mirrored windows, overlooked the lake and woods from atop a small hill.

Andriy closed his eyes, drew in a deep breath through his scarf and let out a blissful sigh. Tilting his head down, he listened to the current murmur under the bridge. 'That sound is enough to keep me warm.'

Dmitriy took in the whole scene: Andriy tranquil in the foreground, the clear night sky twinkling in the back. As he started over towards him, his phone began buzzing in his pocket. Andriy tried to breathe through his irritation at the interruption as he heard Dmitriy rustle around in his pocket for his phone. As Dmitriy pulled the phone out, the call, which was from an unsaved mobile number, ended before he had chance to pick up. He unlocked his screen, intending to set the phone to silent, but just before he did a Snapchat notification appeared. It was a friend request from Victor. He accepted the request and immediately got a video snap notification.

'You have all this and you're piddling around with your phone?' said Andriy, gesturing to the lake.

'One minute – I think Victor wants to speak.'

Andriy let out a surprised huh, opened his eyes and carried on admiring the scenery. Dmitriy opened the video snap and a selfie video of Victor began.

'Fam . . .' he started. His mouth kept moving but the sound cut out. On the screen appeared the message

Are you watching closely?

Three question marks flashed up on the screen followed by the old multicoloured TV test card accompanied by its high-pitched tone. The screen cut to black. White text messages flashed up in quickfire, a line at a time

I've been watching you
I know what you've done

What you are
Soon the whole world will know too
Unless you do EXACTLY AS I SAY
Go to the police and you're done
AWAIT MY INSTRUCTIONS

The video cut and vanished. Dmitriy's face contorted in concerned confusion as he began walking away from Andriy. He opened the Snapchat contact and dialled. The call would not connect. He searched his phone contacts and dialled.

After rings that seemed to go on forever, 'Yoooooooo! What you saying at this hour, fam?'

'What the fuck was that, Victor?'

Andriy turned immediately.

'Chiiilllll bro. What was what?'

'What you just send me on Snapchat.'

'I ain't sent you nothin' on Snapchat, fam.'

Dmitriy grew angrier. 'Just now. You add me and send me . . . I don't know . . . fucking weird . . .'

'Dimmy, I didn't send you a ting. Swear down. I haven't added you; I already got you, innit?'

A moment passed as Dmitriy ran this through his mind.

'You been catfished or somethin'?'

'Are you telling me truth? You didn't send to me? Like a shitty Victor joke?'

'Not a thing, bruv. On my brother's life. What was it?'

Dmitriy's mind raced. 'Doesn't matter . . . Sorry I call so late.'

'No worries, fam.'

'See you tomorrow, yes?'

'You know it. Peace out, Dimmy.'

Dmitriy hung up and turned to a concerned Andriy.

'What was all that commotion about?'

The phone buzzed again in Dmitriy's hand. His eyes darted to it. A Snapchat video message awaited him. He swiped it open. What he witnessed drained the colour from him more with each passing second. Andriy jogged over to take a look at the video but he was too late; it had vanished into the ether. Dmitriy was aghast.

'What on earth was that?!'

Dmitriy stared blankly ahead, his mind whirling. 'I . . . am fucked.'

CHAPTER 4

The players congregated on the training pitch, chatting and limbering up before the warm-up on what was a bracing, bright morning. Cas stood ahead of them, talking his staff through some ideas, illustrating them with magnetic markers on a clipboard. '. . . the striker comes deep so their centre back follows. The left back is slow to cover and we can make advantage. Dmitriy runs into that gap.'

Steve got Cas's attention. 'So are we emphasising the striker or Dmitriy?'

'We work more with the strikers. They're not used to being *señuelos*. . . how you say? To only distract. We build the expectation to break and make advantage later. The first few times, our strikers drop deep, turn and shoot. The defender follows, more each time.' Cas slid the markers to show them. 'Then, we find Dmitriy or our other midfield runner in the gap.'

One of the other coaches meekly raised a hand. Cas called on him.

'It's a great move but doesn't it rely on a midfielder who'll actually pull the trigger?'

Cas looked at him, expressionless.

'Should we be maybe working with one or two of them on getting them to shoot?'

'Dmitriy is the last one working most of the days. He is shooting very well.'

'Oh, no doubt he can hit it but it's rare he does. More often than not he'll look to give it to someone else. Shouldn't we be looking at that with him? His bottle?'

Cas peered down at his boots, using one to scrape a lump of mud off the other. 'Is an interesting point. Let me think about it.'

After a quick glance at his watch, Steve scanned around the players. 'OK, it's time but we're looking short. Who's missing?'

Cas did his own study of the group. 'No Dmitriy . . . no . . . Bryan. Neil, any sick calls?'

Neil, the team's physio, answered, 'No sickies today, boss.'

Cas processed for a moment. 'OK. Jason, warm them up please. Steve, try their mobiles please.'

Steve walked out of earshot of the training group as Jason went over to greet the players and led them to a cone-marked warm-up area. Cas stayed put and made an effort to watch the players, trying not to pay too much attention to Steve's calls.

'Right, fellas. Two equal lines,' said Jason the fitness coach. As the players sorted themselves into lines, a few looked around the group. Victor gave Finney a nudge.

'Yo, Machine. Where's the foreign contingent at?'

'Ha! That's pretty good for you, Easy . . . if you actually meant it.'

Victor looked at him expectantly.

'It pains me to admit it, but for once I don't know any more than you. I don't keep them on tag. I dread to think where half of you get to.'

'You know what day it is don't you, big man? Cone Master Frank was lookin' spooked, fam.'

'I know fine well what day it is and I know there's nowhere better to be right now so chill. They'll just be sick or'll have been banging all night or something.'

Charlie chipped in. 'He's right, mate. If I looked like Dimmy I'd be late every day!' He paused as a vision came to him. 'I feel bad for whatever Bry's smashed. He's probably drilled a hole through her.'

Finney grimaced at the thought. 'He needs to get a grip, that lad. He's gonna get himself in bother chasing every shiny new bit of skirt.'

Charlie nodded.

'He needs to take a leaf out of Vic's book, Chaz. Bangin' wouldn't even *occur* to him as a cause of lateness. All goals, no holes this one. *V is for virgin, blud. God squad ting*,' he said, imitating Victor.

'Chat all the shit you want, Grey Goose. You know EasyMoney gets that easy honey. But nah, fam. Last night, Dimmy phoned me acting all weird.'

'Dimmy phoned *you?* That is weird.'

Charlie laughed.

'Fo' real though, and he never bells me. Man was vexed, sounded . . .'

'SPEAK OF THE DEVIL!' Finney raised his hands jubilantly. As the players began jogging, Dmitriy, unkempt and red-eyed, laboured over to them. 'What brings our man of mystery in so late? My money's on some actress from that advert?'

Dmitriy kept schtum.

'Dish it then.'

Dmitriy eventually broke his silence. 'A gentleman never tells.'

'Fuck that, Dimmy!' Finney slapped Dmitriy's back. 'Sharing's caring. Some of these poor sods score less than I *actually* score! Educate brother Victor. Battyman's confused, scoring own goals left, right and centre. Enlighten him.'

'Piss off, dickhead,' snapped Victor. 'We don't play like that where I'm from.'

'Alright, darling. Calm down.'

'Has Cas said anything about me yet?' asked Dmitriy.

Charlie nodded over Dmitriy's shoulder. 'It's not him you wanna worry about.'

Steve appeared next to them. 'What fucking time do you call this?'

'Sorry, Steve. It's one time. I promise.' Dmitriy stepped out of the line to talk with Steve.

'Best be. Everything alright? Not ill or anything?'

'No. All good, Steve.'

'Good. Expect the level two fine.'

Dmitriy nodded.

'You'd best play better than you look. Get back to it.'

Dmitriy caught back up with the warm-up pack as Steve walked over to Cas, trying to conceal his urgency.

'No answer from Lawler, guv.'

Cas's stomach dropped. 'Right. Cover the start of the session. I'll try – maybe he answers me.'

'OK. Can I throw in some stuff with the defensive block?'

'Is a great idea but today stick to what we talked about, with the strikers dropping to create the space behind.'

Steve nodded with a tinge of disappointment as Cas sped off, trying to maintain an air of calm. Some of the players noticed their boss's hurry.

Cas stormed through the common room. As he passed one of the TVs, he half-heard something that made him slam on his brakes. He turned to see Lawler on the screen walking towards a huge, futuristic black and gold training complex, its doors branded with golden Spartan helmets.

The OmniSports news anchor carried on, '. . . on his way to undergo a medical at Warriors, who will reportedly pay around twenty-eight million for him. We now go live to The Barracks to find out the latest on this massive move. Jordan, what's the news there?'

Pale-faced, Cas spun away from the TV to dash off, but smashed his shin into a chair leg, nearly sending himself flying. He recovered from his stumble and ran, limping, out of the common room, narrowly dodging a cleaner who had suddenly appeared in the doorway.

He flung open his office door and skidded inside, scrambling around his desk until he found his mobile. It showed three missed calls and a text. He opened the notifications to find they were all from McGlynn. He opened the text.

MCGLYNN

I'm on my way. See you in your office.

His hand went limp, dropping his phone to the table. He stood for a few seconds, restless. Adrenaline bubbled around inside him. He took off out of his office, up the hall then back down it, up and down, up and down, in a world of his own. He had no idea how many lengths he had done. He was not even aware that the cleaner kept seeing him pop through the door to the common room then back into it, like a demented mole waiting to be whacked. As he marched past his office, a shout came.

'I said your office.'

Cas halted, took a deep breath, and walked back to his door.

Andy McGlynn, the club's majority owner, sat behind Cas's desk, reclined in Cas's leather office chair. The position did nothing for McGlynn's paunch and moobs, which were accentuated by his tight sky blue crew-neck sweater. A strand of his heavily greased-back hair flopped down onto his face.

'Did we get you this?!'

'I think so,' said Cas.

'Is it Italian?'

Cas shrugged.

'It's like a bloody throne.' He closed his eyes and sighed orgasmically. 'If Alexander the Great himself lived today, this'd be his office chair. Cosy as a cock in a concubine. I'll have to get myself one.'

'Mr McGlynn . . .'

'Andy, Cas. Please.'

'Andy. What's going on? Bryan's missing. I see on the TV he is to leave and now you're . . .'

McGlynn spoke as if pained to be the messenger. 'I got a call at the crack of dawn. They made a silly offer. The lad wanted to go – he's getting a fat signing fee and they're doubling his wages.' He leaned forward, taking on the demeanour of a used-car salesman. 'You don't want to keep a player who doesn't really want to be here. He'd never be the same if you convinced him to stay; always wondering what might've been. We make a nice profit on a fringe player. This way, everybody wins.'

Cas paused for a moment. 'Convinced him . . .? Didn't they meet his buyout price?'

'Not quite. Two million under, but we'd set it artificially high so . . .'

Cas became uncharacteristically animated. 'So we don't have to sell, sir.'

'Andy.'

'Andy. Bryan is a big player. He's part of the future of the team.'

'Cas, Cas, Cas. Don't make this bigger than it is. It's done. He was a squad player barely getting a sniff with The Machine smashing it like he is. The team's flying! We won't even notice he's gone. If you feel like you need another body in, we'll see if we can get something over the line today. If you wait until summer, with the windfall we can get whoever you want. Within reason.'

'Mr McGlynn, Bryan is crucial. He understands our system and was developing every day. We can't get somebody with his knowledge to slot straight in.'

'Cas – it's done. I didn't need to come here. I didn't need to offer you another body. We've got plenty.'

'But you want the league sir, no? Stability is cruci—'

McGlynn leaned forward, resting his palms on the table. 'Cas, you think I'd weaken *my own* team's chance of winning? Who bought these players? Who appointed you?' Having felt his own anger build, he paused and reconsidered his tack. A large friendly smile emerged on his face. 'Keep doing the excellent job you've been doing, keep the lads at it. We're top of the bloody pile! Let's make history here!' With another flick of an internal switch, he oozed benevolence. 'Have a think on another body. We can get one over the line if we act fast.' He admired the feel of his hands on the arms of the seat as he rose. 'And enjoy this. You never know how long something this good will last.'

McGlynn left. Cas stood rooted to the spot. After a few seconds, when the sound of footsteps walking along the corridor faded out, he walked over to his chair and volleyed it; but instead of it toppling it, it rolled away. Scurrying after it, he purposely hooked his next kick under the seat to tip it over. It rocked, but didn't fall. He grabbed the backrest, heaved it in the air and tossed it to the ground. Three deep breaths. He took his mobile out of his pocket, dialled and waited for a ring.

'You know the fuckin' drill – BEEEEEEP.'

Cas hung up and gazed out of his window at the rest of his squad training.

Back on the training pitch, the team was playing small-sided games, zipping the ball around. Finney slid a pass to Dmitriy, who let the ball run through his legs, taking two opposition midfielders out of the game. Victor made a diagonal burst to get between the two centre backs and waved for a killer-ball from Dmitriy, but instead Dmitriy fed it sideways to the wing.

As the winger ran into a dead-end, Victor shouted, 'Yo Dimmy,' pointing in frustration to the space he thought the ball should have been played into.

'Was too tight,' yelled Dmitriy as he ran over to provide an option to the winger. The ball ran out of play. Finney ran past the back of Dmitriy.

'C'mon. You coulda made that.'

Dmitriy clenched his jaw, shook his head to himself and played on.

Cas arrived at the touchline where he slotted in amongst the coaching staff next to Steve, who was shouting for the team to shuffle across and up to defend the throw-in.

'You reach him?' murmured Steve.

'I just saw McGlynn. Bryan's gone. It's all over the news.'

'You what?!' said Steve, restraining himself halfway through the outburst.

Cas scanned around to see if anybody had noticed. He looked straight ahead and barely moved as he gave a hushed response. 'He's been sold to Warriors. They offered just under his buyout price and that's it.'

Steve struggled to keep a lid on his rage but kept his volume down. 'Fucking lactating twat. It's one thing if they meet it; nothing you can do, but under it . . . greedy bastard! How are we meant to do our job if he sells our fucking players out from underneath us? You work fucking miracles for him and he shafts us.'

'I know.'

'What are we gonna do? We're short in the middle now.'

Cas nodded towards the pitch. 'We still have plenty of quality there. Some good young guys. We'll figure it out.'

Steve dug his top teeth into his bottom lip. 'Yeh but, guv, the quality's all offensive. Some of them can do a job there but they're not specialists.'

'McGlynn said we can buy somebody; but we don't have time, not to bring the right quality player.'

'It's surely worth putting the feelers out? What've we got to lose?'

Cas nodded.

The short pause gave time for Steve's rage to bubble back up. 'Leaving us for fucking mid-table mediocrity. What the fuck's he doing?'

Cas shrugged. 'I'll do some calls but I don't think we can find anyone good enough for a McGlynn price. Let's trust in the players except for if we find someone special, yes?'

Steve's eyes bobbed around as he thought it all through. 'Alright.'

'You finish the session. When you're done, tell the guys so they don't find out from TV or the Twitter or something.'

Steve gave a trustworthy nod. Cas turned and started to head back to the complex.

'Yo boss, where's The Animal?' called Victor.

Cas pretended not to hear him and walked on.

'BOSS! Is Bry alright?'

Cas stopped, took a deep breath and turned to face Victor. 'We'll speak later, Victor. For now, play.'

Victor appeared genuinely concerned. 'Is he alright? It's not like him to miss training. To be honest, it's spooking us you running off before the sesh. Is everything OK?'

Cas's face betrayed him and he realised it. Reluctantly, he spoke. 'One minute.' He shouted towards the pitch. 'GUYS . . . GUYS.' The game stopped and he walked onto the pitch. The players and coaching staff gathered in front of him. He slid his hands deep into his pockets, almost poking his fingers through the bottom of them. Everybody waited.

'There is some news.' He peered down at his boots. 'Steve, can you tell them so I can start, yes?'

'Umm, yeh. No bother, guv.' Steve snapped on his game-face as he walked to the head of the group. Cas set off for the complex.

With only fifty yards left to go, a shout came from behind him.

'Gaffer.'

He turned to find Finney jogging his way.

'Gaffer, I've got this. I'll make sure the lads know nowt changes. If anything, now we graft even harder. That little arsehole doesn't know how good he's had it here. We do.' He noticed a tinge of sadness on his manager's face. 'We'll do you proud. I've waited my entire career for a season like this and I won't let that disloyal twat derail it. Watch me turn it up a notch.'

Cas gratefully patted Finney's arm and the two parted ways.

CHAPTER 5

The common room buzzed. A large group of players gravitated around Victor. He picked up a half-full water bottle from next to a stack of fifty-pound notes in the middle of the table and poised himself. The crowd awaited. Victor took a breath, shook his body loose and shouted across the table to Charlie, 'Bro, can you pass me that?' With his free hand pointed towards the cash, Victor did a no-look flip of the water bottle into the air. It rotated and landed standing perfectly on the table. Victor nonchalantly kept his eyes fixed on Charlie, knowing full well that he had nailed his toss.

Most of the crowd erupted, engulfing Victor in celebration. He managed to keep his hand stuck out towards Charlie through the celebratory swarm. Even Dmitriy cracked a smile. The losers shook their heads in bemusement. As the excitement died down, Victor fanned out the wad of fifties on the table and flapped them around like a peacock's tail. He flipped the water bottle with his free hand and caught it.

'Come on then, clever dick,' said Finney. 'One more, at least as hard. Quadruple or bust.'

'Yo' pension dropped today, big man? What's the shot?'

'The money shot.'

Victor rubbed his hands. 'Your mum's favourite.'

Finney shook his head then pointed to the bottle. 'Fool's choice, as long as it's tougher than the last one.'

Victor pondered for a moment. He sauntered over to a stray football, flicked it into his hands and steadied it by the table's edge. He carefully set the water bottle on top of the ball. 'I volley the ball, the bottle lands standing on the floor.'

The audacity of the claim even pulled Dmitriy in. 'Fuck off. NEVER!'

'Big talk, Dimmy! How's about you put your rubles where your ring-piece is?'

Dmitriy slipped off his Hublot and placed it on the cash pile.

'Wooooo! Now we're talking!'

Some of the other guys broke out their wallets and cash, making the pile larger. One wobbled the table so that the bottle fell off the ball. A delighted jeer sounded around the room.

'You sure you wanna do this? That's a fat stack, junior,' said Finney with some concern.

'EasyMoney lives for this shit, Birdseye!'

Finney shrugged. The players crowded in but Victor signalled them to give him some space. He set the ball and bottle back up then took a couple of practise swings at table height. He paused. Stepped back. The crowd silenced. He skipped up to pull the trigger. As he swung his foot towards the ball, Dmitriy's phone rang, startling him. He fluffed his kick and smashed the bottle instead of the ball, sending it flying across the room. The crowd erupted even more raucously than before, howling at Victor, some falling around on their seats, others reaching in towards the cash pile.

'Nah man, that don't count. Ringin' while I'm swingin's bare sabotage, fam.'

Dmitriy scampered away from the group to find some privacy. He nipped into the kit room and accepted the call quietly. 'Hello.'

The voice that replied was distorted through some sort of electronic filter. 'Hello Dmitriy. How are you today?'

'What do you want from me?' snapped Dmitriy, taking care to stay quiet.

'Woah! So blunt . . . I am your friend, Dmitriy. Somebody else who knew what I know may be more loose-lipped. I'm giving you the opportunity to keep your privacy; your dignity.'

'Friends don't blackmail friends.'

'Hmm. We'll have to agree to disagree a little on that. I think every relationship is transactional. I'm just being honest about the nature of the transaction.'

'What do you want?'

'Not big on the foreplay then? Shame. I'd like one hundred thousand pounds cash delivered to me at a place and time of my choosing. I'll contact you closer to that time with details. You have ten working days to gather the funds. It's unbelievable that banks still haven't adapted to the modern seven-day working week yet. Anyway, go armed with some decent reasons for withdrawal so as not to draw suspicion. A nice second-hand set of wheels. Some of that garish bling all you footballers insist on. And don't give me it all in fifties. They're worse to spend than Scottish notes.'

'One hundred thousand and you will delete what you have?'

'Come now, Dmitriy. Don't try to take advantage of me. We both know that wouldn't be a fair deal. By the same token, I'm not greedy. I'll want a few tokens of our friendship but there's more to life than money. If you give me what I ask of you, you'll see that I'll keep our little secret. When the time is right, I'll delete the video and you'll trust that it's truly gone. Do you understand?'

Dmitriy's mind whirred for a few seconds before his mouth engaged. 'I understand.'

'I sense a little hesitation in you, Dmitriy. It's only natural to consider all of this carefully. Maybe you'll even try to hatch a way out of the situation. But I warn you, that would be extremely unwise. I can make your information public at any time. You know what that would do to your existence.'

Dmitriy peered up as the neon strip light above him flickered.

'You won't hear from this number again. Keep your phone on at all times. Any unknown numbers, email addresses, contact requests, et cetera that you receive over our coming time together may be me, so pay attention to them . . . oh, and don't contact the police or anybody of the sort. I found out about you, and I'd find out about that. Quite frankly, I'd find it an insult to my intelligence. Any questions?'

'No.' He sighed.

'Don't sound so glum. This is a drop in the ocean to keep your life as it is. I'll be in touch. Ta taa.'

The call ended. Dmitriy grabbed at the skin of his neck, clawing it raw pink. Hearing the guys frolicking down the corridor, he made his way back out to the common room, texting as he went.

'Are you sure . . .? OK. Call if anything changes. Adios.' Cas hung up his landline, keeping his hand on the receiver, despondent. Eventually, he let go and reclined in his chair, hands clasped behind his head, staring through the ceiling.

*

A large trophy gleamed. Two men's warped reflections fluttered around on its surface. Many others surrounded it in an impressively-stocked trophy cabinet, backed by photos of teams wearing black and gold.

Cas and Cedric Johnstone admired the silverware.

'What are you? Thirty-one?' asked Johnstone.

'In a few months, yes.'

'The way you play, you can still rack up plenty, son. You'll give us an extra creative dimension. We'll give you the strongest support you've ever had so you can get what your talent deserves. You'll be surrounded by winners,' said Johnstone, gesturing to the photos in and around the cabinet. A few were of Gunnar lifting trophies with Krugg and Wascoe. 'You'll *become* a winner.' He let Cas soak in his words. 'What do you say?'

Cas gazed longingly at the trophies. His reflection glinted back at him.

*

The buzz of his mobile snapped Cas out of his reverie. He scrambled to view the text, hopeful for some good news.

AMBER
Honey, you OK? I just read about Bryan.
It must be manic there? X

A knock at the door distracted him from the message. It slowly opened a crack. Steve poked his head around it and came in.

'Any joy?'

Cas shook his head. 'Nobody good enough. Our guys will call if any options come up.'

Steve nodded in reluctant acceptance.

'Nothing more to do. Let's be around the guys; make things as normal as possible.' As he got up to leave the room with Steve, he suddenly stopped, droopy-eyed. 'I still can't believe it. Why has he gone?'

'Money talks, guv. For him and McGlynn. Simple as that. Nothing we could do.'

Cas shook his head then snapped himself out of his drift into negativity.

'*Vámonos*. Big smiles. We're fine.'

The players were still nestled around the TV. With the gambling done, they chatted and half-watched the sports news as transfer deadline day played out. As Cas and Steve approached the group from behind, they met Andriy on their way.

'Mr Velasquez, Mr Frank. Fantastic to see you both.' Andriy heartily shook hands with Cas and Steve.

'Andriy. Looking sharp like usual,' said Cas.

'Thank you kindly,' said Andriy, grinning as he checked his lapels were straight. 'If I'm looking half as sharp as your football at the moment, I'm a happy man indeed.'

Cas turned to Steve. 'Can we get a few more like him around here?'

'What, instead of the slithering variety?'

Cas chuckled.

Andriy restarted. 'I heard about Bryan . . .'

'Do you know of anyone who might fit that sort of profile?' asked Steve.

'Umm, well not personally. I'm still a one-horse stable. But I can put some calls around a few of my more esteemed colleagues if that would be of help?'

'That'd be great!' replied Steve. Cas noticed a jittery edge to his voice.

'How are preparations for the weekend going otherwise?'

'Very well, thank you,' said Cas with an emphatic nod and a look at Steve. 'The guys, they are looking very bright. We have a lot of quality in the squad to make the middle work so we'll be fine. Have you manage to . . .?'

'Yes, we watched a few of those vids together last week actually. He appreciates you holding him in regard with such great playmakers. I know he's keen to do everything he can to bring you more final product.'

Cas nodded. 'Good. I see him staying back more by himself the last few days. Is easy to give it all when the world watches. Doing it when there's no pressure, that's when you see who somebody really is. Thank you for helping him.'

'Not at all. Thank *you* for believing in him and doing what you can to bring it out of him. Gentlemen, a pleasure as always.' Andriy shook their hands again. 'He has an appointment I must get him to. All the best for Saturday.' He headed towards the bulk of the players. 'DMITRIY . . .'

The group turned to identify the voice. Victor's eyes lit up. 'Oh ho hooo! Wagwan, Benson?!'

'Hello gents . . . Victor. Are you all ready for the weekend?'

'Always ready,' said Charlie, clapping his hands together.

'Nearly there, just need my boots shining so I'm looking SUPER superfly. Can you giz a quick polish?' asked Victor, gesturing a polishing motion in front of his crotch.

'Don't mind him, Andriy,' said Finney. 'The gobshite couldn't get a polish in an alley full of shoeshiners with a handful of fifties.'

'Piss off, Birdseye. No one was aksin' you. I think Benson would gimme a *real good* polish, wouldn't ya?'

Finney shook his head as a few of the other players snickered. Dmitriy looked around them, deadpan.

'Chop chop,' Andriy said to Dmitriy. 'We've got somewhere more stimulating to be.'

Dmitriy stood, nodded to the group and headed out with Andriy.

Victor called after them, keeping his eyes on Andriy. '*Stimulating*, Dimmy. Watch yourself.' He exchanged some knowing looks with a few of the snickerers as the pair left. 'Chop chop,' he muttered, chuckling to himself.

'Here's the little dickhead,' said Finney, pulling the attention of the others back around. On the TV, in crisp enough definition to almost be there with them, was Lawler: holding up a black and gold Warriors shirt, with his name and the number four on the back. As the cameras snapped away, he smiled like a hyena.

The news anchor spoke over the video. 'Lawler has signed a four-year megadeal with Warriors. In what's been a busy day for them, they've also brought in Michel Ayissi off the back of a fantastic eighteen months in Alpha League Français. It's believed the young striker cost twenty-three million on a four-year contract. We'll shortly go live for their first words in the black and gold.'

Behind the group now, Cas gave Steve a nudge and nodded at the remote on the table. Steve moved towards it.

Finney spotted Steve swooping. 'Steve, Boss – can we watch this? I know it's done but I wanna hear what he's got to say for himself. I'm guessing the lads are the same.' He scanned around for approval. Many of his teammates nodded. Steve looked to Cas, who eventually nodded too, triggering Steve to retreat.

Finney looked around the group. 'Has anyone even heard from him?'

Quiet 'no's and shakes of the head rippled around.

Finney shook his head. 'You think someone's your mate and then *pooof* . . . gone.'

The TV cut to Lawler sat ready to talk to the press. The Warriors' press officer pointed to a journalist for the first question. 'Bryan, how does it feel to be a Warrior?'

'It's an honour for me to wear this shirt. I grew up a fan and I've come here to help get the club back where it belongs, winning leagues.'

Victor spluttered at the TV. The rest of the room remained in sombre silence.

The next journalist spoke. 'Bryan, congrats on your move. It seems a sudden one. Has it been in the pipeline long?'

'No, to be honest, it's happened quickly. I only found out about the interest yesterday but they came in big for me, which is a privilege given the club's size. They've invested in some quality players and told me their ambitions. I'm proud to be a part of them.'

'Proud to be part of a fucking past-it team with a caretaker manager,' said Finney as the others watched on, their faces sour.

Another journalist took her turn. 'Bryan, you've left the league leaders for their local rivals who sit in seventh. What do you say to those saying this is a money move?'

An uncomfortable moment passed, Lawler looking less than impressed. 'I say they don't know what they're talking about. I love playing. I want to play week in, week out. What good's a winner's medal you don't feel like you've earned? I was waiting for a dead-man's shoes where I was . . .'

Finney scowled through his sunken face.

'Wouldn't have had to have waited that long,' whispered Victor to Charlie.

'. . . it's hard to displace a captain, however good you are. Plus, I really feel that here, I'll grow into a better player than I could've been there.'

'Better than with the team lauded for their revolutionary style and player development?' asked the journalist.

'Yeh. I had a great time there, but everything was forward focused. For a defensive player, I felt like I was always being asked to get further away from what I really am. It doesn't matter how much you run a Rottweiler, it'll never be a Greyhound. Run a Rottweiler too much, feed it like a hound and it gets tired and weak. There, I learned lots but I never quite got what I asked for; what I needed. Here, the chief plays the way I wanna play. Here, I'll thrive.'

His former teammates watched on open-mouthed. Cas was the picture of heartbroken.

Lawler took another question. 'So the manager and his vision played big parts in you coming here?'

'Yes, he was an absolute lege—'

The press officer stepped forwards, rested his hand on Lawler's shoulder and picked up a microphone off the table. 'Michel will take your questions now.'

CHAPTER 6

The black Mercedes swept along the empty country road under the canopy of darkened, dead trees. Ayissi's portion of the press conference played quietly on the radio. Out of the corner of his eye, Andriy noticed Dmitriy sticking a blob of Blu Tack over his phone's microphone and putting it in the glovebox. 'What're you doing?' he asked, trying to stay focused on the road ahead.

'Pass me yours. We can't be too careful,' replied Dmitriy.

Andriy glanced over to check his seriousness. Stern eyes stared back his way. He took a hand off the wheel to fish his phone out and passed it over. Dmitriy typed in the security code, turned it off and closed it in the glovebox with his. Both of their minds whirred away, Dmitriy continually biting at his lower lip.

'What can I do? He has me by the balls,' said Dmitriy.

'We,' replied Andriy in a slow, soothing tone. 'We have to stay calm. Think clearly.'

'That's easy for you to—'

Andriy fired a look across that stopped Dmitriy dead. 'First things first. We gather the money as instructed. It'll give us time to think of a way out.'

'There's no way out of this.'

'There is almost always a way,' said Andriy, his eyes set ahead.

'What? He has video . . . to deny is impossible. I can't run. What am I meant to do . . . just pay and hope he is man of his word?!'

'It's one option.'

Dmitriy slammed his hand against the glovebox. 'NO! I can't live with this on top of me.'

Andriy considered his next words carefully. 'You've done nothing wrong.'

Dmitriy burst into incredulous laughter. 'Tell them that. You know if people find out, it's game over.'

Andriy paused and braced himself.
'Are you certain? What if you . . .?'

'No! This is NOT possible . . . For both of us.'

'I think it's doable.'

Dmitriy glowered, shaking his head with absolute conviction.

Andriy recalculated his approach. 'Fair enough. My father knows people who can deal with this sort of thing.'

'He said nobody messing around.'

'He would never see these coming. They're professionals; very discreet.'

Dmitriy looked out at the gnarled, dark branches reaching out over the road, almost strangling out the daylight. 'No . . . we can't. People like this running around here only makes bigger trouble.'

'We already have trouble.'

The rest of the Weavers were still watching the new Warriors recruits field questions.

The press officer stepped forward and spoke again. 'Thank you, Michel. I'd like to thank you all for your time today, but don't go anywhere just yet. We've got a little something extra for you. You're a hard bunch to surprise but at great effort I think we've managed. Our dealings today don't stop with Michel.' He beamed with pride. 'It is my great pleasure to introduce the man to lead this club into a new era. Ladies and gentlemen . . .'

Behind the advertising boards backstage, a towering, broad-shouldered man dressed in a dark, fitted suit lurked in the shadows. He ran a hand through his slick black hair then sauntered out to meet the crowd.

Cas looked like he had seen a ghost.

The press officer continued '. . . our new permanent manager, Gunnar Magnusson.'

Camera snaps cascaded around the room like a piranha feeding frenzy. Gunnar, cleanly shaven and looking sharp, sat down next to Lawler, nodding at a few of the press. The room was electric with chatter and the flutter of fingers across keyboards. The commotion eventually died down. Gunnar pointed to a journalist.

'This is quite the surprise, Gunnar! How does it feel to be back?'

'Did you miss me, Tommy? Black and gold courses through my veins and now I'm back in time for my firstborn to be born a Warrior too! I am *so* proud to be home. I had to leave to get experience as a number one. Now I'm back to lead us back to the top for our amazing fans.'

The press officer selected the next journalist.

'Welcome back. How long have you been plotting your return? It's not often we're in the dark about something so big.'

'Great to see you, Darren!' It was only when Gunnar mildly trilled his double 'r's that anybody could really hear the Icelandic in him. 'We've been laying the groundwork for a while. Of course you didn't know. It's the business of a general to be quiet and thus ensure secrecy.'

'I was wondering how long it was going to take you to slip a war quote in,' quipped the journalist.

'I have plenty more where that came from. You know you love it.'

The journalists chuckled.

Finney sneered. 'Smug twat.'

The next question came. 'Gunnar, what did you learn while away that equips you for the role here?'

Gunnar sat tall, his torso supremely still, his hands laid wide open on the table. 'I've shown what I showed as a player – I know how to win. I went to a league where defending and physicality aren't focuses, helped my players master those aspects of the game and we won two leagues. Imagine what I can do with players primed for my style.' He grabbed Lawler's shoulder. 'Bryan's a man you follow into battle. He'll give us everything he has.'

Cas's eyelids lolled into his next blink. Everything lost its power, like a fuse had tripped. As he felt himself beginning to fall, he just as quickly jolted back on and righted himself. Steve, just ahead of him, had not seen. Nobody had.

Gunnar pointed along to Michel. 'Michel here is an assassin in front of goal. We have a troop of Warriors ready to fight tooth and nail for this club.'

The press officer pointed to another journalist with her hand up. 'Gunnar, you're twelve points off the top and the club hasn't won a trophy since your penultimate season. How big is your job to return to the top?'

'Great question, Gina. With the signings we've made and my brand of football, we'll hit the ground running. I know the gap's large but the league is weak. With these men and our intensity, we'll build a dynasty.'

She followed up. 'Over what sort of time frame?'

'I'm here to win; win this weekend, win the game after that, win silverware. I'm here to take it this season.'

The press bustled.

Victor flung his hand in the direction of the TV. 'What's this bumbaclaat been smokin', fam? Man is warped.'

The group nodded along. Nobody could believe Gunnar's brass neck.

The journalist continued. 'Is that not overambitious given that we're already halfway through the season? The Weavers are flying, arguably playing the best football the league's ever seen.'

Gunnar reset his lapels and leaned forward. 'It's trendy or there's romanticism or something attached to the belief that attacking football is somehow special and deserves to win. That it's art. Look around. The streets are lined with failed artists, all with their ideas about how the world *should be.* The world is ruled by pragmatists who act based on how the world *is.* My football isn't about ideas or aesthetics. It's about results. The best football *wins.*' He paused and panned around the room, making eye contact with many in the crowd. 'We have fourteen league games before the season ends. We play *them* twice. Beat them twice and we're breathing down their necks. Then we'll see what sort of match silk is for steel.'

Victor slapped his thigh and bumped shoulders with Charlie next to him. 'Woooo! This bitch *crazy*, blud!'

The press officer stepped forward and addressed the audience. 'This'll be the last one, people.' He picked the last questioner.

'You know the Weavers' manager well from your time here. That's rumoured to have ended with a bust-up. How is your relationship now?'

'Ah, my old mate little Cassie.'

Cas's face dropped.

'I'm not sure what you're referring to but I'm sure if anything happened, it was nothing more than a lovers' tiff.'

Chuckles sounded around. Even Lawler smirked.

'He's so close but he's never quite managed it, not even here, surrounded by purebreds. Him and his fancy football had a clear run at it till now. I bet he's been dreaming of lifting that trophy; vindicating his artistry. Now it's my job to wake him up and bring us back to greatness.' He looked directly down the main camera. 'See you soon, Cassie,' he said, finishing with a wink.

Camera clicks crackled and the din loudened as Gunnar stood and led Lawler and Ayissi out.

Cas's face was bloodless. His eyes had welled up. Quickly remembering where he was, he turned away to hide them. The squad looked dumbfounded.

Finney grabbed a remote and hit mute. 'Who the fuck does this clown think he is?! Who even talks like that?' Along with some of the others, he turned to Cas for a response.

Even as more bodies rustled as they faced towards him and the team's silence grew more deafening, he remained turned away from them. After a few moments of silence, he walked away towards the exit. The players exchanged glances, their brows furrowed.

Finney stood up and went after him. Steve blocked him with an outstretched arm and shook his head. They watched Cas walk out of the common room, down the hall and into his office, closing the door behind him.

As the players gathered their thoughts, Finney sat back down and grabbed a remote.

Sssmmmaaasssbhh. The players' heads whipped around towards Cas's office. Inside, a cacophony of destruction ensued.

CHAPTER 7

*

All he could see above him, framed by the blue sky, was the impassive face of Gunnar. A smile spread across it and Gunnar extended a helping hand down. Cas, grimacing, grabbed it and accepted a helping heave up to his feet. He bent forward for a second, checking his knee was in one piece.

'Give these savages half a chance and they'll destroy you,' said Gunnar, joking and serious in equal measure. Cas forced a smile through his pain and hobbled a few yards across the training pitch to retrieve the ball to take his free kick. He doubled over, positioning the ball with his hand as he still struggled with the pain. With his hand barely off the ball and without looking up, he chipped a thickly-spun pass to a teammate that took half of the opposition out of the equation. The teammate, with space and time galore, stuck the ball past the 'keeper. A few of his new teammates applauded, exchanging impressed looks with one another.

'I can't stop them kicking me but at least I can hurt them like this,' replied Cas as he limped past Gunnar back to his position.

'I guess so,' said Gunnar.

Cas could not tell if his gigantic teammate was impressed or annoyed.

Gunnar tapped his temple with his index finger. 'Still, good to let them know not to fuck with you.' A grin spread across his face as he darted off with intent.

The game had restarted and the ball was at the feet of an opposition player, Krugg – a sinewy, stocky man with shaggy hair who looked like a relic from the Stone Age. Gunnar steamed in and bullied him off the ball, crumpling him to the floor. As he sent the ball to Cas, he nodded at him as if to say 'you're welcome', then glared back at Krugg, who scowled his way but did not rush to get up. Cas grinned as he received the ball, took a well-weighted touch out of his feet and floated forwards with it.

An hour or so later, trap music blared out. A few players danced around as others shot the shit. A cloud of strawberry vapour filled a corner. The dressing room vibe was more like that of a club.

Through the hubbub, Cas emerged from the shower area tightening his towel around him and wedging his feet into his sliders. His frame looked barely adolescent amongst his more muscular teammates, most of whom were five to ten years his junior. He tightened the wrap of his towel again and began across the room. A hurtling ball flew his way. Cat-like, he dodged it, nearly losing his towel in the process. He grabbed and rewrapped it, this time keeping hold.

Reaching his locker area, he kicked off his sliders and grabbed his black briefs, fumbling with them under his towel, trying to stay concealed. As he attempted to get his second leg into his underwear, he struggled to keep his balance.

Gunnar arrived at the locker next to him, naked and joking around with Krugg, who was laid on a nearby physio table. As Gunnar grabbed a towel and started to rub his hair, he knocked a small holdall off his bench, not noticing as the banter continued.

Krugg abruptly stopped, sat up and gestured to the pads stuck to his knee. 'You need to turn these up, clever dick?' he said to the physio, Ted.

'It's not muscle stim. You're not meant to feel anything. The cortisone's being transmitted into the tendon.'

Krugg rolled his eyes. 'How long's this gonna take?'

'Another fifteen or so.'

'Fifteen?! I've got places to be. Can't you just bang it in with an injection?'

'We need to be sparing with those.'

Krugg shook his head and laid back down.

'Trust the man, Kruggo,' said Gunnar. 'He's got more PhDs than you have STDs. He knows what he's doing.'

Ted gratefully nodded at him.

Bored, Krugg rummaged around in the physio bag on the stand beside him.

'What the actual fuck?!' Krugg's hand came out clutching something that looked like a nunchuck handle. It was vibrating. 'How can I trust a man who keeps a fucking vibrator in his bag of tricks?' He threw it to Gunnar, who examined its weight.

'Jesus, Ted – that'd give someone a good rattling. Properly heavy duty!'

Some nearby teammates laughed. One held out his hands, inviting Gunnar to throw it over.

'Pass that back, please,' pleaded Ted, just as Gunnar threw it to his teammate. 'It's a prototype.'

Gunnar glanced at him apologetically.

'I hate to break it to you, mate, but they've been selling this shit in Ann Summers forever,' said the guy in possession as he threw it to another teammate nearby. Half of the room was laughing now.

Ted's face reddened. 'Please.'

The vibrating handle was being tossed around the room like a hot potato.

It came back to Krugg who sniffed it like a cigar. 'Where the fuck have you had this, you filthy twat?'

The laughter loudened.

Suddenly, the handle jolted out of Krugg's hand, whacking him in the mouth before dropping to the floor. The room howled. Ted double-tapped his phone screen, stopping the handle vibrating before he picked it up, stashed it back in his bag and stormed out of the room.

Krugg nursed his mouth. 'Surprised he's so sensitive if he likes it *that* rough,' he said, milking a few more laughs from the dying-down chorus.

Gunnar resumed rubbing his hair, his face covered by his towel. He repositioned himself a half-step, bringing him a little too close for comfort to Cas, who was now sat on the bench. Cas averted his eyes and saw Johnstone was doing the rounds, chatting to his players over the far side of the room. Having just finished with a group, he looked over Cas's way and gave a friendly nod. Gunnar was still scrubbing his hair, oblivious to how close he was, so Cas stood and stepped away. From his new position, he caught a glimpse of something shiny on the floor next to Gunnar's bag. It looked like a black gumshield.

Johnstone was making a beeline for him. Cas realised he may see the gumshield thing. As Johnstone glanced down to a ball rolling past his feet, Cas reached a foot out and dragged the gumshield behind the fallen bag. His foot remained out in a ballet pointe-like position as Johnstone reached him.

'Settling in alright, son?' asked Johnstone with a perplexed look.

Cas retracted his foot and stood normally. 'Perfect, Mr Johnstone . . . just doing some balance exercise the physio show me.'

Johnstone bought it with a small nod. 'Gunnar showing you what's what?'

'Affirmative chief,' said Gunnar, turning to them while towelling his back with gusto.

Johnstone tilted his gaze up to just take in Gunnar's face. 'Howay son. You'll have someone's eye out with that.'

Gunnar smirked, slowed his scrubbing, and began to towel his arms.

Johnstone turned back to Cas. 'You need anything, my door's always open.'

'Thank you, sir,' replied Cas.

As Johnstone walked clear, Cas picked up the gumshield. Gunnar quizzically looked his way as he stood and repositioned himself to block Johnstone's view. After a check over his shoulder, he showed Gunnar what was in his hand.

Gunnar stopped towelling. 'Oh fuck. Was that down there?'

Cas nodded.

'Thanks. If he'd seen that, he'd have ripped my dick off!'

Cas passed it over. 'Why do you have this?'

'I do a bit of MMA,' replied Gunnar, rounding out his consonants as he puffed his chest out a touch.

'You fight?!' whispered Cas.

'Yeh, I'm a fighter. You ever done any?'

Cas spluttered a laugh and looked to see if Gunnar was seriously asking. 'No . . . I'm more a lover.'

Gunnar took a moment to conjure up a response. 'I guess it takes all kinds.' He began drying his thighs. 'He really would've fined the shit out of me if he'd seen that so thanks again. Do you mind if we keep this between us?'

'For sure.'

'Good man. I owe you one.'

Cas still did not know where to look but had a little smile to himself as he pulled on his T-shirt.

*

On his knees, Cas swept broken glass off the carpet into a dustpan. Along with the glass, analysis documents littered half of the office. A tactical board on an easel lay on its side, a couple of its magnetic markers scattered by it. His laptop was face down in the far corner. Somebody knocked at the door gently. Cas paid it no attention. The handle slowly turned and the door edged open. Steve poked his head around the door and crept in, closing it behind him.

'You alright, guv?'

'Fine,' answered Cas, not turning to look at Steve, instead paying meticulous attention to gathering up the glass.

'I know he's a mouthy twat but even for him that was bang out of—'

Cas cut him off. 'Let's just concentrate on us.'

'Yeh . . . of course.' He hesitated for a few seconds. 'The fellas . . . they seem a bit rattled . . . they heard you . . .'

'They'll be fine. We prepare for Saturday. Nothing's changed.'

The smoke-grey dressing room held the permanent smell of heat spray. The Weavers squad sat muted, looking to the coaches, all of whom stood except Cas. He sat behind them, scribbling out sentences in his notepad as quickly as he could jot them, seemingly oblivious to the team.

Steve tapped him on the shoulder, nodding towards the waiting players. Cas rose and walked across to the whiteboard. He picked up a marker, removed its lid, put its tip to the board and paused. It was as if somebody needed to pull a string in his back to set him going again.

Finney scanned the room to check on his teammates. Victor peered at his feet. Dmitriy sat back against the wall, his eyes closed. Knowing that the energy needed lifting, he readied himself to stand; but then it came.

'Guys . . .' said Cas, '. . . remember, *we* are top of the league. We should play with confidence. Trust in what you can do. Play quicker. Lift yourselves.' His flat words stopped. Clicking the lid back on the marker and setting it on its ledge, he neither looked at the board nor the players.

A few silent moments passed before Steve realised that was all they were getting. He started a lukewarm applause.

Finney stood. 'C'mon lads! One goal is nothing. We can't let these bang-average fucks end our run. Who are we?'

'Weavers!' chanted back his teammates.

'Who the fuck are we?'

'Weavers!!'

The applause escalated. The players livened, jumping to their feet, exchanging back-slaps. The staff dispersed to speak with them. As Steve walked towards a cluster of defenders, he looked back to see Cas stood alone, staring at his notepad, only snapping out of it as Charlie asked him a question.

STEEL TOWN 1-1 WEAVERS

FT
(HT 1-0)

Brownrigg (42') Ezemonye (74')

COLIN SAMSON, OMNISPORTS' LEAD COMMENTATOR
That was like a different team wearing white today.

PETE GOSSAMERE
Yes. When Ezemonye got them back in the game, I thought that'd ignite them, but they just fizzled out like a damp squib. It just goes to show that even the best can have an off-day. They still managed something from the game. Velasquez will be glad of that.

COLIN
One man who hasn't had an off-day today recently swapped white for black. Let's go to No Man's Land to see how the new-look Warriors did against the visiting Engineers.

Lawler peeled his sweaty Warriors shirt off his black base layer, balled it up and lobbed it into the laundry bin in the middle of the dressing room. A large pair of hands grasped his shoulders.

'He shoots, he scores,' said Gunnar as he let go and circled Lawler to face him. 'That was brilliant, Bry. You were meant to be a Warrior.'

Lawler grinned bashfully.

'That was game one! Imagine what you'll be like in a few weeks.'

Lawler's grin widened into a fully-fledged smile.

'Settle in, listen to me and we'll destroy this league.'

'Sound, chief. I'm all ears. I wanna soak up everything I can from you,' said Lawler, somewhat starstruck.

'That's what I like to hear. I really appreciate you took that yellow for the team today, taking him down on that breakaway. Don't worry about the yellow.'

'Ta, chief. Owt I can do better?'

'Always; but for now just enjoy the win. There are harder battles ahead that we'll have to reach much deeper for. Those who reach the deepest climb the highest, Bry.' Gunnar patted Lawler's shoulder and made his way towards another of his players.

His eyes wide, Lawler nodded and mumbled to himself, 'Those who reach the deepest climb the highest.'

CHAPTER 8

The blinding winter sun glistened off the wet stone steps of the monolithic building. Andriy trotted out of the oversized doorway and down the steps, a coffee in one hand and a briefcase in the other. As he opened the door of his black Aston Martin and shimmied into the driver's seat, Dmitriy abruptly locked his Blu-Tacked phone and shoved it into his pocket. Andriy passed him the briefcase and the coffee then started the car.

'If anyone asks, today's was for jewellery.'

Dmitriy blankly looked at the items.

'No thank you?' asked Andriy.

Dmitriy kicked into gear and began fumbling with the case and cup. 'Sorry . . . thanks.'

'You weren't looking at the ratings, were you?'

'No . . . no. I don't want to look. I just . . .' The sentence drifted away from him.

Andriy nodded as he drove them down the road. 'I know this is hard. Have you given any more thought to bringing in . . .'

Dmitriy raised his finger to his mouth, imploring Andriy to be quiet, then pulled out his phone, showing it was powered down.

Andriy pulled his phone out, showing it was already off. 'I know. So, thoughts?'

'I don't know. I don't know anything now. I can't sleep, can't play. I'm scared whatever I do. I am mess.'

'Look; I've made enquiries. My father's organisation uses people who deal with sensitive matters from time to time. We could have somebody here within a day or two. They'll find whoever did this and clean it all up. We can get on with our lives as we were.'

Restless, Dmitriy slapped his hands onto the glovebox and shoved himself back against his seat.

Andriy reached over, laid his hand on Dmitriy's arm and encouraged him to lower it and relax. 'I will *not* let this happen. I'm your manager. Let me manage this.'

Dmitriy withdrew from his touch. 'He said he find out if anybody tries to make trouble. I can't make the risk.'

Andriy put his hand back on the wheel, tapping it a few times before letting it settle. Eventually, he nodded.

'Look. He only has one player in the space,' said Cas as he directed his laser pointer at the relevant player on the projector screen. The auditorium was full; its seats occupied by Weavers players and staff watching on intently. 'Making yourself in the space is like a communication. The less we communicate, the less we understand each other. We lose the harmony. We make mistakes. We are less dangerous, they are more. When your mate has the ball, find the space. Communicate.'

Cas turned off the video and brought the lights up, signalling that the players could leave. They started filing past him as he shut his laptop down and unplugged it from the projector. He said his 'goodbyes' and 'see you tomorrows' until everybody had left except Steve, who stopped by him.

'That was shite the other day. I can't remember seeing us so slow in our build-ups then so vulnerable on the counter. We were just . . . flat. Are we going to do anything with them this next few days to shore up the back?'

'We'll make it faster again. They know now.'

'Surely it can't hurt to do a bit with them to make them more solid in case we play like that again?'

'It was one time, Steve,' said Cas. 'We'll be fine. Just maybe some fatigue.'

'OK,' replied Steve with a tiny shrug.

Dmitriy stepped his upper back under the barbell, unracked it and began squatting. Victor and Finney doddled over from the far side of the gym towards him.

'By yourself in here. On the furthest rack away. I can't decide whether to be proud of your dedication or wounded that you don't like us,' said Finney with a grin.

Victor waved off his comment. 'Speak for yourself, Birdseye. Dimmy loves Easy. Slipping me dem balls left n' right, me smashin' in bare goals, making him look like a boss man.'

'He only slips you the balls?'

Victor sucked his teeth in disgust. 'You've got serious problems to be thinkin' o' that shit on the double.'

Mid-squat, Dmitriy chimed in. 'It's not personal, ladies. I just like to get in and get out.'

'Yes, brudda! That's how we roll!'

Dmitriy finished his set and Victor stepped in for his, offering his fist for a bump as the two passed. Dmitriy looked away as he walked past him, leaving him hanging.

'Bro?!'

Dmitriy turned back to Victor, who gave one solid rattle of his fist.

'Tag me in, fam.'

Dmitriy saw Victor wasn't going to shut up until he got one, so he gave him a half-hearted bump to set him on his way.

'Can one of you throw some beats on? Man needs some rhythm up in here.'

As Dmitriy walked to the adjacent rig and grabbed a weighted vest off the floor, Finney fetched the sound-system remote from a nearby plyometric box. He pointed it at the system and pressed the power button. Nothing. He pressed again. Nothing. He pulled the back off the remote, popped one of the batteries out and back in and tried again. Nothing.

Dmitriy, now in his weighted vest, gestured for Finney to toss him the remote.

'Batteries are buggered,' replied Finney.

'C'mon. My mother is from near Ukraine so maybe I give it some Chernobyl power.'

Finney grinned as he tossed it over. One press from Dmitriy and the gym flooded with music. Finney shook his head in disbelief as Dmitriy jumped up, clasped a bar and began a set of chin-ups with a rapid pull.

Without any weight yet, Victor squatted down part way and began winding his hips around to the music. 'Yes, Dimmy! Now man can get loose. The groove might oil them old tinman fingers too, Machine.' As Victor stood up, unracked the barbell and stepped it out to start his set, Finney walked into his line of sight, held his fist up towards him and slowly extended his middle finger.

'Well-oiled enough for you, gobshite?'

As Victor bashed out a few reps, Finney watched Dmitriy as he still cranked out chin-ups. His chest was meeting the bar with the same thrust it had during the first rep.

Even as Victor re-racked the bar, Dmitriy was still going.

'Dimmy,' said Finney, 'I know you gotta keep those guns polished for those Sex Panther ads . . .'

'What the fuck is Sex Panther?' asked Victor.

Finney shook his head in disbelief. 'You're beyond help. Dimmy, just don't go too heavy on them mirror muscles. We need you quick, not thick.' Finney shoved another twenty-kilo plate on one end of the squat bar then turned to Victor. 'Think you can manage putting one of those on for me, buttercup?'

'No probs, Werther's OG.' Victor slid one on. 'You gots to be careful there, Dim.'

Dmitriy finished his final rep and jumped down from the bar, a little puffed out. 'Why?'

'Bi's for the guys, innit? Don't wanna bring yo'self . . . unnecessary attention, you know?'

Dmitriy stared expressionlessly at Victor.

'I don't think anybody knows what the fuck you're on about,' said Finney as he walked the much heavier bar out and squatted it. He dropped into his first rep and exploded up so hard that the plates rattled against the bar. It was nothing that the others had not seen before, but they were still transfixed by how easy Finney made it look. He slammed out another two reps, re-racked the bar and turned to Victor. 'Tin Man's plenty well-oiled, Easy. Eat your kale, say your prayers and *maybe* at my age you'll be half the specimen I am, still running the show.'

'Here's your prayer, big man,' replied Victor whilst making his custom 'sign of the cross' with his right hand, touching his left shoulder, his stomach and then his right shoulder to finish the V-shape before cupping his balls. 'Sign of the boss.'

Finney shook his head, smiling. 'Bet Chuka loves you.'

'Fuck Chuka. Till some big man in the sky starts scoring for us, if you wanna pray to someone, pray to me.'

Finney, pleased that he had gotten a bite out of Victor, smirked at the still-expressionless Dmitriy.

Victor shook his legs off and walked over to some stacked plyometric boxes. 'If you're such a specimen, I'll bet you cash money right now I'll beat you at a box jump. Bet's good for you too, Air Dimmy.'

'One minute you're calling me a fossil, next minute you think I was born yesterday. That's some Wesley Snipes *White Men Can't Jump'* hustle shit.'

Victor laughed. 'My man . . . Woody dunked in the end!'

'Once in the whole film! I know when the house has the game rigged.'

'Spoken like a true pussy'ole. How are we meant to believe you when you won't even back yourself, captain?'

Finney turned to Dmitriy. 'Can you believe this juvenile's attempt at reverse psychologising me?'

Dmitriy remained stony-faced.

'You OK, man?' said Finney. 'You look like you could do with cutting loose. A few of us are off to play this poker thing tonight. Fancy it?'

Dmitriy un-Velcroed his weighted vest and dropped it to the floor. 'Thanks but I don't feel one hundred per cent. I go now, hope I feel OK tomorrow. See you guys.' He took off towards the exit, his teammates watching with raised eyebrows.

'Man was smashin' out those reps before we came, then was giving me the dead-eye. You reckon he cool with us?'

'The guy's not feeling well and it's still all about you. C'mon. Let's strip some of this weight for you, small fry.' As they started to slide a weight plate off each end a thought popped into Finney's mind. 'Air fucking Dimmy,' he said, shaking his head and glaring at Victor.

'What?'

Hacer más espacio was etched on Cas's notepad. His home-office desk was littered with files and stationery, barely any of which was in the terracotta and mosaiced pots and holders. He flipped to a clean page and locked his eyes on half-speed game footage running on a projector screen that filled the wall ahead of him.

Amber poked her head around the office door. 'Darling, haven't you eaten yet?'

After the few seconds it took the words to penetrate the zone he was in, he responded without taking his eyes off the game. 'Not yet.'

'I'll put something on for us now. Set a timer for say . . . quarter past so I don't have to interrupt you?'

'*Sí, sí*,' he said monotonally, entranced.

'Set it!' she said, flashing a big smile. As she disappeared, he reached for his phone, barely glancing away from the screen.

Amber set two pristinely finished bowls of spicy clam and asparagus broth on the candlelit dining table and sat down. She poured herself a small glass of white and tapped her finger against the table, eyeing the empty glass across from her.

Eventually she took a sip. A smile spread across her face and she poured the other glass as Cas wandered into the dining area and over to the table. '*Buen provecho*,' she said, sitting tall as she gestured to their bowls.

'*Muchas gracias, mi amor*. It looks delicious.' He inhaled its flavourful aroma and picked up the bowl.

'Oi! Where are you going?' she said, assuming he was joking.

'I'm sorry. I need to finish the analysis.'

'Can't you at least give me fifteen minutes?'

'I can't. Not tonight, my love. We were so bad the other day. I have to find the reasons. I'll make it up to you soon.'

Amber's face sank for a split second before she pasted a weak smile back on. 'Alright. Can I at least get a kiss?'

Cas nodded, put his plate down, walked around the table until behind Amber's chair and wrapped his arms around her. She squeezed them in for an even tighter embrace. After pressing a few kisses firmly against them, she reluctantly let go. He stepped away to pick up his plate and cutlery.

'Do you want a little glass to go?' she asked.

'No, thank you. Have to be sharp to really see it.' He started out of the kitchen.

Resigned, she called after him, 'Come find me if you get done. I know the transfer window's closed but the little Velasquez one is open.'

Cas look over his shoulder at her, thinly smiling and nodding before leaving.

Amber pulled over the candle and gazed at its flicker. The slender golden teardrop swayed gently in the ambient air currents. Eventually, she slid it back towards the table's centre, then pressed her fingertips down on a nearby placemat and slid it towards her, bringing with it the bottle of wine that sat on top.

Victor shovelled a pile of casino chips towards himself.

'You've gotta be fucking kidding me,' said Finney, as he shook his head.

'Ain't no one kidding, Birdseye. You know Easy don't miss. Scoring's in my DNA. You know what D-N-A stands for?' said Victor, lightly chopping the table with his hand in time with each letter.

Finney and Charlie, sat the other side of Victor, braced themselves for the answer.

'Don Nigerian Ancestry.'

Charlie blurted out a laugh and joined Finney in his head-shaking as Victor picked up a chip and expertly played with it between his fingers. As the cards were passed along, to be shuffled by the next dealer for a new game, Charlie stood up.

'Where's your pasty ass going, Charles?' said Victor.

'I'm out. My money's buying no more Jordans for you, you jammy bastard.'

'Chaz. Fam. Don't hate the player!'

Charlie left the table, walking past the American pool table behind them and over to a snack table. The dingy room, with its red and gold wallpaper and dragon carvings, looked like a repurposed private-dining room of a Chinese restaurant.

Finney and Victor received and examined their new cards. Finney's face did not move a muscle. Victor, on the other hand, eyed the other five at the table as he bobbed his head to the ambient trap music. He gestured for them to show their cards. Winked at them. Blew a kiss the way of a hench, bearded guy dressed head-to-toe like a cowboy – Jack. Even beneath his ten-gallon hat and shades, Victor could tell he had gotten a little bite out of him.

As Charlie arrived back at the table, there were four players left in the final round of betting. Victor pushed a pile of chips in. 'Five, pagans.'

Finney threw his cards in, folding. Victor watched the next player, Jack, as he decided what to do. Eventually, Jack pushed a larger stack of chips forward. 'Ten,' he grunted.

Victor laughed. 'Yes, Woody! Who else wants it?'

The next player mumbled something and threw his cards in. The last player, Erdar, a Kurdish guy in a leather jacket with a medallion on show, pushed an equal-sized stack forward. 'Call.'

All eyes landed back on Victor, grinning from ear to ear. 'Game on!' He went silent, eyeing everyone as he bobbed away to the music. 'I'mma raise . . . let's go twenty Gs.'

Everyone else became still. Victor examined the guys left in the hand, grinning their way. The cowboy checked his cards.

'You hoping they've changed, blud?' said Victor. 'What you sayin'?'

Jack pulled the rim of his hat down a little then pushed forward a fat pile of chips. 'Raise to thirty.'

Victor's head bob evolved into a full-body groove. Erdar threw his cards into the middle of the table, folding.

'It's just us now, Brokeback,' said Victor with a wink as he pushed more chips in. 'Forty Gs, Butch Assidy. Your move.'

The others watched on, dead still. Jack studied his cards. Victor shuffled some of his remaining chip stacks around, like cups he had hidden a ball under. Jack slid another ten thousand in.

'Woooooooo! Big game, man, but the question is . . . are you a big . . . game . . . playa . . . like . . . the King . . . here?' Victor paused. 'Meet my queens,' he said as he flipped over his cards, 'RiRi and Cardi B.' With his black queens, Victor had a full house. Jack flicked his cards into the middle of the table, stood up and stormed off.

Victor leaned as far forward in his seat as he could and scooped the huge haul of chips towards himself. Finney and Charlie looked at one another, shaking their heads.

Victor shouted towards the exit that his opponent had just walked out of – 'So that's what walking like John Wayne means' – then addressed the remaining players. 'Thanks for the royal treatment, fellas.' He bowed before picking up one of his chips and kissing it.

CHAPTER 9

A ball smashed into a cool box at the side of the training pitch with an almighty thud, rattling but not toppling it. Lawler retrieved the ball from nearby, kicking it back into play. As he returned to the pitch, Gunnar waved his way, beckoning him over. Lawler jogged over to him while Gunnar instructed some of the other players. 'Manage the overload, blacks.'

'How's it going, Bry?'

'Proper boss ta, chief.'

'Boss. I like it! Just wanted to congratulate you on a superb start. You've grafted, you've been tidy technically. I knew you'd give us those things when I signed you. But I also know you've got a lot more under the hood. You fancy a development opportunity?'

'Bring it on, chief.'

'That's the sort of enthusiasm I like to hear! And that's part of the reason I see the potential for you to be captain here one day.'

Lawler almost grew an inch as he tried to contain his smile.

'Captains lead by example. They push everyone around them to do better. They even do things for the good of the team that people don't like them for sometimes. Captains sacrifice. Do you follow me?'

Lawler nodded.

'Superb. I need someone to give Michel a hand.'

The pair looked out onto the training pitch where Michel was haring down one of the channels with the ball under close control.

'Look at him; he's a flying machine, but we'll only see the best of him if he toughens up a bit. He's not in France anymore. You know what he'll face in this league, back to goal. If you're up for helping him and the team, I want you to show him how physical it can be. Keep pairing against him and keep giving him a few bumps; nothing too serious. Just to build up his tolerance. You don't have to – I can get somebody else to do it – but you'd be doing us a big favour.'

'Yeh, no bother all at, chief.'

'Excellent. You're a trooper,' Gunnar said, patting his shoulder before nudging him to rejoin the game. As Lawler jogged back on, Gunnar watched intently.

*

The autumn sun was bright, but the day was brisk. Gunnar slid a long-sleeved golden training top over his head but left the zip neck open. He stood on an empty training pitch where the halfway line met the touchline. A few bag-loads of balls were emptied out next to him. He scooped one up into his hands, rolled another a few yards in front of his feet then strongly passed that one along the deck in the direction of the goal. As it rolled, he popped the ball in his hands up in the air and volleyed it. Looping through the air, it eventually bounced around ten yards from the rolling-goalward ball.

'Very nice.'

'I'm not just a hoofer, you know,' said Gunnar as he turned to see Cas walking his way, wrapped up in a training jacket, gloves and a snood. 'No hat too?' he asked sarcastically.

'I couldn't find one,' Cas replied. 'You know where they are in the kit room?'

Gunnar laughed to himself as he shook his head.

'I know you're not a hoofer. I saw you out here yourself a few times.'

'You been spying on me?'

'No, no,' Cas replied, not sensing the playfulness behind Gunnar's stern demeanour. 'I just saw you. You like to practise by yourself?'

Gunnar pulled up his right sleeve to show Cas his tattooed outer forearm. Cas squinted for a closer look. Entwined within a war scene from feudal China were the words '*Can you imagine what I would do if I could do all I can?*'

'By myself; with others: makes no difference to me. The work needs doing and I want to do everything I can while I can, before I close this chapter. Giving it all on matchdays is only the edge of that. It's easy to give it all when the world's watching and the goal is obvious. Giving it all here every day, when there's no pressure to, is the bulk of the work. These extra hours I put in are what separate the men from the boys.'

Cas nodded emphatically. 'You don't have to be alone to do that.' He trotted to a small cluster of balls and drilled one out towards the goal before turning and scooping another up with the outside of his foot in Gunnar's direction. Gunnar smashed a looping volley towards the goal that came a yard closer to hitting the rolling ball than the last time. 'I'm here to win too.'

'Too gifted for extra practise though?'

'No, no. Not too gifted. I like to do some extra trainings but sometimes it's too much.'

'With light stuff like this, there is no too much,' said Gunnar.

'For me, I play the best when I have trained good, all nice and then I am empty.'

'Empty?'

'Yes, like . . . how do I say . . . when my mind is empty, my reactions are the best and my touch is the softest.' He closed his eyes for a moment, breathed in deeply, exhaled forcefully and shook his body. His eyes snapped open and he kicked one of the nearby balls goalbound before waving for one from Gunnar. Gunnar obliged, scooping a ball in the air for him to side-volley with his right foot; arguably his weaker. With heaps of spin and bend, the ball bounced around five yards from the rolling one.

Gunnar nodded, trying to conceal his irritation. 'So go on then, how do you make your mind empty.'

'I like to meditate.'

Gunnar peered at him.

'Have you ever tried?'

'Nah.' Gunnar hesitated. 'To be honest, looks like a whole bunch of sitting round, doing fuck all to me.'

'No, is very active, mentally. The thoughts, they come up, you let them go. If you don't stay active, you fall asleep or the thoughts take over your mind.'

'Nothing taking over my mind, mate. I know what I need to do to lead this team and I do it, simple as. There's no room for anything else. The narrower I live, the sharper I am to protect you all from everyone coming at us, trying to take what's ours.'

Cas, head down, rolled a ball around with his studs. 'I don't need to be looked after.'

Gunnar's eyebrows raised a little before he nodded.

'I don't,' said Cas, lifting his head to look Gunnar in the eyes.

'Mate, you're a talented, talented player but you need players like me to do the shit you can't do. And won't do. I've seen your little grin when I've let people know not to fuck with you. You might look down at us doing the dirty work, but you know it needs doing.'

Cas clenched his jaw, staring off into the distance as he carried on rolling the ball around. He stopped and looked back at Gunnar. 'I don't look down at you.' With his sole, Cas rolled the ball towards Gunnar – who adjusted to receive it – but stopped it before it left his foot in a fake-pass. 'I *wish* I was more like you. Look at me. All my life I got kicked all over but there's nothing I can do about it.'

'Bullshit.'

'Is easy for you to say. You're like two of me,' said Cas.

'You ever heard the phrase about it not being about the size of the dog in the fight but the size of the fight in the dog?'

Cas shook his head.

'It doesn't matter. We can put a little bit of the fighter in you if you're willing to roll your sleeves up and get your hands dirty.'

Cas tried to pull his jacket sleeve up, bringing a huge smile from Gunnar.

'Ha, you can leave that. Come over here.'

Cas backheeled the ball at his feet as he walked over.

'Look, first things first. Are you willing to hurt your opponent?' asked Gunnar.

'Hurt like how?'

'All the way. Are you willing to end a man's career?'

Cas frowned. 'No, of course not.'

'You're lying.'

Cas raised an eyebrow. 'How am I lying?'

'You wouldn't step on the pitch if you weren't willing to deal with the potential consequences of playing. You know as well as I do that it doesn't take much sometimes to really hurt someone. A little bump or a clip, somebody lands funny and it's six-to-twelve months out.'

'Yes but it's different if you mean it.'

'Is it? Out is out. Look – you can hurt somebody without meaning to, with the most innocuous touch, or you can fly in with the intention to break bones and do nothing. These things aren't black and white. You just need to know that whether you want to admit it or not, if you play, you could end a career. It's something worth embracing if you don't wanna keep playing with the handbrake on and being a target.'

Cas eyed him.

'I know you think this is just a game but this is fucking war. Anyway, the philosophy can wait. Let's talk practicalities. You're on the small side so a few things become crucial. One of them is picking your targets. Not all pain points are created equal. Some places don't need much contact at all to let them know not to fuck with you. Less contact equals less chance of refereeing repercussions.'

'You think a lot about these things?' asked Cas, his brow and nose wrinkling into each other.

'Of course. This is *my* art. It can be as simple as this.' Gunnar positioned himself diagonally in front of Cas's left foot, hovered his right studs over his instep for a moment then took them away. 'An accidental step on a foot will let someone know you're there. Doesn't matter how big they are compared to you, feet are fragile. They hurt. You know how long the fuckers take to heal, even if it's just bruising. But here's the thing. You have to be subtle. It definitely can't be a stamp. It's best it's not even really a tackle. You just wanna run across them. Don't reach a foot out. Don't slow down or speed up. Just run across them like you're gonna dribble the ball straight off their foot. Look.'

Gunnar took a backwards step then walked forwards. Without looking down, his right foot stepped against the border of the bigger toes of Cas's left foot. Any closer and he would have trod on them. 'Casually walk over somebody's toes or heels a few times and they're gonna start to get the drift. C'mon, have a go. You don't have to stand on me but just walk past me like I did. No change of pace, no movement of your foot away from yourself towards mine, no looking at me. Use your peripheral vision and just brush past me.'

Cas nodded and positioned himself to start. He strolled past Gunnar, slowing slightly on his way and missing by six inches.

'Closer,' said Gunnar.

Cas turned and walked back past, this time passing by an inch.

'Good. A little quicker now.'

Cas turned and slowly jogged back past him, brushing past Gunnar's front but stepping past his feet. 'You'll get it. It's just practise like anything.'

Cas nodded, surprised at how something so simple had never occurred to him.

'You can take that same target area and really do damage with some leverage. Position your body relative to your opponent's so that they feel it as much as possible with you doing as little as possible. Essentially, it's about setting up a situation where their body does the work. We do it all the time in jiu-jitsu and judo. Last time you walked past me so that your right foot caught my left. Try now to come almost face on to me so that you walk with your left over my left.'

They both took a few steps back and Cas walked obliquely towards Gunnar, narrowly missing his left foot and knee.

'You pin that foot at a bit of an angle and that knee isn't gonna like it. Hinges don't like twisting . . .'

'But if I step on you like that, do we not hit knees?'

Gunnar nodded. 'Maybe. But the likelihood is they're gonna come out of that worse than you. Plus, if you're down nursing your knee, a ref's more likely to see it as a clumsy coming together. Yellow at worst. See if your marker gets as close after that.'

Cas laughed to himself and shook his head. 'Thank God I'm on your team now. I hated playing against you.' He side-footed a ball hard towards the goal and quickly flicked another up towards Gunnar to smash. His volley bounced around twelve yards from the rolling ball. 'It's the adrenaline,' he said, gesturing towards the balls.

'What is?'

'You missed worse. It's because of the adrenaline and the testosterone and the this and that rushing round in the body. The thinking of hurting; it makes you like a storm inside. Close your eyes.'

'Nah, I'm alright cheers,' replied Gunnar with a quiet snicker.

'Trust in me. I show you something now.'

Gunnar gave in and skeptically closed his eyes.

'Notice the cool air against your skin . . . and how your feet feel against the ground.'

Gunnar's eyes flickered under their lids as he followed the instructions.

'Don't close the eyes so tight. Relax them. Relax all of your face. Your mouth.'

His mouth stayed closed but he separated his teeth a few millimetres.

'Can you feel your laces on top of your feet?'

'Course I can.'

'Is OK, you don't need to answer. Just notice those places . . . the lines down your feet to your toes . . . feel them awake . . . and breathe. Breathe.'

Gunnar's shoulders rose and fell a little as he deepened his breath. He felt a pair of hands gently settle on top of them.

Cas's voice grew softer. 'Don't let the breathing move you here. Just your belly.'

Gunnar let his shoulders loosen as he directed his next inhale down.

'Good. Feel your belly grow and empty.'

In and out, in and out, Gunnar's face softened.

Cas softly squeezed his shoulders. 'Slowly let your eyes open.' He let go and wandered towards a cluster of balls as Gunnar peeled his eyes open as if from a restful nap. After watching Gunnar breathe a few cycles, he looked at him for signs of approval or disapproval. A small smile spread on Gunnar's face as he gave his shoulders a tiny shrug. Cas spun and knocked a ball out towards the goal then immediately spun back around and scooped one in the air towards Gunnar. Gunnar flowed forward and smoothly struck it. They both watched as it looped through the air and bounced a yard from the rolling ball. Smiles spread across both their faces.

'Do you have plans tomorrow night?' asked Cas.

'Nah, just resting, staying fresh for the weekend.'

'Come to my house. I cook for you, thank you for welcoming me here, for teaching me.'

'No need to thank me.'

'No need to help me. Plenty didn't but you did.'

Gunnar mulled it over for a few moments as he fetched another ball. 'Well, when you put it like that, it'd be rude not to.'

Cas smiled and nodded before Gunnar closed his eyes for a moment and deeply inhaled.

CHAPTER 10

Dmitriy, head down, slid out of the dressing room without saying a goodbye. The players that were left in the half-empty room were slipping on their jackets and grabbing their bags, ready to leave. The door opened from the outside. In walked McGlynn. If the room's atmosphere was a buoyant balloon, he was a pin prick.

'How are my guys? That was quite the ride you gave me there!'

The players gave an appeasing chuckle. McGlynn zeroed in on Victor, who hugged the match ball under his arm.

'Here he is . . . the golden boy. Brilliant, Victor! Shake my hand.'

Victor swapped the ball to his left hand and reached out his right.

McGlynn almost slapped his hand into it, clenching it hard before dropping his free hand on top of it. He shook it like a magnum of champagne he was desperate to spray. 'It's performances like that that'll bring this home for us. Keep it up, *Easy*!' he said, trying to sound cool.

'I will, Mr McGlynn,' replied Victor in the tone of a pupil trying to get out of the headmaster's office.

'Call me Andy.'

'Alright . . . Andy. Peace out.'

Victor, Charlie and their posse grabbed their gear and headed for the door. On their way out, Charlie, with a smarmy look on his face, mouthed 'Call me Andy' to Victor, who rammed a finger-gun into his mouth.

Only a few remained in the dressing room. McGlynn made a beeline for Cas and Steve.

'Just wanted to show my face after our riveting comeback. A little close for my liking but that's part of the appeal of our beautiful game, I guess.'

'Yes, today was close, Andy, but the guys showed character to come back,' said Cas.

'Let's hope they needn't show it too often! Keep it up, fellas.' McGlynn insistently offered his hand to both of them, and one by one they complied. As he headed out of the room, he held the door open for the last of the leaving players.

Steve invited Cas away from the remaining staff in the room. 'That was bloody close,' he whispered.

'Yes but we got through it. Victor was so strong in the second half.'

'But we were so weak in the first. We gave ourselves a mountain to climb.'

'I know, I know but we climbed it.'

'We can't make a habit of that. Play like that next week and the mountain'll be too steep for us. You've seen them since he took over. It'll be more than steep. They'll be lobbing boulders at our fucking heads.'

'Next week is just another game, same like always.'

Steve folded his arms.

'Let's just enjoy this win for now and begin to prepare after recovery day,' said Cas.

'What about Dimmy? He was an absolute passenger today. Has been for a week or two now.'

Cas unconsciously nodded as he lost himself gazing through the fixture at the bottom of one of the dressing room benches.

Steve jumped back in. 'I mean, he just looks a bit low in confidence. Maybe we just need to give him some sort of lift.'

Cas's gaze shifted towards Steve. An epiphany had landed.

After an active recovery day and a day off, the players had a spring in their step as they walked out to the training pitches. Layered up for the frosty February morning, they stood in the warm-up section, the coaches ahead of them. Cas flanked the group and positioned himself ahead of them; a big, confident smile on his face.

'*Buenos días*, guys. How was everybody's day off?'

'Sensational, boss man,' replied Victor. 'Just hangin' and bangin'.'

The squad cracked up. Even the coaches couldn't contain their smiles.

'Let's hope Victor's left something in his tank. Everyone else ready to go?' shouted Cas, followed by a clap of his gloved hands.

'Yeah!' boomed the team, with some whoops and claps thrown in for good measure.

'Excellent. We have something special for you today.'

A few of the players made an 'ooooOOOOoooo'.

'Steve made an excellent point the other day. The game this weekend is a bit different from most of the games. You probably saw them the last few weeks. They try to make the games very physical. We have to prepare for that.'

Steve's eyebrows raised and an optimistic smile emerged.

'We fight the fire with fire, yes?'

The players exchanged some pleasantly surprised glances and clapped.

'No no. We burn ourselves. That is not us. We fight the fire with the water.'

The applause dampened.

'We have a special guest for a few days to help us be like the water. Give him a warm welcome.' Cas began a clap, signalling the team to applaud, before extending a welcoming hand past the side of the group.

A short, stocky man with a topknot jogged up the side of the group. He was kitted out in a blue and white Weavers training snood, sweatshirt and shorts but wore nothing on his feet. No socks, no boots or trainers. Nothing. His bowling-ball calves bounced as his bare feet trotted along the barely thawed turf.

As the players noticed him, a ripple of eyebrows raised. Someone in the pack spluttered. Jason the fitness coach folded his arms.

'Daft bastard needs a warm welcome running in like that,' muttered Charlie to Finney and Victor.

'Yo, I seen this don on Insta doing fuckin' cartwheels and ninja shit. G is sh-redd-edddd,' whispered Victor.

'Guys, this is Vasily Kalashnikov. World expert movement coach. For those who don't know him, he'll maybe tell you some things about himself and then get you warmed up. Vasily!'

Their guest took his place in front of them.

'Life . . . is . . . movement,' announced Vasily; his manner solemn, his posture almost yogic. 'From the womb, to the cradle, to the grave, movement is how we express ourselves in this life. If we cannot move it, we cannot prove it to the world around us. It just lives inside us, festering, unfulfilled.'

Victor nudged Dmitriy and whispered to him, 'Man, between him and Dre, I'm starting to think your place is full o' dese fruity dons. You won the genetic lottery, fam.'

Dmitriy barely even glanced Victor's way.

'My life has been dedicated to full self-expression and actualisation through movement and my control of it. From dancing in the Moscow Ballet to fighting in the World Sambo Championship to breaking the world record for standing still atop a hundred-foot pillar for forty hours, I have explored many facets of my own movement. I'm here with you for a few days to facilitate a delve into your own so that you can, to borrow a famous quote, "float like a butterfly, sting like a bee" so that your opponents "can't hit what their eyes can't see". You will become more nimble and more supple: so that you can avoid some of those hits; and with the ones you must take, you'll bend and not break. Let us get moving. Who will be my first volunteer?' Vasily looked towards Dmitriy, who pretended not to notice, then continued searching the players for a willing participant.

'Yo. Easy'll represent,' called Victor as he strutted out of the pack.

'Very good. What's your name, comrade?'

Victor turned towards his teammates in mock disbelief. 'Man doesn't know me! The name's EasyMoney, Frodo.'

His teammates tried not to laugh.

'Kalashnikov – your dad the Russian Howard Stark?'

'Ah, this must be the English humour your nation is so famous for,' replied Vasily, barely smiling. 'No – a *kalach* is a bread. My family is from the peaceful profession of baking.'

'So you're the only fucking weapon here, Easy,' shouted one of his teammates, breaking the squad into a fit of laughter.

'Very good,' replied Vasily humourlessly, trying to bring the group's attention back to him. 'EasyMoney – I want you to gently push me.'

The group's attention focused like a forward-facing arrow.

'Push you, blud?'

'Yes, push me. Anywhere you please.'

Victor eyed him suspiciously, saw that he was being serious, then squared up to him. After a moment, he pushed his hand out towards Vasily's left shoulder. Vasily twisted away, causing Victor to miss by millimetres.

'Again, Easy.'

Victor went for the other shoulder, only to be evaded again by a smooth swivel of Vasily's spine.

'Faster, like you're trying to really push me. Anywhere.'

Victor grinned and launched a palm at Vasily's sternum. A swift backbend later, Victor had a handful of fresh air but saw Vasily's pelvis was now closer to him. Before even fully retracting his extended arm, with his free hand he went for the left crest of Vasily's pelvis. With his feet fixed to the ground, Vasily quickly curved sideways out of his backbend and circled into a hinge at the hips, avoiding Victor's hand again. The nimble move drew a jeer from the team.

Frustrated, Victor swiped his other arm at the side of Vasily's shin, only for it to be hurdled with a swift tuck jump, leaving Victor off balance to stumble to the floor.

Most of the squad swarmed Victor, piling on him and cheering as Vasily stood by, watching impassively down his lifted nose. Even Cas and the coaching staff laughed at

Victor's fail. After the commotion calmed, Vasily addressed the group again.

'Mr EasyMoney tried to walk before he could crawl, but you see the game.'

Victor shifted his jaw.

'The target keeps his feet planted, unless he must lift them, and avoids contact by the smallest margin possible. Go slowly, let your partner learn how to bend without breaking, then start to stretch them. Find a partner, two minutes each. Go.'

Dmitriy, Charlie and Finney watched Victor make a beeline for Vasily. Victor asked him something. Vasily shook his head and turned away, leaving Victor in a sulk, much to the guys' delight.

Seeing their grins, Victor paced over, zeroing in on Dmitriy. 'Dunno what you're laughing at, fam. I knew your people were behind the times but man's walking round here with no shoes. Real caveman shit. Embarrassing.'

Dmitriy eyeballed him, deadpan. 'Says the African.'

Finney and Charlie erupted in a fit of laughter and shook Dmitriy in celebration. He cracked a smirk at Victor, who for once was blushing. Victor sucked his teeth and stormed off to find a partner, the duo almost crying hysterically on Dmitriy's shoulders.

As the team finished cooling down and headed towards the training complex, Cas called Dmitriy over and patted his shoulder. '12:15 outside the old psychologist's office OK?'

'Uh . . . yes. Not the video room?'

Cas grinned. 'Not today. I made something special for you.'

Arms folded and an ankle resting on his other thigh, Dmitriy, back in his regular clothes, sat back deep in his armchair.

'I'll just be a jif,' said Brygg, the man across the office, in his melodious Scottish accent.

Dmitriy said nothing.

Brygg spritzed the far corners of the room with a spray, dimmed the lights halfway and rolled up the sleeves of his floral dress shirt as he made his way over to sit in an armchair around the coffee table from Dmitriy. As he rustled around in his travel bag on the floor, Dmitriy pulled his phone out and began scrolling. The scent of lavender hit him.

'We're just about . . . ready,' said Brygg.

Dmitriy looked up to see he had put a box of tissues on the table.

'You'd be surprised what comes up in these sessions.'

Dmitriy rested his phone on the arm of his chair and refolded his arms.

'Oh, I'm sorry. You'll have to turn that off and put it away. We need your full attention right here.'

Dmitriy stiffened. 'I need it. I'm expecting business calls.'

'I'm sorry. This was all in the pre-session email. It's non-negotiable. You want a result, this is how we get it.'

'I see no email.' Dmitriy examined the Scot's face to see if his explanation had softened his stance. Not one iota. He leaned forward, picked up his phone and stood. 'Then we have to make another time.'

'That could be a fair while. Today was only available because of a last-minute cancellation. My waiting list is nine months long.'

Dmitriy stopped. 'The club has paid you?'

Brygg nodded. 'And flew me down private. To open up your entire future.'

Dmitriy clenched his jaw and took a look at his phone. Its notification light remained lifeless. 'OK,' he said, unlocking his phone then powering it down, 'we do this now.' He showed Brygg, who nodded in satisfaction, then sat back down.

'Fabulous. Let's begin.'

'. . . and now as the film projectionist, play that black and white movie again and again, backwards, at double speed. Hear that Cossack music playing at ridiculous speed.'

Dmitriy's eyes flickered underneath his closed eyelids as he followed Brygg's instructions in his imagination.

'Run that over and over, faster and faster . . . STOP!' shouted Brygg, clapping simultaneously.

Dmitriy jolted, his eyes snapped open.

'Now, if I ask you to think about taking a flight, how does that feel now?'

Dmitriy's eyes flickered around as he pictured the scene and examined his feelings towards it. 'I don't know. Maybe not so bad.'

Brygg studied his face and his demeanour intently. 'Do you think you could fly to a European away game next season?'

Dmitriy's strategic cogs turned for a moment. 'I think so, yes.'

'And how does it make you feel to know that you'll help out your team in the biggest competition they've ever played in, having made this breakthrough?'

'Proud,' said Dmitriy, allowing a slight smile to appear.

'And to know that the whole world is more open to you to explore and holiday in?'

'Good, yes.'

'So how about today?'

The smile fell away. 'What you mean *today*?'

'Would you fly today?'

'For what?' clipped Dmitriy.

'To know that you can. We have use of the private plane that brought me here for the rest of the day. We can do a quick fly around and have you back home for tea.'

Dmitriy rigidified. His throat tightened.

'Can you feel that? What you're feeling and what I'm seeing lets me know we've got just a wee bit more work to do to demolish this phobia once and for all. Are you familiar with the term *secondary gain?*'

Dmitriy shook his head.

'So sometimes, we develop protective behaviours like phobias for fairly small reasons. As we dwell on them, the phobias become more intense over time. Those sorts of fears and phobias can be cleared without delving around in the mind much. Sometimes though, we have phobias for very good reasons. Big reasons. Bigger than the things we're obviously afraid of. Phobias like these can be easily undone too, but only when we realise what those larger reasons are. Let me ask you a question – *can you think of any benefit you get from not flying?'*

'What you mean?' Dmitriy snapped back, more colour in his face than usual.

Brygg softened his tone even further. 'If you were perfectly fine with flying, how would your life be worse than it is right now?'

Dmitriy was flummoxed. Brygg watched him rack his brain for an answer.

'It not be worse. I like to travel to most of world if I can.'

'Is there some of the world *you don't like to travel to*?'

A wave of heat hit Dmitriy.

'Dmitriy, everything in here is confidential. I'm legally bound to keep everything we talk about between us unless you give permission otherwise. *I* know how hard it can be for somebody in *your* position to open up, but here you can be completely open about your thoughts and feelings. You can be completely yourself in here.'

Dmitriy's face burned hotter. He was unnerved by the therapist's knowing expression.

'You know what? I just being pussy. You help me. I let go of the fear. We can fly today.'

A wave of sadness washed over Brygg. He paused. 'You can?'

'Today, yes,' said Dmitriy as he jumped to his feet and pulled his shoulders back.

Brygg rose slowly and summoned a smile. 'Fabulous.'

CHAPTER 11

The sound of his knocking reverberated through the arena corridor. Finney backed away from the door, running his hand through his grey fleck and tapping his heel against the floor. The sound of the door latch rattling made him stand to attention. The door opened a foot. Out popped the half-shaven, half-dreadlocked head of a young Japanese guy in his early twenties. Finney peered down at him and his wooden ear spacer and drew his shoulder back.

'Yes?' asked the guy in his Shoreditch accent, guarding the opening.

'Is Nova here?'

'Who are you?'

'Ian Finney. Her husband,' he replied, hitting his final two words hard.

'Oh, the cricketer?'

'Footballer.'

The guy looked over his shoulder. 'Nova – wanna see your hubby?'

Finney raised an eyebrow.

'Come in, dude.' He opened the door, welcoming Finney in, revealing himself to be wearing a white string vest and white cargo pants with PVC strips down the sides. Nova, still in full stage make-up and hair, wearing a white PVC and Lycra costume, sat on one of two yoga mats on the floor, butterflying her knees towards the ground.

'Darling! What are you doing here?' she said, beaming at him.

He walked over as she continued stretching and kissed the crown of her head, before labouring down to sit by her. 'I said I was gonna come see you play, Princess. Wanted to give you a nice surprise.'

She smiled and wrapped an arm around him, kissing his cheek. He kissed her on the lips and cradled the back of her neck with his hand.

'Are we OK to finish off these stretches before we get moving?' asked the guy, taking Finney out of his tender moment. Nova waved him over.

Finney whispered to her. 'Can it wait?'

'Would I come to your changing room after a game and ask you if yours can wait?' she whispered back.

'Fair enough,' he said, his voice trailing off as he glanced away.

As the young guy reached them, Finney heaved himself up off the floor. 'What's your name, fella?' He offered his hand for a shake.

'Jiro,' he replied, bowing instead.

Finney awkwardly took his hand back and nodded his head.

'Dude, I love your hair,' he said as Finney watched him effortlessly squat and kneel ahead of Nova. 'Where'd you get that done?' He pointed towards Finney's hairline. 'The highlight?'

Finney's face dropped momentarily. 'Mother Nature.'

'Oh. I don't know it. Are they on social?'

Finney rolled his eyes as he glanced away. As he turned back, Jiro was leaning forward, pressing Nova's open knees down to the ground, helping her deeper into her groin stretch. Finney gnawed his bottom lip.

'You were amazing out there, Princess. If it's possible, you sounded even more unbelievable than usual. The way you moved. Your interaction. Everything. It's like you've found another level I couldn't have imagined existed.'

Nova smiled through the grimace of her deep stretch, her eyes shut tight. Jiro let her knees go. She took a deep breath and looked at Finney.

'Yeh, it's been a while since you saw the full show. I feel like I've come on leaps and bounds. The voice work, the choreography and the physical work.' She nodded towards Jiro. 'It's really helped me evolve. I'm in a new place.' A beatific smile lit up her face.

Finney came back towards her and laid his hand on her hair. 'I couldn't be happier for you.' He gazed into her eyes and started bending forwards to kiss her.

'Bridge and done?' asked Jiro.

She nodded and rolled onto the floor just before Finney's lips reached her forehead.

'Sorry, just one minute, darling.' She pressed herself up into a gymnastic bridge with slightly bent elbows.

'No problem. Do what you need to do.' Finney watched on as Jiro grabbed a yoga strap from a chair across the dressing room.

He strolled over, stood just in front of her hands, looped the strap under her upper back and grabbed the other end of it. 'And press,' he said as he gently pulled and leaned back. As she pressed through her hands, her elbows straightened, her chest opened and her head lifted a little closer to Jiro's crotch.

Finney's brow furrowed.

'And press.'

Her head came higher.

'And squeeze those cheeks.'

She squeezed her glutes, pushing her pelvis up and her head came higher still.

'Really squeeze those buns and open your chest.'

She squeezed with all her might, holding her breath.

'Annndddd . . . release.'

She gasped and he gently took away his support as she lowered back to the floor and hugged her knees to her chest.

Finney also took a deep breath, silencing it as best he could. 'Intense stuff,' he said as Nova rolled into a squat and stood.

'Yep, that heart chakra's the one, dude. Open that and the whole world opens up to us,' said Jiro as Nova hugged him. 'A little more gentle forward-bending and you're done. I'll see you on the bus.' He let go and bowed to Finney. 'Go with love, brother.'

After Jiro left, Nova linked eyes with her husband, strode over to him, pulled him close and buried her head in his chest.

Finney wrapped his long arms around her petite frame. 'I miss you. We both do.'

'I know.'

Finney waited. 'You miss us too?'

'What sort of question is that? You know I do, just I have things I want to achieve too.'

'I know. I know, Princess.' They held each other a while longer. 'And him?'

She leaned back and looked him in the eyes. 'Jiro?' she said, sounding mildly insulted. 'I think he likes boys. And look at him. You know my type.'

'Oh.' Finney chuckled at himself.

'Look, I've got a break for a few days so I'm going to nip back early Saturday, see baby Lu. I'll be home after your game.'

Finney lit up. 'Good. I've felt a million miles from you lately. I just want you back with us, where you belong.'

A knock sounded at the door. 'Bus is ready, hun,' shouted a woman outside. Nova loosened her hug. 'Saturday. Love you, Daddy.'

He pecked her on the lips and let her go. 'Me more, Princess.'

Lawler pulled his cap down as he paced through the opulent lobby. Ten p.m. meant only a few guests milled around. He reached the elevators, keeping his head down as he waited for one. Ping. The door opened. He entered and hit the button for floor twelve. The doors closed and the elevator descended. 'Bastard.' It went down to B2 and the doors opened. Lawler's face dropped. Stood there in black gym gear was Gunnar. He got in and walked right up to Lawler, like a boxer at a weigh-in.

After what seemed like an eternity for Lawler, Gunnar, a little grin on his face, rumbled a few words. 'What're you doing here on a school night, Bry?'

Lawler broke eye contact then mumbled, 'I've got a date.' The doors closed and the elevator began upwards.

Gunnar didn't bat an eyelid. 'Blow on me.'

Lawler squinted then understood. He blew gently towards Gunnar's face. Gunnar's glare immediately fell away, replaced by a huge warm smile. He patted Lawler on the shoulder, pressed for floor fifteen and stepped around to stand beside him. 'As long as it's just your missus on the merlot, I wish you both a wonderful night.'

Lawler sheepishly nodded.

'You stayed here before?'

Lawler shook his head.

'The rooms are amazing. We're in the penthouse for another week or two yet until our place is ready. My missus loves it. How about Suzy? She been here before?'

Lawler shook his head again.

Gunnar's could see he was still tense. 'She already up there?'

Lawler stared at the floor. 'She's not here.'

Gunnar nodded matter-of-factly and paused for a moment. 'Can't say I trust a man without an appetite.'

Lawler looked his way, an eyebrow raised.

'We're winners, Bry. We embrace the animal in us. We work hard, we play hard.'

Lawler did not know what to say to him.

'Just keep it quiet. The club doesn't need the hassle. As long as you give me it all on the pitch, I couldn't give a toss.' Ping. Floor twelve. 'Here's where you get off.' Gunnar winked his way. 'Enjoy yourself, son.'

'Ta,' replied Lawler. He scuttled out of the elevator and glanced back. Gunnar nodded as the doors shut. Lawler pulled his cap down again and marched off along the corridor.

Andriy pulled down the blinds, shutting out the lake and the rest of the outside world. The bedroom glowed with warm yellow light from a few lamps and a sleek fireplace built into one of the walls. The babble of water echoed from the adjoining bathroom.

A torn-open box and packets from Prime Now laid by the bed. In his T-shirt and boxers, Dmitriy stood in the doorway where he tested the sturdiness of a portable chin-up bar hooked onto the doorframe. He hung from it, rotating his torso to stretch out his shoulders, chest and spine. His vertebrae clunked and the spaces between his ribs expanded as he twisted. As Andriy slipped off his suit jacket and lit some tealights on the windowsills, Dmitriy got off the bar, strapped on a weighted vest from the floor and hung again.

'Enough for today?' asked Andriy.

'Yes, I just check it takes the weight properly.'

'Can't it go somewhere else?' asked Andriy as he pointed a remote control at a wall opposite the end of the bed. Out of the wall appeared a TV.

'Maybe. Anywhere with the door like this. Vasily said it's good to have so you can hang whenever you go past. Make the chest a good stretch, the shoulders strong.'

'That's good but you have enough on your shoulders for now. Leave it. It's been a stressful day. The bath'll be ready in a few minutes. I managed to find those salts. Nothing like a nice bath to wash the worries away.'

Dmitriy smiled gratefully, ripped open the vest's Velcro and removed it.

'I can't believe he put you on the spot like that to just hop on a plane.'

'It's OK. Doesn't matter this season. Nobody else knows and Cas wants me fresh so he says nothing. I have until summer to make the excuses again.'

Andriy nodded. 'Yes, we'll cross that bridge when we come to it. For now, let's forget that and forget everything else for the night. All is calm and nothing can be done about anything right now. If you fancy really turning the brain off after your bath, I bought us a classic to watch – *Masters of the Universe.*'

Dmitriy chuckled, walked over to Andriy and hugged him tight.

Andriy savoured the embrace. 'Let me check if it's ready yet.' He let go, headed into the bathroom and dipped his hand in the bathwater.

Dmitriy peeled off his T-shirt, dumped himself onto his bed and stretched out like a starfish. He closed his eyes and listened to the tub filling. The sound lifted the hairs on the back of his neck. Air filled his open ribcage. He breathed it out fully. *Bxxxt.* His eyes snapped open and peered at his phone on his bedside table. Its notification light blinked. He scrambled over to it, picked it up and opened it. There was a WhatsApp message from an unsaved number.

Oh Dmitriy. What a naughty boy you've been.
I tried calling you several times this afternoon to check in.
I told you to be available at all times.
Instead of next Wednesday, it'll now be Saturday night.
See you soon.
P.S. ask Andriy where he got that sexy black shirt from for me x

Dmitriy dropped his phone, scooted off the bed and ran to the bathroom where his eyes immediately darted to the windows. The blinds were down on all of them.

'He just message me. He must be outside somewhere! You have to go,'

Seeing Dmitriy's panic, Andriy shut off the water. 'How do you know?'

'He just message now. He can see you.'

'Dmitriy,' he gestured to the windows, 'nobody can see me. Mirrored by day, blinded by night.'

'He did. You have to go.'

'If I go, he sees me coming out. Not that it's a crime for a friend to be leaving another friend's house late anyway. Or even to crash in a guest bedroom in a house this large.'

Dmitriy stormed out of the bathroom and the bedroom, grabbing his T-shirt as he went.

'What are you doing?' Andriy called after him in Russian. A few moments later, he heard the front door slam closed. He ran to the window and rolled up the blinds.

Dmitriy, in his boxers and tee, marched down the lawn, arms outstretched, screaming at his invisible enemy in Russian. His voice strained as he veered left and right, trying to goad them out. After a solid minute of bellowing into the nothingness with no movement in sight, he dropped his arms and slumped to sit on the grass, silently watching the water ahead.

CHAPTER 12

Cas side-footed the ball up into the air and it dropped into one of the six plastic bins lining the edge of the pitch. Steve and three of the other coaching staff raised their hands and cheered, with Steve running towards Cas and scooping him up in a fireman's carry. Slung over his shoulder, Steve and the group ran around maniacally, the other teams of five players stopping their collective juggles towards their bins. Steve set Cas down and ran off towards the nearest team of five to taunt them about how the coaches had won the game. A big smile on his face, Cas walked in their direction, players coming over and congratulating him and the other coaches.

The game wound down with everybody in high spirits, exchanging fist bumps and hands slaps on their way towards an area where Jason and Vasily waited with mats laid out and a pile of wooden broom handles.

'Lovely finish that, guv,' said Steve, patting Cas on the shoulder.

Proud, Cas gestured towards his jovial squad. 'Great finish to *their* week. They're ready.'

Steve smiled. 'With finishes like that, you look ready too. Don't fancy showing some of these jokers up and putting yourself on the team sheet?'

Cas laughed, strolling off the pitch.

A spring in his step, he strode along the corridor and knocked on an office window before reaching the open door.

'Cas! I was literally just about to come to fetch you,' said Clive, the assistant press officer, as he stood to greet him. 'They're waiting.'

'*Vámonos* then,' he replied with a big smile on his face, playfully beckoning with his hand. The assistant grabbed a folder and the two headed out and down the corridor. As they approached the entrance to the press conference, a journalist stood outside with one earphone in, laughing at something she was watching on her phone. 'Julia!'

Startled, she whipped her earphone out and locked her phone.

'Sorry, I didn't mean to scare you. How are you?'

'Yeh . . . fine thanks,' she blurted out as she whirled her earphones around her phone and shoved it in her pocket. She stood sheepishly for a moment, wrestling with whether to say something, as Cas paced back and forth and Clive texted somebody. 'Cas, have you . . .?'

'They're ready, Cas,' said Clive.

'OK!' replied Cas, clapping his hands together and halting. Friendly faced, he turned to Julia. 'Time to go on. You ask me in there, yes?'

Flustered, she nodded and opened the double doors to the room. All of them headed in. The audience of journalists was buzzing as Cas headed around them. He climbed a few stairs, passed a big screen bearing the Alpha League's wolf logo and the Weavers badge and took his place behind the desk, centre stage, smiling out to his audience.

Sue, the head press officer, received a nod from Cas and started to head to the side of the stage. 'Cas is ready to take your questions now.'

'Good day everyone!' he said.

The crowd echoed his greeting. Sue pointed to the first questioner.

'Good morning, Cas. Can we start with your team news and any injury updates?'

'Of course. Xavier is back in full training and available for the squad. Luka's rehab goes well. We still think March, maybe the middle. Apart from them, everybody is fit and ready.'

Sue pointed towards his next questioner.

'Good morning, Cas. The word is that you've had a guest in this week – Vasily Kalashnikov, the movement coach. He's probably most famous for his work in the mixed martial arts world. Have you been gearing the team up for a physical bout tomorrow?'

'Well yes, all the games are physical, a very high intensity. But we bring Vasily in to mix things up a bit for the lads and look at how we can make our movements more fast and smoother. We're here to play beautiful football, not to do fighting.'

The crowd rustled with anticipation. Sue scanned those with their hands up and selected Julia.

'Good morning again. What do you make of Gunnar saying that a fight is exactly what you're looking for tomorrow?'

Cas's face contorted. 'I don't know about what he said so I can't tell you about that.'

'This morning at his press conference, he talked in detail about how you were going to –' she paused to read from her phone '– "abandon your principles and try to fight the fire with the fire".'

'Well, like I said, I don't know exactly what he said but he's free to say as he likes. We know who we are and what we do and we stick to ourselves.'

Without being prompted, another journalist piped up. 'He flat out disrespected you, Cas.'

Sue tapped on her microphone. 'Excuse me. Let's have a bit of decorum please. Only speak when you've been selected.'

The journalist raised his hand in apology then waved frantically towards Cas. Cas saw his urgency then glanced at Sue and nodded. Sue pointed to the journalist. Cas shifted in his seat.

'Cas, he did a big chunk of his press conference in character as you. The video's gone viral.'

Cas's innards plunged like he'd just sped over the crest of a roller-coaster, but he tried not to let any sign of it spill out. 'Like I said, I don't know about this. I'm here to talk about my team, our preparations, what we want to show.'

Suddenly, a voice came on over the speakers. Cas looked to the side of the stage. On the big screen was Gunnar's face. Somebody in the audience had cast a clip from Gunnar's press conference to the TV. The picture zoomed out from Gunnar's face to show that his head was barely above the desk and microphones in front of him, like a toddler sat at an adult's table. He must have been sitting on something half the size of a regular seat. Then came the voice. A caricature of Cas's thick Spanish accent.

'Well, eeeeaaaahhhh, we reconise-eah the challenge-a they-a pose-eah. Tip tap tip tap is not-eah gonna cut it. I don't even think-eah a nice-eah pre-match strumming of 'Kumbaya' with-eah mis amigas will-eah do. I think-eah, we're gonna have to-eah, *smash them,*' he shouted in a whiny voice as he banged his palms down on the table, knocking over an open water bottle.

Some of the audience spluttered as cameras snapped Cas's mortified face. Sue indicated to the AV guy at the back of the room to cut the TV, which immediately powered down. She walked onto the stage and whispered something in Cas's ear. He shook his head.

'Ladies and gentlemen, I have to insist there'll be no more of that. Cas, graciously, will continue with questions on *our team* only.'

Cas gave her a nod and she headed off the stage again.

His body felt numb as he turned to the next questioner. He heard them and answered every question that followed, but he did not know what he was saying; he was barely even there.

From behind the door came a high whir, a gentle pounding and the tones of Lionel Richie's 'Easy'. Amber cracked it open and crept in. Across the dimly lit room, Cas – his hair up in a bun – cantered away on the curved treadmill, his feet causing the belt's motion like a hamster wheel.

Facing the window that overlooked their expansive garden, she could see in the reflection against the dark sky that his eyes were closed. With a bottle of sports drink in hand, she light-footed across the space towards him. 'Honey,' she murmured, to no response. '*Honey.*'

He opened his eyes and mustered a smile at her reflection as he kept his pace.

She arrived beside the treadmill, showed him the bottle and went to put it in the cupholder in the treadmill's control panel. There was not one. She laughed to herself and set it down on the floor. 'Been a while since I've seen you in here.'

'Ten more seconds,' he panted, as the perspiration poured down his forehead.

She nodded and stood by as he finished, slowed to a walk and took a few breaths.

'How was your day?' he asked.

'Decent thanks,' she said, almost apologetically.

'Good. Work OK?'

'It was thanks.' She hesitated. 'How was training this morning?'

'Ah, you know, light. They look very good. Loose. Confident.'

'Fantastic!' She paused. 'What brings you in here at this time?'

'What time is it?'

'Nearly ten.'

He checked his heart-rate on his watch. 'Nothing. Just the movement coach, he said to run with the eyes closed is a good exercise. Like a meditation.' He kept his eyes straight ahead.

'Why not just meditate?'

He checked his watch again. 'Huh?'

'Is it not a bit dangerous going so fast with your eyes closed?'

'Ah, maybe a bit but it makes you pay attention to now.'

'Takes your mind off other things?'

Cas walked on. Amber looked at his face. She could not tell if he was oblivious to her attention or ignoring it. She offered her hand to him over the side of the treadmill, in front of him where he had to see it.

'I'm soaking.'

'So?'

He slowed and put his hand in hers. She pulled it towards her and kissed it tenderly. His eyes dropped a little from the horizon but still stayed forwards. She squeezed his hand and kissed it again, harder. He gave a sad smile. Then she licked his hand. He turned towards her, bemused. She let go of his hand, picked up the sports drink and handed it to him, deadpan.

'You defo need those electrolytes.' She beamed a beautiful smile at him.

He could not help but crack and smile back.

'Gotta be hydrated for tomorrow and our after-party. What should I get out for it? The Cantabria?'

'Can we do another one please?'

'Of course. We'll go for the Hermanos and candlelight.'

He gestured for her hand and gave it a grateful kiss and squeeze. Keeping hold of it, he took a swig from his bottle with his other hand. 'Hermanos and candlelight it is, *mi amor*.'

CHAPTER 13

Black and white, almost shoulder to shoulder, the teams lined up side by side in the cramped tunnel. A few of the Weavers looked across to Lawler, trying to catch his eye. Victor nudged him. He stared dead ahead.

Finney saw his ignorance. 'Bry?!'

Lawler barely blinked.

'C'MON LADS!!!' bellowed the Warriors' captain at the top of his lungs. His troop behind him exploded in a racket, smacking teammates' shoulders, a few of them ragging each other around. The Weavers patted each other's upper arms. A few yells of encouragement failed to pierce the Warriors' din.

The teams walked out to the ovation of the predominantly white and blue crowd, around 29,000 strong. Cas trailed his team. His opposite number was nowhere to be seen.

As the players ran onto the pitch, Cas stopped between the dugouts and waved all around to the fans. As he waved at the last stand, a heavy hand landed on his shoulder. He turned to find Gunnar towering over him, uncomfortably close. Gunnar offered his hand to shake. With all eyes on them, he shook it. Gunnar gripped it tightly and raised his other hand to shield his mouth from the cameras.

'What soft hands you have. All the easier to pull that fucking trophy right out of.'

Gunnar abruptly dropped Cas's hand then spun away to greet the travelling fans, his hands in the air and his smile from ear to ear. They burst into a chant of his name. Cas started towards the dugout.

'Guv!'

Cas halted and turned. Steve was almost behind him in the home dugout. Cas had headed for the Warriors' dugout. Red-faced, he turned and headed to his seat.

COLIN

We're moments from kick-off here at The Cooperative, where sixth place Warriors are attempting to do what no team has yet this season – win against the Weavers on their remarkable unbeaten run. How do you see this one unfolding today, Pete?

PETE

Well, the Weavers have swept away all-comers so far this season so my money goes on them but I think the Warriors have looked a different proposition since Magnusson took over so they're going to push the hosts hard today and cause them a few problems.

COLIN

That black pocket of away fans are really making their presence known.

PETE

I think we can expect plenty of the same from their team today given Gunnar's antics yesterday.

COLIN

Yes, it's pretty safe to say there'll be no love lost between these teams today. It's incredible to think that just four years ago today, Warriors were top of the table and the Weavers were sixth place two leagues below. *What a game this is!*

And the Weavers get us underway, with Allen to Ezemonye, who plays the ball back to Finney. Finney lays the ball off to Lebedev who plays it out to the right. Only Ayissi has ventured into the Weavers' half so far – probably a sign of things to come. The ball goes back to Allen who drives one long looking for the knockdown from Ezemonye. Oof!

Hardison's came right through the back of him there but the ref hasn't given it. Velasquez and the Weavers' bench are up in arms. Hardison plays it to Lawler. The home fans are making their feelings known as he carries it forward. He spreads the ball out to their right only for

Finney to cut it out and restart the Weavers' forward motion.

*

COLIN

. . . and Lebedev takes that beautifully in his stride through the tight gap between them but Botterill grabs a handful of shirt and the whistle goes. The foul count is totting up already.

PETE

Yes. They're sharing them out tactically. We saw this at Sporting. Magnusson's teams don't allow you to build any sort of flow against them.

COLIN

Lebedev plays it back to Allen for a one-two and Allen sets off for the overlap only to get checked by a black shirt. Nope. The ref waves play on. Steve Frank is out on the edge of the technical area letting the fourth official know what he thinks about the refereeing so far. There's a lot being let go. Lawler looks for Ayissi down the channel but finds a white shirt again. It's very disjointed isn't it, Pete?

PETE

Very. The Warriors are breaking up lots of the Weavers' moves, keeping compact, limiting the space and being aggressive – but they're lacking quality in possession and giving it straight back to the Whites.

COLIN

Who are starting to drag the Warriors around and find a few gaps. Here's Finney, threading it to Lebedev, who's got the wrong side of Lawler. Lebedev dribbles across the wall of black on the edge of the Warriors' area, evading one, then another. Allen is supporting him on the right but he's just been hit by a hefty challenge from Sweeney before he could get his pass off. That certainly looked a foul to me, but the play goes on. The ball goes to Massingham who breaks forward. Wow. What a tackle from Finney. He's managed to slide across, wrap one of those long legs around the ball and slide back up into his stride in one motion. That's one for the young defenders to watch. He plays a one-two with Lebedev and then feeds one into Ezemonye's feet. He's down; absolutely pole-axed. That looked like an elbow to his back. Surely we've got to see a card now?

PETE

I'd guess so. Velasquez has sprinted to the edge of his technical area. He's counting his fingers in the air towards the ref. There have been plenty of cynical ones so far and yep, there's the first yellow of the game. He doesn't look surprised and they're not arguing with it. Gunnar's out at the edge of his area, helping them organise to defend the free kick, which is in a pretty dangerous position.

COLIN
Is that a little smirk across to Velasquez?

*

COLIN
We've got about two minutes to go here and we're still at nil-nil in what has been a bitty first half. Weavers have been the better side, but Warriors have managed to frustrate them so far. Your take, Pete?

PETE
It certainly hasn't made for the best watching but nobody has managed to stop the Weavers scoring in the first half here yet this season so Magnusson should be fairly happy with what his team has done. Velasquez's team might find a way through in the second half if they stick to their guns but if they can't, do they have a plan B?

COLIN

Lawler, who's still being given an inhospitable reception here by his old fans, turns on the ball and takes it towards the sideline trying to get away from Finney, who's never been too far from him this first half. Lawler stops and starts again to try to make a yard for himself, but Finney's read that like a book, nicked it and turned away. Can they do something before half-time? Velasquez is urging his team forward. The ball goes up to Ezemonye who takes a lovely touch away from his marker. He's been buffeted off the ball by another – surely that was a shove rather than a shoulder. The ref waves it away. Lawler picks up the loose ball. First-time, he's sent it long. They're high. Ayissi's outmuscled his marker. He's through. They're not gonna catch him. Can Cope stop him? Ayissi smashes it past him into the roof of the net! One-nil Warriors! What a hammer blow just before the stroke of half-time! Velasquez is remonstrating with the fourth official about that challenge on Ezemonye but it's no use. White shirts have surrounded the referee who's signalling for a restart and telling them to back off. Lebedev's being dragged away by Finney, who's imploring his teammates to leave it.

PETE
Lawler has just sprinted forty yards to join in with the celebrations. He's kissing his badge. Listen to the home fans. And look! Magnusson's right on the edge of the Weavers' technical area, pumping his fists towards the travelling fans! Steve Frank has just shoved him away. His staff are up. Velasquez is pleading for them to sit back down but now the Warriors' staff are up. All hell's breaking loose down there!

The empty whiteboard was a beacon for the players as they tried to calm themselves, sipping recovery drinks and stretching off. Only the odd nervous shuffle broke the silence.

'Lads, forget that shit just then,' said Finney. 'They're just trying to rile us. Before that, it's been all us apart from that one break and *they know it*. How the fuck the ref didn't give that on Vic, I don't know.'

'That *and how many others?!* The ref's a wasteman, fam.'

Cas sat alone in his stadium office, tapping the tip of his pencil on his empty notepad.

In the away dressing room, the Warriors players sat to attention. Gunnar commanded the space. 'We've executed perfectly! They want space; we smother them. They play soft; we smash them. They prod and probe; we gut them.'

Finney held the floor from his bench in the Weavers' dressing room. 'They can't keep hold of the ball. Keep doing what we're doing, we'll find a gap and make them pay. The gaffer'll have seen where they leave themselves open.'

He noticed a few of his teammates still looking towards the empty whiteboard and knew he had to draw them in. He began again, louder and gesturing towards them. 'Just remember, this ref won't give us a fucking thing. It's up to us to let them know we're no easy touch. It's up to us to make our superiority pay and get back into this.'

Cas stared at a few scribbled-out sentence beginnings.

Gunnar's ferocity was ramping up. 'Not a second, not an inch. If you really want to give our fans what they deserve, reach deep inside yourselves for more intensity. We can't just beat these; we have to *destroy* them. I want us to humiliate them *so* badly that their fans never look at them the same way again. That's how we dismantle their season and make our fans proud!'

His team erupted, ready for a second-half onslaught.

A few seconds after Finney had finished, Cas entered the muted room. Relief washed over many of the players' faces. They dropped everything. He walked to the whiteboard, took a pen and peered at its lid. Without removing the lid, he set the pen back down and turned to the team.

'More of the same, guys. Our football is better; the real football. More chances will come.' He clapped to rouse the players, who began a trickle of applause. They looked around at each other. *Is that all?* Steve went to interject but the applause loudened and his moment was gone.

'Oway! We're better than these!' yelled Charlie. The ovation grew louder still.

As it eventually began to tail off, Finney called out to Cas. 'Gaffer . . . gaffer . . . any tweaks?'

'No. This is nothing special. We play our game.'

Steve clasped his mouth.

'Our quality will find the way through. They are just thugs. We are too much for them.'

Finney got up and marched to the centre of the room. 'You heard him, lads. We're better than these. Just keep it going!'

The others rose, patted backs and bumped fists as they headed for the door. As Dmitriy stepped away from his locker area, he heard the short buzz of a text and froze. He slowly peered back towards his gear. A hand on his shoulder snapped him out of it.

'Let's go!' said Finney, wired for the half ahead. 'We've got a midfield to boss.'

The door opened, letting in the distant wail of war cries.

About to be last out of the away dressing room, Lawler felt a hand grasp his arm.

Gunnar spoke softly, 'Bryan, I need you to reach the deepest of all this half.'

Lawler eagerly nodded.

'Finney's controlling the middle for them. He's their only hope. I want their hope gone.'

'I'll do better with him, chief.'

'I need you to do *a lot* better; or better still, I need him gone.'

Lawler examined Gunnar's expression.

'With him on the pitch, they can get a foothold back at any time. With him gone, they'll crumble.'

Lawler looked down at his boots.

'Son, I'd rather not ask this of you, but this is what it takes sometimes to climb highest. You think I won so much without getting my hands dirty sometimes? Like I said, leading is about doing things others won't. If it isn't for you, Bry, fine, but it needs taking care of one way or another.'

After a few moments, Lawler looked back up to meet Gunnar's gaze, sheepishly nodded and turned for the door.

'Reach deep, son. Win here and your daughter doesn't just have a Dad that plays, she has a Dad who's a winner at the end of the season and for the rest of his life.'

CHAPTER 14

COLIN

It's going to be interesting to see how the Weavers respond after that fracas before half-time.

PETE

It is. They're on the ropes here for the first time in nearly eighteen months but Cas is a cool customer. He'll have got everyone together, calmed them down and laid out what he thinks they need to change this half to find a way through.

COLIN

With that one-goal lead, you can bet the Warriors are going to make the spaces tighter and their tackles more ferocious. Can the Weavers win the war ahead and keep their unbeaten run intact?

PETE

The war's started before we've even kicked off. Magnusson has just waved Velasquez's way. You can see his face – he's trying to get a rise out of him. Steve Frank is up to the fourth official again.

COLIN

He's not happy about this utter lack of sportsmanship. What do you make of all this?

PETE

We all know what Gunnar Magnusson brings to the game. He's more interested in gamesmanship than sportsmanship. As such a highly decorated player and manager, can we really argue with him?

* *

COLIN

Ten minutes into the second half and the Warriors are clinging onto their lead. It's one-way traffic. As well as the Blacks are closing the space, the Weavers are starting to find gaps, aren't they?

PETE

Yes. I don't know what wisdom Velasquez dropped during half-time but they've responded exactly like you'd expect the league leaders to. Finney is still dictating the pace of the game and at some point one of these forwards is going to get a shot off that doesn't meet a last-ditch block.

COLIN

Allen plays the ball infield to the safe feet of Lebedev. He switches the play to Nixon, who's been nothing but a nuisance to the Warriors' right-hand side all evening. What's he got up his sleeve here? I spoke too soon – he's bamboozled himself with his own trickery and turned the ball over. It comes into the Warriors' midfield. Can they build some possession? There he is again – Finney with those telescopic legs, winning the ball back, carrying it forward. Lawler comes steaming in but thinks better of it and stays on his feet. Can he outmuscle his larger, more experienced counterpart? Oh dear. Finney's left him for dead with a delicious nutmeg to the delight of around twenty-eight thousand Weavers fans. Lawler's not going to have liked that one little bit. Finney plays the ball to Lebedev and carries on his run. Oh – he's just ran his hand over the top of Lawler's head. Lawler nearly slapped out at him there but the referee's not seen it. There's activity on the Warriors' bench. Magnusson's sent out a few midfielders to warm up.

Nixon plays it in to Ezemonye and carries on for the return. Has he got the beating of his man this time? He's got a yard, he drills one in. A black body gets it clear, only as far as Finney. He plays it to Lebedev and goes for the return. Ohhh! That looks like a bad one from Lawler on Finney.

PETE

Yeh, that could be nasty. Lawler's came across him like a freight train. He's not even really went to tackle him, you know. On the replay it looks like he's just ran across his foot and they've knocked knees but Finney's knee has twisted. Knees do not *like twisting.*

The crunch was so loud, he didn't know exactly where it came from. As he crumpled to the ground, black flashed before his eyes. There was no pain. He instinctively clutched his knee and yelped. It felt odd in a way he'd never felt before, but he knew it was disaster.

As the whistle went, a swarm of Weavers rushed past Lawler – who also grabbed his knee – to their captain. Charlie frantically waved over to the bench. The physio was already sprinting on, treatment bag in hand. Finney was writhing around by the time the physio reached him.

The anguish was so severe, the physio's words weren't registering.

Neil tried to examine his knee but as soon as he managed to convince Finney to let go of it, the slightest attempt to straighten it out brought a wail. His teammates stood by, pale-faced. Neil waved towards the dugout – the stretcher was already being rushed on.

Finney's face pressed firmly into the turf. A barrage of soft, reassuring words washed over him, but none sank in. Deafened by his agony, eventually he rolled as he felt they wished him to and was carefully placed onto the stretcher.

As the stretcher was lifted, Lawler, back on his feet now, watched on vacantly. The crowd bombarded him with shrieks and whistles. His eyes peered past the stretcher and met with his manager's. They looked at each other for a short eternity before Gunnar shouted over to his substitutes. They stopped their warm-ups and headed for the bench.

Lawler was violently jolted out of his stare by a shove in the back. He righted himself to find Charlie in his face.

'Fuck you, you turncoat cunt!'

Lawler clasped his hands behind his back as he stepped forward into Charlie's space and took a strong shove in the chest before the referee made it over to break them up. The yellow card was brandished towards Charlie and then Lawler, who skulked away. Four Weavers players circled the referee, incredulous at the colour of the card he had shown. As Lawler reached a cluster of his teammates, he watched the stretcher disappear off down the tunnel. His eyes flickered to Steve on the edge of the Weavers' technical area, who stonily stared his way.

Steve broke away to look over at Gunnar. 'Control your fucking players!'

Gunnar glanced back at him blankly.

Steve marched back over to Cas in the dugout. All of the subs were out warming up. 'Who's going in?'

'Alex.'

Steve's brow raised. 'Won't that leave us a bit open? How about Xavier?'

Twenty yards away, Xavier ran behind Alex towards the technical area as they warmed up. With Xavier being the much taller of the two, Cas could see his slick black quiff and stubbled face bobbing up and down over the top of Alex.

'No. We go with Alex.'

Steve bit his lip as Cas waved over to Alex to ready himself.

Cas continued to the edge of his technical area and shouted for Dmitriy, waving him over. As he waited for Dmitriy to arrive, he fetched something from the kitman.

'Dmitriy, drop in for Ian and take this.' He laid a captain's armband in his number ten's hand.

Dmitriy's jaw tightened.

'I *know* you can.' He closed Dmitriy's fingers around it then patted him on the back and nodded. Dmitriy Velcroed it on and raced back onto the field.

Alex stripped off his training gear, readying himself to be subbed on.

Steve eyed him and turned back to Cas.

'It's been all us, Steve. We'll be fine.'

WEAVERS 1-4 WARRIORS

FT

(HT 0-1)

Ezemonye (87')	Ayissi (44', 62')
	Nixon [OG] (69')
	Strmcnik (74')

White shirts streamed down the stairways and out. Only the black shirts remained in their section, chanting down towards

Gunnar and his team. Lawler returned the applause, aware that it was the first time he had ever cheered to this section in the ground. A firm congratulatory pat landed on his shoulder. He turned to find Gunnar stood beside him, almost imperceptibly nodding. His smile dampened.

The Weavers undressed in silence. Dmitriy un-Velcroed the armband. Victor thumbed clean the name on one of his boots. Steve sighed, shaking his head to himself. Finney's spot was empty.

Back in his stadium office, Cas lifted his head out of his hands. His reddened eyes searched the desk until he found the remote. On went the TV.

'. . . we controlled the game. I think this performance shows our fans what they can expect from us,' said Gunnar.

'The game swung dramatically after Finney's injury. What did you make of the incident?' asked the reporter.

'Bryan went in honestly, took the ball and unfortunately in the process their guy took a knock. Sadly, these things happen in football sometimes. We obviously wish him a speedy recovery.'

With a grunt, Cas launched the remote at the screen. It smashed open, the batteries scattering. Now unable to get Gunnar off his screen, he ripped open his desk drawer and pulled out a frosted glass ball-shaped Manager of the Month trophy. As he cocked his arm, the door knocked. He lowered the trophy to the desk and tried to calm his breathing. 'Who is it?' The door partially opened and through the gap popped the head of McGlynn.

'Don't you ever let me be embarrassed with a performance like that here again.'

He popped back out and slammed the door behind him.

Cas clenched his jaw and his eyes closed, waiting for McGlynn to get away from the office. As the heat bubbled up inside him, all he could hear was Gunnar's voice. His eyes snapped open and he hurled the trophy at the TV. It cracked the screen and thudded against the floor. Gunnar's warped face and voice remained.

The players' lounge was more lifeless than it had been after any game all season; only half full and quiet as a wake. Andriy sat chatting with Charlie's wife, Tiffany, as Charlie talked to a waitress. Dmitriy wandered over to join them.

'What do you want, Dimmy?' asked Charlie, gesturing to him with an empty glass.

'Not for me, thanks.' He waited a moment for a break in Andriy's conversation. 'Hello Tiffany.' He leaned in and they kissed cheeks. 'Sorry to be so short but we must go.'

'C'mon, Dimmy. Just one?' pleaded Charlie, glummer than usual.

'Next time. We have meeting later.'

Andriy downed the last of his pear juice and slid his arms into his jacket.

'When are you coming round?' asked Tiffany. 'You still haven't seen the new place. You're more than welcome too,' she said to Andriy. 'Bring some dates if you like. The more, the merrier.'

'That'd be lovely. We'll sort something,' said Andriy as he stood and edged to Tiffany for goodbye kisses.

Charlie and Dmitriy wearily shook hands.

'Catch you tomorrow, mate.'

Dmitriy and Andriy headed for the exit, exchanging nods with plenty around the room on their way.

'Here he is,' a voice bellowed from behind them in Russian. They froze, looked at one another out the corners of their eyes, then turned.

Approaching was a man in his mid-fifties with weathered skin, small dark eyes and a fur-collared leather jacket. 'Our prime export.' He heartily shook Dmitriy's hand, then Andriy's. Still in Russian, he carried on, 'Today aside, how are you?'

'Very well thanks, Kazimir,' replied Dmitriy, trying to hide his surprise. 'What brings you here?'

'You think I can get this news and not come see you?'

'What news?'

'That you have your wings now!'

Dmitriy's stomach almost sunk through him.

'Your manager called me with the good news. Now our prime export can import himself too and help make his nation even prouder.'

Andriy watched the colour drain from Dmitriy's face. 'Mr Volkov, I'm Andriy Romanov – Dmitriy's manager. We hadn't been in contact with the good news yet as it's early days. A little thirty-minute circular flight is quite a different proposition to the four-hour flight home. We were thinking of making sure he's OK with shorter haul before letting you know he could definitely represent the national team.'

'Mr Romanov – I understand your concerns, but they're misplaced. I called the gentleman who helped Dmitriy and it turns out that, although he couldn't remark on Dmitriy specifically, he has never had one relapse with any of his clients. That justifies his extortionate prices! Plus, if you would like, we can make it a private flight and stop off halfway. We want nothing but comfort for your man.'

Dmitriy's forehead glistened, coldly clammy.

'Come celebrate with me! My hotel is near the finest caviar restaurant in the city. I'll be more likely to get our Beluga here that back home with all that Chinese imitation shit we have now.'

'We actually have an appointment to get to,' said Andriy.

Kazimir checked his watch and scrunched his brow. 'She can wait a few hours, playboy. Come, come. I want to tell you my plans for you at the heart of my team.'

'We really can't,' said Andriy.

Kazimir addressed Dmitriy. 'Where did you find this one? He'd have me travel all this way to eat alone just so you two can get some pussy faster. Do what you must, Mr Romanov. You're not going to have me go back to our FA headquarters with a dinner receipt for one are you, Dmitriy?'

Dmitriy swapped glances with Andriy and gulped.

CHAPTER 15

*

The front door opened revealing Gunnar warmly smiling. From behind his back he revealed a bottle of red wine and a small wrapped gift.

'How did you know?' asked Cas, gesturing to the wine.

'Educated guess.'

'Come in, come in.' Cas stepped aside and welcomed Gunnar in. '*Nuestra casa es tu casa.*'

'I've not heard it said quite like that before.'

'It's a lovely language, isn't it?' said Amber, popping out impishly from round the corner. 'It's so lovely to meet you.' She welcomed him with a firm hug and kiss on the cheek. 'Look at you. Even bigger than you look on the tele!' As she detached from him, her hand lingered on his arm. 'Bloody hell. He's made of steel.'

Gunnar smirked. 'You flatter. Cas never told me how beautiful you are.'

'Men! All you ever talk about are your toys and your games,' she said before spotting the bottle in his hand. 'That stuff is my absolute fave. Your new pal gets the Amber seal of approval, honey,' she said, winking at her husband.

The three sat around the dinner table, their plates empty. Amber, a tad tipsy, waved the almost empty wine bottle at Gunnar. 'You sure I can't tempt you?'

Gunnar held up his palm. 'I'm sure. I'm an absolute lightweight. One glass and I'm anybody's.'

Amber giggled. Cas forced a polite smile.

'How aren't you?' asked Amber.

'How aren't I what?'

'How aren't you somebody's?'

Cas interjected, '*Mi amor*. Maybe people don't like to speak about these things.'

'It's alright, soldier. I'm a big boy. It's fine.'

Amber put the bottle down and rested her chin on the backs of her hands.

'Not much to tell. You know, haven't met a good one yet. You've seen the relationships most footballers end up in and out of. The types we attract. I guess I won't be a footballer soon so maybe it's part of my next chapter. Till then, it's eyes on the prize. Full focus on one last medal for the mantlepiece. Unlike some,' he nodded over towards Cas, 'I have to graft for every ounce of quality I have.'

'Well, on behalf of ladies all around the world, let me say that football's loss will be our gain. They'll be licking their lips at the prospect of having such a strapping man!'

Gunnar noticed Cas rake his teeth across his top lip. 'How did you two meet?'

'Us?' Amber sat up, posed one hand on her waist, one behind her head and pouted. 'Cas was my official holiday photographer.'

Gunnar looked at her quizzically.

'Me and some pals were on our hols in Barcelona, walking in this park in the hills – Parc Güell; it's like some place out of a Disney film – and we stopped to take a photo in front of this amazing balcony thing that looks out over the city. Selfies just weren't cutting it, so I handed my phone to the first kind face I saw walking past.'

Gunnar smiled.

'And the rest is history, like they say,' said Cas, smiling too but looking away.

'Our history. We went back there a year later and he proposed to me on that same balcony.'

'That's a lovely story,' said Gunnar.

'Have you ever been?' said Cas.

Gunnar shook his head.

'You must. There is no place like it. On the yellow hills, designed by an amazing Catalan architect with crazy structures and art from tiles everywhere. It was meant to be a garden city where many beautiful houses would be, but they only end up building two.'

'But one day, we'll build another,' said Amber, raising her empty glass towards Gunnar.

'You're going to move to Barcelona?' said Gunnar.

'No, we're just gonna make a Güell-style playhouse, all mosaiced – like our own part of that hill, in the garden – aren't we honey?'

Cas nodded.

'Soon, I hope,' she said.

He straightened his cutlery on his plate and reached for hers. Her smiling cheeks dropped a little.

Aware of something going on, Gunnar picked up the gift from the seat beside him and offered it across to Cas.

'A small thanks for having me over and for saving my arse from Johnstone the other week. Hopefully this helps you on your way.'

'Thank you. Is very kind. You didn't need to,' he said, smiling warmly as he took it, appreciating the grainy texture of the wrapping paper.

'Well don't just bloody stroke it. Open it.'

Cas chuckled and carefully ran his pinky underneath one of the wrapping paper's seams to keep it as intact as possible. Inside was an antique red hardback book – *The Art of War* by Sun Tzu.

'It's my favourite book of all time; the greatest thing ever written on winning. Call it the companion book to the stuff I showed you.'

Cas put his hand over his heart. 'Is very kind of you.'

Gunnar replied with a stoic double thumbs-up.

*

The door slammed downstairs, breaking Amber's focus from the book she was reading. She glanced at the clock – 23:15. The game had been done for nearly four hours. Putting her book aside and sitting up straighter, she listened out to try to figure out what he might be doing downstairs. She pulled the cover from over her and cautiously shouted, 'Honey . . . I'm up here.' No reply came. She heard nothing until suddenly footsteps came running up the stairs. Cas entered the room and almost jogged around the bed, his eyes wide. 'You OK?' she asked.

'Fine, *mi amor*. Give me five minutes.' He took the lamp off his bedside table, set it on the floor and briskly started emptying the drawers. Then he lifted the table and marched out of the room with it. Something slid and bumped around inside of it.

Amber, perplexed, listened to him tread down the stairs. A few moments later she heard the patio doors open. She got out of bed and walked over to the window.

Cas was in the centre of the garden. The table was laid on its side in front of him. He took a yellow tin from his back pocket and doused the table with its liquid. Next, he took out a candle lighter. He flicked on a flame and lit the table.

Amber's jaw dropped. Cas stepped back as the table was engulfed by flames. He stood absolutely still as he watched the glow dance and flicker for a few moments, then headed back for the house.

Amber dived back into bed, her mind whirring, as she heard the stairs again.

As Cas arrived in the room, his face now calmer, she pulled the cover back on his side and patted the bed. He came over, sat down and began unbuttoning his shirt. She racked her brain, searching for the perfect words. There was nothing she could say. She sat up, got out from underneath the sheets and hugged the back of him. He grabbed one of her embracing hands and went to kiss it but instead just gave it a squeeze.

'Leave it behind you and move on. It's just one game,' she said.

He moved as if to reply then just nodded. Still wrapped around the back of him, she looked towards the window.

'You sure you're OK?'

'You asked me one time already. I'm fine,' he said straightforwardly. 'I just think about the future now.'

'To the future.' She squeezed him again, tighter, then pecked a couple of kisses on his neck, then a longer, softer one. Her breathing deepened. She stroked his chest and ran her hand up around the other side of his neck as she kissed him again, closer to the back of his ear.

'Did you eat yet?' he asked.

She stopped kissing him but carried on stroking. With her voice low and full, 'Yes, you didn't message back so I had a bit of something.'

'I need something before bed.' He shifted forward, breaking her hug, then looked back to her. 'You want an omelette? I think there's some chorizo and the sweet peppers.'

Her heart sank. 'No, I'm alright.'

'You want to come down? I'll be quick.'

'Umm, I'll just read till you're done.'

'OK.' He stood and took his unbuttoned shirt off, leaving him in his vest. 'Happy reading.' He reached back to her for a small kiss and headed out, then started to whistle Marvin Gaye's 'Let's Get It On'.

As his tune vanished down the stairs, Amber picked up her book and got back under the covers, tucking herself in tightly. Her lips fidgeted as she flipped the pages hard against each other until she found where she had left off.

The blacked-out Mercedes crawled through the dark streets of the derelict industrial estate. It slowed to a stop under one of the few working sodium orange street lights outside a haggard warehouse.

Out of the car climbed a flustered Dmitriy with a black backpack in hand. He checked over both shoulders. Not a soul in sight. As he walked towards the warehouse, he scanned around for something on the floor. His eyes landed on two interlinked white chalk circles with arrows off them pointing towards a large metal sliding door. He crept towards its handle, which was wrapped with a chain and an open padlock. Grabbing it, he had to lean to get it moving, such was its weight. It screeched as he pulled it a few feet ajar. That was all he needed.

He turned on his phone's torch and lit ahead into the gap before stepping through it. In he edged, turning the beam like a prison patrol light, searching for unwanted movement. The place was like a graveyard for flatpack furniture. Battered sets of drawers. Stacks of dusty tabletops. A filthy cabinet with a broken door.

He stopped his search on a candy pink wardrobe. As he inched over to it, the pounding of his heart in his chest rattled him. His armpits grew sweatier. He peeled open a door. Inside was a small pink envelope. He took the backpack off, placed it in the wardrobe and picked up the card, noticing its flap was covered with a red lipstick mark. As he slotted it into his pocket, a loud metallic groan came from above. He looked up into the blackness. A cold drip fell on his face. Then another. Suddenly, music blared out – The Weather Girls' 'It's Raining Men' – causing him to jump. Then a downpour. The sprinklers had sprung to life, soaking everything in the warehouse. He spun and sprinted for the door as the music taunted him. Skidding out of the gap, he turned, yanking the door closed with an ear-piercing shriek that momentarily drowned out the music. His trembling hands managed to fumble the padlock through the chain and lock it. He jumped into his car, slammed the door and sped away, tears streaming down his wet face.

The distant sound of an alarm stirred him. Finney's eyelids groggily peeled open. He tried to roll onto his side but something stopped him. As he oriented himself, he was shocked to see his leg in traction, engulfed by cables and braces. As memories of the night before rushed back to him, the pain descended.

A slender doctor wearing glasses and a high ponytail entered his private room. 'Mr Finney. Good morning.'

'Doesn't look that way to me,' he muttered, his throat dry.

'No, of course not.'

Finney licked his lips and spotted a jug of water on his bedside table. He shifted to reach for it but winced and gave up, cursing under his breath. 'Could you grab me some, please?'

'Of course.' She walked around, poured some into a sip-cup and handed it to Finney, who slurped it dry through its inbuilt straw.

'Go on then. What's the deal, doc?'

'We don't know for sure yet as we have to wait for the swelling to subside before we scan.'

'Come on. I know you know more than that.'

The doctor shifted her glasses. 'Our initial orthopaedic tests showed possible ACL, MCL and meniscus damage. The X-rays show no breaks.'

Finney covered his face with his hands then raked them up through his hair. 'That sounds like, what, a year?'

The doctor paused. 'If it is compounded like we suspect, that wouldn't be an unlikely prognosis. I'm sorry, Mr Finney.'

Finney's face greyed as the parts of him supported by the bed flattened further onto it.

'You're in the finest hands here to get you back fit as soon as humanly possible.'

'Is it still Ratcliffe who does the knees here?'

'No, Mr Ratcliffe retired last year. I'm the knee specialist here now.'

'Oh right,' he said, his voice rising.

'Unless you would like us to explore other options?' she asked, matter-of-factly.

'No, no. Sorry, no,' he bumbled. 'Just you're a lot younger than the older gents who usually do these sorts of things.'

'What do they say in your game? If you're good enough, you're old enough?'

He smiled wryly.

'I'll be back with you shortly.' The doctor started out of the room then turned back. 'Oh, the desk is holding a lot of messages for you. Shall I get them sent through?'

'From my girls?'

'I'm not sure. I know some are from your team.'

'Have my girls been?'

'No. No visitors yet.'

'Aren't they allowed?'

'We'd have allowed family.'

Finney sighed. 'Can I get my phone, please?'

'Of course. I'll get a nurse on the case. I'll get them to bring the messages too.'

'Leave them. I just want my phone.'

The doctor nodded and left. Finney buried his face in his hands.

Steve slid the statistical report to Cas, who moved it to one side.

'We should take a look, guv.'

'Why? We know the important numbers. They finish with eleven. We have one man in the hospital. He's thirty-five, Steve. Thirty-five.'

Steve's eyeline sunk. 'I know.'

'And one of *our* boys who did it.'

'He's not ours anymore,' said Steve, shaking his head.

'He will always be one of ours.'

'Well, we're not the ones in his ear now.' The pair sat silent for a while. 'McGlynn was skating on thin ice selling him and now we're freezing our fucking nuts off, drowning in the icy waters. What we gonna do in the middle now?'

'We're off tomorrow. I'll have a big think and we talk about it after the tactical review on Tuesday.'

'Good. A bit of headspace before we dissect the lot. Do make sure you have a read. For what it's worth, I think Xavier's better in there than Alex. He's like-for-like. Plus Dmitriy isn't a specialist there and he's not been at the races the last few weeks.'

Cas drummed his fingers on the report. 'I understand.'

Dmitriy scrambled his phone away as Andriy entered the living room.

'I know you need it close by but it's not healthy to be glued to it. Just turn it up to full volume and leave it across the room.'

Dmitriy gave an appeasing nod.

'Feeling any better for the recovery session this morning?'

Gazing out of the floor-to-ceiling window at the lake, Dmitriy shrugged. 'A bit.'

'Good good. Hopefully last night's the wors . . .'

'I need to get out,' said Dmitriy. 'I can't sit doing nothing, waiting for the next thing.'

'Of course. Where shall we go?'

Dmitriy fiddled with his car keys in his hand. 'I go myself . . . clear my head.'

'Of course,' said Andriy, his tone dropping. 'Whatever you need.'

Andriy started over to hug him but Dmitriy simultaneously turned and headed out. *Had he just been blanked?* As he pondered, his phone vibrated. He crept to the corner furthest from the door and answered in a whisper. '*Da*?'

CHAPTER 16

'C'mon, Mr Finney. We can't be having that, not today,' said the nurse. He laid motionless for a moment then removed the pillow from over his head. His face hadn't seen a razor for days, nor his hair a comb. 'Sit yourself up then,' she said as she loitered in the doorway.

'Why? They're coming for me soon.'

'They are but look who's here no-ooow,' she said, gesturing like a magician's assistant towards the reveal. Into the doorway walked Nova, dark cap pulled down and plainly clothed.

Finney snatched at the buttons on the side of the bed to incline the top half. 'Princess!'

'I wish my hubby was that happy when I walked in the room! Lovely meeting you, darling. Bell me if you need anything, Mr Finney.'

Nova stepped in and took her cap off as the nurse closed the door. The bed inclined at a snail's pace as Finney tried to tidy his hair. 'I'm so glad you're here.'

She examined the traction rig, put her handbag down by the bedside and took his hand. 'I'm so sorry you had to be alone through this. Between losing the phone and then having already went to . . .'

'You're here now. Where's Lulu?'

'I left her with them. She's pretty upset. I wanted to check how you were before I brought her.'

'Oh, OK. Tell her Daddy'll be alright and that her magic hugs'll help get me back on my feet.'

'I will.'

'Can't say one right now'd hurt either.' She leaned over and wrapped her arms around him. He let out a deep sigh. 'This place is so bleak. I'm in here by myself most of the time, bored out of my skull. The nurses are nice enough when I see them but the doctor . . . I dunno what to make of her. As long as she does the biz I guess I can't complain. I just can't wait to get back home, cosy, for some real TLC with my girls while I get through this.'

Nova let go of him and stood up. 'We're not there anymore.' Her face quivered.

'I know, Princess,' he said, trying to soothe her. 'Don't feel guilty for one second. You weren't to know I was gonna end up . . .'

Her expression hardened. 'I'm leaving you, Ian. We're done.'

'What are you talking about, Princess.'

'I'm not yours and I'm not a fucking Princess.'

'Whoa!' Finney shoved himself further upright. 'Where the hell is this coming from all of a sudden?!'

'This isn't sudden, Ian. This has been coming for years. You just have no awareness of me and *my needs*.'

'What are you talking about?! We have Lulu. We've made a home together.'

'You snagged me, Ian. I was *nineteen*. I didn't know what I wanted.'

He grew more incredulous. '*You* wanted me. *You* pursued me!'

'But you were a grown man. You knew what you were doing and you trapped me. You wanted the family. You wanted to settle. I'm twenty-six. Twenty . . . six. Do you know how much of the world I haven't experienced yet?!'

Finney's volume rose. 'This is about that pineapple-headed fuckboy, isn't it?'

'Keep your voice down!' she hissed. 'We don't want the entire ward knowing our business.'

'What, that you're banging your teenage back-up dancer, you fucking nonce?'

'Grow up. He's two years younger than me. But it's fine that you're ten older than me?'

'Nine! You're really gonna walk out on your husband when he's laid up in the hospital, his career in tatters?'

'I'd left already. I moved my stuff out on Saturday and left you a letter. I didn't want all this. I know it hurts. It's hurt me too.'

'Boo-fucking-hoo. Hurts you too. You're *really* gonna do this with me here like this?'

'You want me to stay out of pity? We're not right for each other, Ian. There's a whole world out there I have to explore and there is for you too. You'll find somebody who likes the things you like, who wants to be more settled.'

'You fucking child. Bring me my daughter so she can live a *settled* life with somebody who doesn't have their fucking head in the clouds while you go let that dippy cunt and the rest of the Jap Street Boys run a fucking train on you.'

'Speaking like that to the mother of your own daughter. Patriarchy and pre-school all in one aren't you, you dickhead? Lulu's good with me for now, while you calm down and get back on your feet.'

'She is fucking not!' he seethed. 'You bring her here. I'll make sure she's taken care of.'

'I'm not going to discuss this while you're being so aggressive.'

'Aggressive? Aggressive?! You come in here with this shit and you don't like my tone of voice and my fucking word choice. Fuck you. Bring Lulu here to somebody who's not fucking wishing her existence away.'

'Fuck you, Ian,' she said shaking her head as she reached down for her bag. Pushing through the pain, Finney twisted his upper body and grabbed its handle at the same time.

'Get off it,' she hissed, yanking it.

'Tell me you'll bring Lulu.'

Nova took it down a notch. 'Of course I'll bring her, just after your op.'

'You'll bring her back for good? To live with me?'

Nova's face dropped. 'She needs her Mum, Ian. She's coming with *me*,' she said as she yanked again.

'She's not going globetrotting with you while you *find yourself* on a Cocks of the World Tour.'

'You're vile.'

'Yeh, I'm the vile one.'

'Just give me my bag, Ian.'

'Over my dead body.'

A sharp knock at the door sounded as it opened. The feuding couple both shot out of their skin, with Nova yanking her bag free. Finney stared a hole through her.

'Good morning, Mr Finney!' chirped the hospital assistant. 'Let's get you down to pre-op. You want a minute before we go?'

Nova retreated from the bed and wedged her cap back on. 'No, we're done thanks,' she said, backing towards the door as Finney stayed tight-lipped and sour-faced. 'I'll bring her in a few days. You'll get through this, stronger,' she said to him before vanishing out of the doorway.

As the assistant started to take him out of traction, he glowered at the space his wife left.

The players hushed as the auditorium lights dimmed.

'I hope you're all well-rested. We have hard work ahead,' said Cas from centre stage. 'First, I have news about Ian. He's had the surgery today. He'll miss the rest of the season and some of next season.'

The players slumped in their seats like a reverse Mexican wave.

'I know, I know . . . Now, we have to focus on our performance. We have to bring the league home for him.'

A gentle applause built around the room.

'Firstly, with him out, I want no uncertainty about what we do with his place. Alex; you play the next game. You and Dmitriy share the defensive responsibility.'

Near the back, Steve threw his hands up and clasped them behind his head as he watched on.

'Second, the other day was a one-off. After Ian went, that wasn't us. We draw the line underneath. We won't analyse it here. Please, don't watch it outside.'

Steve stood, shuffled out of his row and headed down the stairs. Cas watched him, trying to keep his flow.

'Forget it. We just concentrate on *our* game. We move the ball, we find the space, we work honestly with ourselves, we trust in each other.'

A few metres away, Steve walked out of the door.

'We show the world why we are top.'

Drip. Finney glared at the pump as he jabbed away at the button. No more morphine fell. He threw the button down and raked his stubbled face before closing his bloodshot, glassy eyes.

'They got you on the good shit, big man?'

Finney's eyes snapped open as he turned his head away from the door. He quickly wiped his eyes and looked back towards it. There was Charlie, Dmitriy, Steve, Cas and Victor, who was walking towards the bed holding a bunch of robot balloons.

'For The Machine, to come back stronger. Terminator knee 'n dat,' said Victor as he tied the balloons to the bed frame while the mechanical contraption strapped around Finney's knee slowly flexed and straightened it.

Finney watched his leg being moved for him, unconvinced.

'C'mon man. You got this.'

Finney did not respond, entranced by the sliding pistons.

'Big man. *Boss* man. Who'd have this better than you?'

Finney's gaze turned towards Victor. 'No-fucking-body but it still fucking happened, didn't it?'

Nobody answered.

'Look!' He pointed at his mechanised leg. 'You tell me anyone you know that looked after themselves better than me. Go on.'

Nobody responded.

'Fucking model pro. But here I fucking am. Nine months fucking minimum. May as well be twatting dog years at my age. I'm gonna pick up the biggest trophy of my fucking career on fucking crutches knowing that by the time I get back, *if* I get back, some other younger model'll be bedded in there. Nobody's needing me after a year out . . .'

'Ian . . .' said Cas, his tone low and pleading.

'You tell me one thirty-six-year-old centre-mid in our league.'

Cas could not. None of them could. The only sound came from the contraption.

'Stop talking that weak shit, man,' said Victor. 'You're our motherfuckin' captain.'

'Captain fucking *Birdseye*?'

'Pfff, c'mon man. That's a mark of respect! You all fucking distinguished 'n dat.'

Finney swatted away his comment. 'Piss off.'

'Really, big man. Which other Clooney motherfuckers you see running the game?'

Finney almost grinned.

'Which other Clooney motherfuckers you see picking up medals in any top leagues across the globe, fam?'

Finney's eyes began welling up.

'Which other Clooney motherfucker gots the fish fingers from the baddest, pengest young ting on this motherfuckin' Earth?'

Finney's face dropped 'Get out!'

The gang's faces contorted in confusion.

'Go on. You heard me. Go,' said Finney.

Dmitriy glared at Victor, shaking his head.

Cas spoke up. 'Ian, he's jus—'

'Gaffer. Don't. Please,' said Finney. 'All of you. Just leave me.'

Charlie chimed in. 'Fin – if there's owt we can do . . .'

Finney held up the morphine button. 'Unless you can make this spit out drops like a fucking PEZ dispenser, there's nowt you can do apart from going home, Chaz.' He looked at them all. 'Please.'

The gang reluctantly mobilised to leave.

'Giz a shout if you want some company anytime, fella,' said Charlie.

Finney half-heartedly nodded as he looked away.

'Peace out, big man,' muttered Victor as they began heading out.

Cas hung back and walked over to the bed, putting a hand on Finney's shoulder. 'You are strong. You will be back.'

Finney couldn't bring himself to look his manager in the eye.

As Cas left, Finney looked back at the pump and hit the button a few times. Still nothing. He squeezed his eyes shut, praying for the sound for a drip.

Lawler turned off his engine and put his thumb on the seat-belt button. Eventually, he clicked it, took a deep breath and opened his door, only to yank it back closed. Across the car park at the private hospital's entrance, Victor stormed out, trying to ignore a tirade from Dmitriy. Dmitriy grabbed him but Victor shook himself loose, accidentally slapping the phone out of Dmitriy's other hand in the process. Dmitriy scrambled over to his phone on the pavement, mouthing off at Victor, who was walking towards his car. Charlie ran out after him as Steve and Cas appeared out of the door. Steve said something to Dmitriy, who pointed over to Victor. Steve yelled after him to no avail then looked to Cas for some interjection. Cas stood quietly, hands in pockets. Shaking his head, Steve strode off leaving Dmitriy nursing his shattered phone and Cas beside him looking lost.

Lawler fastened his seat belt, scrolled through the contacts on his dash screen, tapped one and started the car. The phone began ringing as he pulled out of his space.

'Hello handsome,' answered a flirtatious female voice. 'Are you wanting something this evening?'

'Yeh . . . you got any friends?'

Magnetic markers dotted the whiteboard, linked by lines and arrows. Cas slid one of the markers left. 'We need you a bit closer to our box when Dmitriy makes the forwards move. Can you do it?'

Alex nodded earnestly. Off to the side, Steve squeezed his mouth shut as he shoved his hands into his pockets.

'Dmitriy. It's good. You're keeping the good possession and breaking the lines. When you can, pass for Victor even quicker.'

Victor glanced over to him and nodded.

'If they block that line to him, then make past one more and don't be scared to shoot yourself. When you make that space, it's all the same as the training. The ball. The goal. Just the goalkeeper is different but if you hit it the same, it doesn't matter, he can't stop it. I just want to see the training Dmitriy here for the second half. Can you bring him?'

Dmitriy nodded, towelling the sweat from his face.

'Good.' Cas turned his attention back out to the entire group. 'For Ian, guys.'

The team rose to their feet in ovation. Charlie changed the rhythm of the clap and began the whole dressing room off in a fan song, to the tune of the Motown classic 'Love Machine':

'Ian Finney
He's a football machine
Bossing our midfield, ball control's obscene

(Oo-oo-oo – yeh)
We call him The Machine
(Yeah Finney)
A Weavers tackling fiend

Laa-l-la-la-laa-l-la-laa-la-laa-Fi-i-nney
Laa-l-la-la-laa-l-la-laa-la-laaaaaaaaa'

The robot balloon hovered low, partially deflated. Finney, his stubble thick and his hair a shaggy mess, shook his head as he watched his team on TV, leading one-nil against a team in red. His gourmet hospital dinner, with the exception of the raspberry-topped panna cotta, was going cold on the table over his bed.

'You're too bloody high, kid,' he shouted towards Alex onscreen, as his team turned over possession to the reds before luckily immediately retrieving it due to an awful pass. Seven minutes remained.

The doctor walked into the room. 'Mr Finney. Do you have a few minutes for a word?'

'All I've got is time, doc,' he said as he reached for the remote, eyes glued to the screen. He hit mute and eventually tore his gaze away from the screen. 'What can I do you for?'

'Well, it's not so much a case of that as what we can do for you. We're basically at the end of our post-surgical processes now. There's nothing we can do for you here now that you can't do with the help of your club medical staff and in the comfort of your own home.'

'Yeh, the nurse has been pecking my head about it. Like a waitress in a busy restaurant asking me if I want anything else, over and over. You need my table for a bigger tipper, doc?' he said as he glanced past her at the screen.

'Not at all. We're not shy for space and I think your club's a generous tipper, to use your terms. My only concern is your recovery. We have fine sports medics and physiotherapists, but all the evidencc shows that recoveries are improved when patients can return to their everyday lives and support networks.'

'Honestly, doc, this is a home from home for me now. It's nice and quiet. The lumbar support on this mattress is outstanding. I've grown quite attached to these jelly cups,' he said as he picked up the panna cotta and dinged its ramekin with the accompanying teaspoon.

'Hartley's have really upped their game,' he said before taking a bite.

'Very funny, Mr Finney. I can't make you leave here but I will keep advising it. We have some excellent people you can speak to about adjusting to life after an injury if you think they might help the transition back home.'

'I'm grand where I am for now, thanks.'

'Try eating some of the grown-up food too while you're at it,' said the doctor, smiling wryly as she headed out.

On the TV, Alex passed the ball forward to Dmitriy and followed his run.

'No need, kid.'

Dmitriy played the ball out to Nixon. Alex continued his forward run.

'No *need*.'

Nixon played a poorly weighted pass to Alex, who got to it first but whose overstretched touch saw him then dispossessed.

'Fuck off,' he called out, leaning forward.

The opposition played to ball to a red in the gap in front of the back four.

'No. Get out at him!'

One of the Weavers' centre backs raced out to the man in possession, who dropped his shoulder and shifted the ball half a yard the other way.

'Block it!'

The red wrapped his foot around the ball, which grazed past the leg of the centre back, bent towards the top corner, hit the bar and went in.

'FUCK OFF!!!' he yelled as loud as he could as he flung the ramekin at the TV, cracking the screen. The ramekin smashed all over the floor, wobbly cream splodged everywhere. 'MotherFUCKER!'

The doctor shot back into the doorway, her eyes darting around the room to figure out what had happened. She frowned at Finney, who snapped out of his rage and realised where he was. 'I'll replace it, I promise,' he said, like a kid whose ball had smashed a neighbour's window.

CHAPTER 17

*

The foamy fingers dug deeply into their flesh as they rolled back and forth over the knobbled rollers, their hips flexors loosening a little at each pass.

'Invite the tackle but only go to ground if there's contact. And don't flail like an idiot. Falling naturally is an art just like everything else. You have to practise to make it look convincing,' said Gunnar.

'Be extremely subtle, even to the point of formlessness,' said Cas with a pronounced rhythm.

Gunnar stopped rolling and turned to Cas with an impressed smile. 'Yes! You've been reading.'

'A little bit.' Cas stopped rolling, got off the roller and kneeled up. 'Just one page or two when I wake up. It's hard for me to read the old English.'

'I think Sun Tzu himself would agree. But make sure you finish it. You'll never look at the world the same way again when you realise we're always at war; we just have those with us and those against us. Once you know how to bring the ones you want onside and deal with the others, you'll be bulletproof.'

Cas nodded in uncomfortable agreement.

'I know you're not convinced yet. I know it doesn't feel right. You're battling against the habits and thought patterns of a lifetime, thinking you can just be good and prance around and get what you want. You've seen what that's done for you so far. Finish the book. You'll be surprised how a change of perspective can take something foreign and make it feel comfortable, even good.'

Cas chuckled to himself and shook his head. 'How will you stop the playing? You love to battle too much.'

'I do but I'm tired. This has been my path for thirty years to the exclusion of all others. It's time to walk some of those others next. Knowing me, I'll probably find some serene paradise and manage to find a fight there anyway. Speaking of scrapping . . .' Gunnar nodded across to the far side of the gym where Krugg and Ted were bickering. Ted was sat in a leg press machine that had two independent foot plates and was seemingly demonstrating a slow single-legged repetition, explaining it as he went. Krugg stood next to him, arms folded, shaking his head and speaking loudly enough for them to hear his aggressive tone way across the room. Krugg reached down for a sports bottle while Ted tried to talk him around.

Cas shook his head as they both lunged forwards into a hip flexor stretch.

'What will you do after you finish?' asked Cas.

'I might move abroad, start fresh. Maybe find somebody and have something like a normal life.'

'Where will you go?'

'Somewhere they don't give a shit about football and won't know who I am.'

'Like where?'

'Maybe Oz or New Zealand or Canada. Not ruling out Thailand either.'

'Oh wow. Half the way around the world.'

'Well yeh. It's hard to live a normal life here. The profile. The money. The preconceptions. I don't want it to define me anymore. I don't know how to meet somebody under the shadow of all that.'

'It's possible.'

'I don't think so for me. I know you have but I think all that's insurmountable for me.'

'Love is not easy anywhere,' said Cas, a heaviness in his voice.

'You and Amber seem to have it pretty well-drilled.' He caught Cas navel-gazing. 'Don't you?'

A yell came from across the gym. Krugg was squirting a stream of drink out of his mouth, fountain-esque, onto Ted's crotch as he was pushing out a rep on the leg press. Bearing weight, there was precious little he could do about it. Eventually he racked the weight, got up and raged at Krugg, who stood there laughing to himself for a moment before his demeanour transformed. He squared up to Ted – a scrawnier, meeker man – who quickly quietened. Krugg headed away. Ted called after him. Krugg turned around and quizzically pointed to the GPS tracking vest he was wearing. Ted nodded. Krugg peeled it off and dumped it in a nearby bin before heading out of the door. Ted, purple in the face, plodded over to the bin.

'Why is he like this?' asked Cas as he shook his head.

'Some people are wired differently. Great when they're on your side but a fucking nightmare if they don't like you for whatever reason. I think he doesn't like the clever ones. I'll have a word.' Gunnar changed the leg he was stretching. Cas followed suit.

'Are you and Amber alright?'

Cas closed his eyes and reached an arm skywards to deepen his stretch.

'Sorry,' said Gunnar. It's none of my business.'

'No, is OK.' Cas opened his eyes, twisted side-to-side and settled. 'I don't know . . . I love her . . . I really do but I think she wants something . . . different.'

'How do you mean?'

Cas dropped his arm with a loud sigh. 'I think she wants more of . . . a man. I see how she looks at the strong, confident, successful guys. I know she loves me but I think deep down she wants something . . . stronger. Like who can fight if he needs to and chop the wood and build the things.'

'What the fuck are you talking about? You are a man. You're a fucking Warrior.'

'On the team sheet, yes.' He wrapped his hand around his opposite biceps. His fingers nearly touched his thumb at the back. 'Look at me. Who wants a child with my genes?'

'What are you talking about?! She's lucky to have you. We're lucky to have you here too. This year, with some power next to you, you'll be adding silverware to your talent and she'll be even luckier. If she doesn't recognise that, there are plenty who will.'

Cas gazed down. 'With some power next to me.'

Gunnar realised what he had said. 'Look. I'm nearly a foot taller than you. I must weigh four stone more than you. You can't do what I can do. Doesn't mean you can't learn to use a slingshot and be a little bit more like David against the other Goliaths.'

Cas nodded a little, but Gunnar could see his words had barely dented his state.

Gunnar sighed. 'If I was your size, do you think I could do what you do?' His chin scrunched as his answer tendrilled out in his mind.

'Fellas, am I alright to grab those vests from you please?' said Ted as he arrived by them.

'Of course,' said Gunnar. They both peeled theirs off and passed them over. 'I saw that before. You alright?'

Ted nodded unconvincingly.

'I don't know what his problem is but he's well out of order. I'll be having a word. With Johnstone too if I have to.'

'He just doesn't want to listen. I spend my life making myself an expert but he thinks he knows better. The ego of it!' A vein bulged out of his forehead. 'All I'm trying to do is help him, help all of you, and he treats me like shit. "Goggles" this, "You nobody" that. They don't pay me enough to take shit from people who earn in a week what I do in a year.'

'Well, we appreciate you, Ted.'

'The lengths I go to to look after everyone. These vests – next-level analysis wear! These know who you are just by how you move around in them! The fucking work I put into these and he throws it in the fucking bin and goes on at me like we're still in the playground.'

'I know, mate, I know.' Gunnar stood out of his stretch and put an arm around Ted. 'There are plenty here who appreciate your talents and understand how fortunate we are to have you looking out for us. As I said, I'll have a word.'

Ted took off his glasses and wiped the condensation off the inside of the thick lenses.

'Tell him yourself too,' continued Gunnar. 'Sometimes people just need to know you're not a soft touch. Let them know you're there and they'll shut right up.'

'Cheers, Gunnar.'

'You need any help, you let me know.'

Ted nodded. 'Thanks. See you in a bit, chaps.' He walked off a few steps then turned back. 'Oh Cas. Unbelievable the other day.'

Cas gave a proud little nod his way as he left then turned back to Gunnar. 'That was good of you,' he said as he maneuvered out of his stretch.

'Just performing my captainly duties.'

'I wish I played with you earlier,' said Cas.

Gunnar's face softened for a split second before a simper took hold of it. 'You and every other luxury player.'

*

Andriy set a paper bag and a large glossy designer shopping bag on the coffee table then slipped off his tie and unbuttoned his collar. As he heard footsteps bouncing down the stairs, he tore open the paper bag, putting some pastries on display. 'I come bearing gifts!'

Into the living room walked Emily, the model from the whiskey advert, flushed and beaming. 'Hello Mr Manager!'

Andriy sat bolt upright. 'Good evening.'

'Lovely thanks!' she said as she zipped up her jacket. 'How's yours been?' She fished a lipstick out of her bag and pottered barefooted over to the mirror.

'Educational, thanks.'

'Good good,' she said before refreshing her lipstick. 'My mum says every day's a school day. Always good to learn.' She checked her pout.

'That it is.'

Dmitriy skulked in, avoiding Andriy's gaze. He walked over to Emily and spoke in her ear. She rubbed the back of his neck and pulled him closer for a snog. Andriy turned away at the sight of tongues.

As she peeled off Dmitriy, she waved cutesily. 'Nice seeing you again, Mr Manager.'

'Safe journey.'

'Ooo, what's that?' she asked, pointing to the open bag on the table.

'They're our people's pastries.'

'They look lush. Can I have a bit of one?'

'Take a full one, darling.'

'You sure?'

He nodded and gestured towards them. She came over, took one and took a bite. 'Yummy.' She turned back to Dmitriy. 'Text me later, babe.'

He nodded and she made her way out.

Dmitriy, his lips stained red, nursed his cracked phone as he gazed out of the window. Only one of the swans sat on the lake.

'*Really?* You think you can manage the situation like this?'

Dmitriy continued.

'It doesn't even make sense. Make a new mess to cover the existing one. We pick girls *together*. You know nothing about her.'

Dmitriy put the phone in his pocket and stayed staring out.

Andriy's volume rose. 'You think this is just about you?'

'No . . . but it matters more for me.'

Andriy stopped. He slid his hands out to the sides to steady himself. 'That may be so . . .' His voice petered out. 'That may be so.' He stood, walked over to the mirror and restored his collar and tie. 'Good job one of us is willing to take responsibility.' He paced back over to the coffee table and took a *piroshki*. 'For you . . . if you still have the appetite.' Rustling the larger glossy bag next to it – 'And a little something else. Although maybe it's a bit late now.' He marched out.

Dmitriy glanced over to the doorway and then to the bag, out of which poked a patch of scarlet. He remained rooted to the spot, gutted.

Tiny rainbows threaded through the players' boots brightened up the otherwise drab dressing room.

Cas tried to gee up his players. 'We're better than this. Than them. We had all the ball and they catch us once. We need to work the ball faster, make the spaces to find the last quality pass more easily.'

A towel draped over his head, Dmitriy stooped a little further forward, his eyes on nothing but the laces decorating his usually all-black boots.

'We need to play our game, show who we are this half!'

The players cheered their boss's words and carried on their preparations for the second half as he went to talk with some of his staff.

Victor bumped shoulders with Dmitriy. 'Bro, you good?'

The towel nodded as Dmitriy started to untie one of his boots.

'C'mon, fam. We need some fuckin' Dmitriy dynamite. We can't let these fairies do us. Their five keeps pulling at my shorts bruv . . . my shorts! What sort of violation is that?'

The towel nodded. Victor snatched it off Dmitriy's head.

'Get your head out from under there and into the game, D.'

'I'll be OK,' said Dmitriy as he pulled off a boot and reached up into his locker shelves. 'Need the better grip.' He pulled out a pair of the same model of boots but with studs for harder ground and put them by his feet. They had his customary black laces.

'Tell you what, fam. The rainbow looks fly on those black-outs. Fucks up my gold vibes though,' he said, pointing to his own boots.

Dmitriy began to wedge his free foot into one of his fresh boots.

'You re-lacing?'

'No time,' said Dmitriy as he removed his other boot.

'Best make time, rudeboy, or you'll have McGlynn up your crack.'

Dmitriy paused for a moment, yanked his foot out of the new boot and began to pull the laces out of it.

Victor lowered his voice. 'You think I wanna wear these? Where my people are from, they lynch and stone these motherfuckers. But here, we stay woke or go broke. Wear dem laces, cash dem cheques.'

Dmitriy started to thread the rainbow laces into his fresh boot, tugging them taut.

'They can make us wear their silly shit all they want. We know what we're about.'

The howl of a wolf almost drowned out the sound of the door closing but she heard it. Amber turned the wildlife documentary down and braced herself. Cas eventually wandered into the room and sat in the armchair across from her. She looked over to get his attention, but his eyes were fixed on the screen.

'I know it's not what you wanted but it's not a loss,' she said.

'I know.'

'It takes character to come back. It's a positive.'

'It is.'

'You had most of the play.'

'We did.'

'Well, at least you have the break now. Some time to breathe. To think.'

'We do.'

She tapped the remote control on the arm of the sofa. 'Why are you sat all the way over there?'

He finally glanced her way. She nodded for him to come over. He mustered a sad smile. After heaving himself up, he wandered over and sat at the far end of the couch.

She tilted her head and mirrored his smile. 'That's not by me. Come hug me.'

'Not right now. Can we just watch?'

She dropped the remote to the floor. 'Oh . . . OK.' She forced her eyes back to the TV.

'Can you turn it up, please?' said Cas.

She tried to smile as she nodded but then couldn't find it. She hunted between the arm and the seat cushion, then stood up to see if she had sat on it, eventually noticing it on the floor. Up she turned it.

A sanctuary worker stroked a wolf. The majestic beast blissfully cuddled up to her as she rubbed its ear. Suddenly, a growl sounded off-camera. It panned rapidly.

'The confidence and comfort are short-lived as the alpha reappears,' said the narrator. The alpha prowled over and stood against the first wolf, neck to neck, seeming affectionate until it bared its teeth and rumbled a low growl. The first slightly smaller wolf laid before it. 'Here we see the pack hierarchy firmly reinforced as the beta wolf rolls over, showing its throat to the alpha in an act of submission.' The alpha snarled. The beta quivered underneath.

Cas popped up to standing. 'I'm going to shower and go to bed. End this day. *Mañana es otro día.*'

'It will be. You sure you don't wanna watch the rest with me? It's done in fifteen minutes or so. I just have to see what happens with the cubs.'

Cas watched the beta trembling under the alpha's fangs. 'I know you do. I say goodnight now in case I'm sleeping when you come up, *mi amor.*'

'Night, honey.'

As he left, he glanced back to see her fixated on the alpha prowling away victorious.

CHAPTER 18

The plane's door opened. Out onto the airstair stepped Dmitriy. The airport lights burned bright against the biting, black sky. As he descended the stairs, his freezing breath swirled in front of him. He pulled the zip of his scarlet down jacket right up to his chin. After checking left and right along the mostly empty tarmac, he nodded to himself and blew out a deep breath.

The sounds of his solitary footsteps and his suitcase wheels whirring filled the corridor. He checked his watch – 00:37. The upcoming sign, written in Russian, said:

NO RETURN TO BAGGAGE RECLAIM AFTER THIS POINT

He swished through the first set of automatic doors, then the second opened.

'*Der'mo*,' he cursed inaudibly, before slapping on a huge smile. A large crowd holding signs and flags cheered as he walked into the arrivals lounge. A few security guards tried to keep them at bay as they snapped photos and held objects out for autographs. He took and signed a few items before the guards ushered him forwards, to the dismay of the hungry horde.

Two saw him out to a waiting black Aurus. As the trunk popped, and before the driver could get out, one of the guards had picked up Dmitriy's case.

'You don't need to do that,' said Dmitriy in his mother tongue.

'It's my pleasure, Mr Lebedev. Welcome home.'

The hotel was sublime. The food had been sorely missed. His new international teammates welcomed him like a long-lost brother. If anything, they passed him the ball a little too much in training. His new manager built their play to maximise their new premium player.

There it was. LEBEDEV 10 on the back of the Russian red. He had not seen it for six years, since his youth international days; before he had stopped flying, all-bar his yearly 'tranquilised' trip home. He lifted the shirt by its shoulders, heeding every little detail of the design before slipping it off its hanger, making sure the hook did not catch the shirt and came out as smoothly as possible.

The team-talk, the chants, all in his language. It was utterly surreal. The whole game felt dream-like. The realest he knew it to be was during the goal celebrations, when his teammates bumped him and one jumped on him for a piggy-back following an assist.

At the final whistle, he could have sworn he had drifted off again. He clapped the sea of red shirts as they sang his name. They already had a song for him. Kazimir's sturdy mitt gently slapped his face as he left the pitch. As heavy as it felt, he still was not sure.

Pride beamed from their faces as she opened her arms.

'My boy,' she said as she embraced him. 'And now a man of our nation.'

'It's good to see you, Mama,' he said, kissing her cheek.

'My boy!' His father opened his arms and welcomed him in for a thumping hug. 'Back where you belong,' he rejoiced, pounding his back heartily.

'Hello, Papa.'

'Mr Volkov, lovely meeting you,' said Dmitriy's mother, extending her hand towards him.

'The pleasure is mine, Mrs Lebedev,' he said as he shook it and kissed her cheek.

'Great meeting you, sir,' said Dmitriy's father, shaking the manager's hand.

The maître d' walked over to them and opened her body, inviting them into the executive brasserie.

'I will leave you to catch up. You should be very proud. Your son will lead us into a new golden era.' He turned to Dmitriy. 'Fantastic work. Keep that up and we have big things ahead.'

His father sliced the Tomahawk off its bone.

'This is so good,' said his mother, tucking into her stroganoff.

'I can't believe with everything on the menu, you ordered that. It's like somebody in England going to a Michelin star place and ordering fish and chips,' Dmitriy said with a chuckle.

'Well, firstly, there's nothing wrong with the traditional dishes done well. There's stroganoff and then there's *stroganoff*. And secondly, I didn't mean the food, Dima. I meant having you here and knowing you'll visit more often.'

He smiled cautiously.

'I'm so glad you can fly now without all that carry on.'

'So am I. But I'll still love to have you come visit me too.'

Dmitriy's father shaved the gristle off the bone before he started on the meat. 'Anywhere with that murky piss-water as its national drink isn't somewhere I can get excited about visiting.'

Dmitriy smirked. 'Have you tried the *Khrabryy* yet?'

'I have.'

'And?'

'Not bad.'

Dmitriy's chin tilted up as the hint of a grin appeared.

'Maybe more to your mother's taste though.'

The grin passed.

'I liked it very much! Speaking of us ladies, am I still the only one in your life?' she asked with a twinkle in her eye.

'Maybe,' he replied coyly.

'Ooooo! Tell me more,' she said.

'You got pictures?' asked his father before he had a chance.

Dmitriy rolled his eyes, pulled his cracked phone out and began to find her picture.

'Her name's Emily. She's a model trying to get into acting too.' He passed the phone over towards his parents, his mother rubbernecking a glimpse as his father keenly grabbed it.

'She's *beautiful*, son,' said his mother as his father squinted and moved the phone away from himself to arm's length, tucking his chin back as far as possible.

'I want to see your girlfriend and you give me this junk to look at her on?'

'It's your eyes that are junk, Papa. Mama saw just fine.'

She reached down to her purse.

'And she's not my girlfriend. We've only been out a few times.'

His mother passed a pair of spectacles to his father.

'He won't wear them even though he *clearly* needs them.'

His father tutted as he put them on. 'But if I wear these too much, you run the risk of me seeing you're not the fairest of them all, dear.'

'Charming, isn't he? Just no Prince Charming anymore!' Her and Dmitriy laughed.

'You have your father's taste, son. Look at her!' he said, a growl in his throat.

His wife shook her head.

'Meat in all the right places.'

'Alexei! You wonder why he never brings anybody home!'

He barely heard her, inspecting the photo. 'Good hips.'

'Here we go,' said Dmitriy, covering half his face.

'What? What's wrong with a man appreciating the female form? A beautiful woman is nature's purest art for a man.'

Mother and son exchanged glazed glances.

'And the form is not purely aesthetic. Like this bone is perfectly evolved to hold this juicy meat, the beautiful woman has perfectly evolved to attract the man and carry his children.' He leaned towards his wife and kissed her cheek tenderly. 'We were made for each other, my love. We knew it from the first time we laid eyes on each other.'

She smiled and lay her head on his shoulder.

'Leave him, Alexei. He has plenty of time.'

Her husband nodded, reached for his glass and lifted it for a toast. His wife followed and Dmitriy obliged.

'To our boy. Now our nation's man.'

Dmitriy smiled and gratefully nodded, leaning in to clink glasses.

'And the Lebedevs of the future.' He clinked Dmitriy's glass and winked.

Dmitriy's insides sunk as he kept his smile high and raised his glass to touch his mother's.

CHAPTER 19

'So this is the shape we practise this week,' said Cas, pointing up to the tactical drawing on the screen. 'The extra player in the back will make us more solid while we adapt the system.' He turned the lights up. 'Before you go, I have news on Ian. He's good, he's home now but he's asking for no visitors yet . . .'

'Bullshit, fam,' Victor whispered to Charlie. 'That's ain't him. That's poontang thumb-down shit all day long. A man needs his boys around.'

'. . . I know, I know,' said Cas to the audience's groan, 'I'll tell you when he says is OK. That's all. We start on the new shape tomorrow.'

The players stood and began to file out. Bringing up the rear, Steve invited Cas off to one side.

'Five at the back. Is this really what we're doing?'

'Yes. You suggested we make it tighter,' replied Cas.

'You haven't been reading the reports, have you? Just shoving an extra body back there won't help. It'll just give the full backs even more license to get forward. We both know the issue is in the midfield. Alex isn't tough enough. I know you wanted to give it a go but you've seen it yourself. Him and Dmitriy just don't give us the cover we need. Why don't we just swap him out for Xavier? He's exactly what we need in there. His physicality. His bite.'

'I respect your opinion but I make the final decision,' said Cas, straining to sound neutral.

'I know it's your call. I just wanna know why you won't make the change that's so glaringly obvious to everybody? The answer is there grafting away right under your nose.'

'You want bite?' snapped Cas. 'We're not in the wild, Steve. You want tough?! We're not at war. We're *playing football.* We will win by *playing football.* Our way.'

'*Your* way, you mean. Why are you the only one here who won't accept that sometimes war's part of the game?'

Cas would not meet his gaze.

Steve shook his head and made for the door. As he opened it, he called back, 'What's more important, guv? Winning or doing things your way?'

The door swished closed leaving Cas all alone.

Scrolling down a social media feed, his finger stopped on a selfie of a student-aged fan with Dmitriy and Emily, all smiling, outside a high-end restaurant. The caption read:

OMG. How perfect are these two together? #couplegoals #weavers #playbyyourownrules @dmlebedev @emilycara

Andriy closed his phone, putting it down next to Dmitriy's, which, with its pristine new screen, was plugged into a laptop across Dmitriy's coffee table. Typing away was Feofan, a large, ungainly man in a three-quarter length leather jacket. Thick, black-rimmed glasses magnified his pin-prick eyes, which sat too close to one another.

'Does he have a landline in here?'

'If he does, it's probably next to the gramophone.'

Feofan looked at him deadpan.

'I'm not sure.'

'I'll take a look. OK. Aside from that, I have all the data I require. The perpetrator never uses the same mode of communication, so depending on his contact frequency this may take a while. I will find him. Your data will be recovered and deleted.'

Feofan reached across the table and unplugged the phone from his laptop cable. Andriy reached back across, sliding a bulging envelope Feofan's way. 'Thank you so much. As agreed, the rest upon completion.'

'My pleasure. There's not much I hate more in this world than blackmailing scum.'

COLIN
Today we saw the Weavers adopt five at the back for the first time. What's your verdict, Pete?

PETE
I don't think it worked. Velasquez had to change something but it's the soft centre, not the back.

COLIN
It's been quite the double-whammy, hasn't it, losing Lawler and then Finney within a

few weeks of each other? And one directly at the hands of the other.

PETE

I know, it was tragic. We hope Finney's rehab is going well . . . Just look at the team's form these past few months without him and Lawler. It's bordered on catastrophic really. That decision to let Lawler go was baffling even before Finney's injury. He was a rough diamond – a bit too rough at times – but if they could have rounded out his aggression and given him some of that Velasquez finesse, he would have been a massive part of their future. Now, he's an integral part of the Warriors' charge up the table, absolutely bullying midfields left and right.

COLIN

He's just received a one-match suspension for his fifth booking of the season, four of which he's received since February. It doesn't seem like Magnusson is trying to round that aggression out?

PETE

No, it doesn't. He's feeding it. He'll make him into a formidable player, just a different sort than he would have been. Aggression is probably the defining characteristic of a Magnusson team and I think he accepts his players are always going to be playing on the edge.

COLIN
And the Weavers are on the edge of disaster at the moment, aren't they? Through a glut of draws, they've squandered most of their substantial lead.

PETE
Absolutely. If it weren't for Ezemonye's golden touch, they'd have fallen away completely. They need to hope his streak continues because their other goals have dried up. Their main creative spark Lebedev's gone missing these last few months when they've needed him most.

COLIN
Yes, he's suffered a massive dip in form. What do you think is going on there?

PETE
I'm not entirely sure. The lad has it all – we've seen that over the last year or so – but he doesn't look himself at the moment. Maybe it's the lack of quality and experience around him. Maybe more defensive responsibility is putting him in areas where he can't find those incisive passes so quickly and he's less inclined to break forward. Maybe it's just the

pressure of the business-end of the season. Whatever it is, they need him to step up and be the game-changer we know he can be for them.

COLIN

Most of the challengers have been faltering too. Who do you think will mount the largest challenge to the Weavers now?

PETE

Given their momentum, my money would go on the Warriors. If the Weavers don't stop their slide, the season finale between them at No Man's Land that looked completely unremarkable when the fixtures came out could be a title-decider.

COLIN

Given that this is still all in Weavers' hands, that makes the million-pound question 'will they stop their slide?'

PETE

They have the ability to stop it, no doubt about it, but I'm not sure they have the psychological strength. Something's not right there and as talented as Velasquez is, I'm not sure he's dealing with it. Don't deal with whatever it is and it will expand and create cracks. Put further pressure on those cracks and teams can collapse. The question really is 'will he honestly take a look at himself and his team, identify whatever's going on and deal with it?'

Everybody continued on their trajectories over the coming few weeks.

Home, mostly alone, Finney could not muster his usual discipline to attack his rehab. He missed a few of his scheduled sessions at the club, found himself busting or booming in his self-care at home and spent most of his time watching his old games or Nova's music videos with a bottle of something strong in his hand. When Lulu visited, he pulled it together somewhat. His newly dark mane drew no comments from Nova.

Lawler received his first red of the campaign for two yellows, either of which could have merited red. It was not always his shoulder the half-time hand would land on, but he had proven himself capable when it was. Between Lawler's general ferocity and the Warriors' growing reputation, the half-time hand often wasn't necessary, as they dominated – or were at least given extra unearned half-yards here and there – in games that came almost as thick and fast as Lawler's hotel rendezvouses.

Game after game, it rained goals and chips for Victor. His goal-a-game ratio kept the Weavers off a losing streak, while his poker winnings – larger by the week in Finney's absence – bought him yards of gold chain and the confidence to draw out negotiations on a new contract. Still on a youth player contract with just over a year left, he knew he held all the cards for a megadeal.

Andriy saw less of Dmitriy while Dmitriy saw more of Emily. With her modelling profile, his growing presence in the Russian media, the release of their sensual black-and-white advert and their public outings, they were shifting into the category of celebrity couple. As Dmitriy's agent and manager, the traction that #dmlebedev was gaining across social media should have been cause for celebration for Andriy. Scrolling most nights through the mentions with a large glass of *Khrabryy* in his other hand, he was anything but celebratory.

Dmitriy's form remained flat. While he became more efficient in his new role, he played even more within himself, not playing forward as quickly and not dribbling at as many openings. The armband seemed more like a shackle to him. The few times shooting opportunities presented themselves, he tried to force cutbacks that were not on. On a few occasions, Steve had to break off his condescending rants at Alex and remind him to lead the team's clap to their fans at full-time. For all his smiling while out with his girlfriend, his eyes deadened as the weeks passed. The antacids he had recently started chugging did nothing for his growing queasiness.

To Amber's despair, Cas's working hours grew ever longer. Thunderous treadmill workouts to sultry soul jams and footage analysis would go late into the night, sometimes spilling into the next day. For the first time during their marriage, he had taken to occasionally sleeping in the guest room, saying he did not want to wake her even though she insisted she didn't mind.

Steve grew quieter with Cas and more vocal with the players as Cas grew quieter with everyone but himself. Steve sometimes saw him walk off into corners to have words with himself. He occasionally noticed how Cas, during conversations that desperately needed the manager's contribution, stood silently apart – moving his tightly closed mouth as if he was uttering words he did not want to let out.

Draws were not as piercing as losses, but a team could still die by the cuts of a thousand of them, or even six from their last seven matches. And maybe the pain of a loss, a real wound, would have caused him to snap out of his haze and stop the bleeding. But it did not come.

As the hope bled out of their season, nobody was more drained than Cas. Under the spotlights of the media, the fans' expectation and the analysis auditorium, he appeared gaunter and smaller than usual. He had never been one to pay attention to the papers but the differences around him were palpable. The supporters' gazes were duller. Though they still sang, their voices were weaker. In analysis meetings, Steve sat in the back corner, unimpassioned. The players, who used to sit as a unit filling the front half, were spread throughout the auditorium, their attention more divided. As he tried to examine their faces to see whether they were still with him, the spotlight blinded him.

In the silence between his words, he was tormented by internal chatter and a strange hyper-focus on the sounds of his breathing and heartbeat, which seemed, through some illusion, to grow infinitesimally faster.

During the words themselves, which seemed to lose their volume as they left his mouth, he could feel his blood being pushed out into his limbs. As it swished back to his centre, he could swear it felt lighter, as if with every beat he was losing one more drop.

CHAPTER 20

*

Crack. A cluster of ice cubes was smashed apart and scooped into a glass by a bartender, who then filled it with sparkling water. She served it, politely smiling with her unnaturally luscious lips, to Cas who sat alone at the bar. He looked over his shoulder to his teammates: all in tuxedos, scattered in an expansive black sea of evening wear. He turned back and took a sip. A hand landed on his shoulder.

'Life and soul, aren't you?' said Gunnar. 'You on the strong stuff there?'

'Ha, no. I need to be one hundred per cent focused for the weekend.'

'Good for you.'

Gunnar waved the bartender back over.

She flipped her hair, leaned forward and smiled at him for a solid second before speaking. 'What can I get you, Mr Magnusson?'

Gunnar shuddered. 'Don't call me Mister, darling. I'm not my dad. Call me Gunnar. What's your name?' He extended his hand for her to shake.

'Bella.'

'That's literally a gorgeous name,' he said as their handshake lingered. 'Hmmm . . . what'll quench my thirst?' he asked, eyeing her and then scanning the bar. 'Give me a double G and T please.'

Her face braced. 'I'm sorry. I'm not meant to serve the players alcohol.'

'Aren't some of the best things those things you aren't meant to do?' He grinned.

She raised one of her pristinely curved eyebrows a smidgen and bit her bottom lip. 'As long it's just between us?'

'It'll be our secret, won't it?' he said, twirling a finger towards all three of them as he turned to Cas, who raised an unimpressed eyebrow. 'What am I doing? Make it a treble, just fill it as high as his,' he said, pointing to Cas's sparkling water. He grinned at Cas. 'C'mon . . . let me enjoy my last gala.'

The bartender smirked as she readied the drink. Cas sat back in his seat, not knowing what to say. She fiddled around under the bar before sliding Gunnar's glass over on a napkin.

'There you go. If you need anything else, just call.' She idled for a moment as they smiled at one another before moving off to serve another party-goer along the bar.

Gunnar took a long drink. As Cas watched him, he noticed a name and phone number written on the napkin below and snickered. 'Ridiculous. Did you even notice?'

Gunnar finished his mouthful and noticed the napkin. 'Ha, original. Sexy girl throwing it at a sexy rich footballer.' He sarcastically smiled over at the bartender then raised his glass to Cas. 'Here's to going out with a bang and to the next chapter.'

'Cheers.' They clinked glasses.

Gunnar downed his drink, put the napkin in his pocket and stood up. 'Come on. Accompany my last schmooze.'

Cas got up and followed Gunnar into the crowd.

The duo sat back at the bar. The now-tipsy Gunnar swirled his ice cubes around an almost-empty glass.

Cas spied Johnstone doing the rounds across the room and looked back at Gunnar's reddened cheeks. 'You want to go soon?'

'There's nowhere I'd rather be . . . than right here. But somewhere else. You know what I mean?'

'Umm, not really,' replied Cas, still with half an eye on Johnstone.

'You know, my dad got me my first Copas when I was like, three?'

Cas shook his head with a small smile.

'*He* made this my game . . . I was like a science project for him . . . drilled me every day with ball work . . . constant video analysis. You know, he read me *On War* as a fucking bedtime story? He had little mnemonics and rhymes for all sorts of shit. *Destabilise, dominate and destroy* – the three Ds of psychological warfare.' He knocked his index finger against his temple a few times. 'He got right in there. What sort of fucking childhood is that? He made me so good I basically didn't have a choice. I had to do this. I had to have this life. Without all that, I'd have gone another way . . . but here I am . . . to my cunt father!' He raised his glass a touch but waited for no clink.

Cas looked at Gunnar's sullen face. 'You've had an amazing career. How many people won so much?'

'Look . . . I know people would kill for it . . . but was it really winning if it wasn't my path?'

Cas pondered his point. 'If this wasn't even your path, imagine how good life will be now you can choose your own.'

'But what if I can't? What if walking this path has made it impossible for me to walk others?'

'You're *Gunnar Magnusson*. You can walk any path you want.'

Gunnar swirled his glass again, watching the ice melt. The bartender reappeared, glowing. 'Can I get you anything else there, Gunnar?'

Gunnar swirled his glass, sinking further into himself.

'He's OK for now, thank you.'

She twinkled a smile and moved on.

'In a few days, you'll have one more winner's medal in your collection and you can leave this behind you forever. You'll have all the opportunity to do whatever you want and be with whoever you want because of who you are.'

Eyes down, Gunnar was as despondent as Cas had ever seen him.

'I'm sad you won't be here every day, but I'm excited for you.'

Without a word, Gunnar heaved himself up and headed in the direction of the toilets, leaving Cas at a loss.

Nursing his glass, Cas checked his watch. Ten minutes had gone by. While he thought, a deep frown emerged. He got up and made his way through the crowd.

*

The suited doorman scanned a pair of ticket QR codes and waved the couple, who were dressed to the nines, past him through the Weavers' hospitality suite entrance. With nobody else queued behind them, he took a moment to straighten his tie then looked down at his left shoe. He lifted its inner edge.

The leather upper was starting to gap away from the sole. Aware of somebody approaching, he autonomously put his hand out for their tickets. As he looked up, he was instead handed a stuffed brown envelope.

Inside, beautiful people dressed to impress mingled and danced. Dmitriy, looking perfect but feeling far from it, introduced Emily to Charlie and Tiffany. Finney sat alone at a table, his leg in a brace and his crutch on the floor. While passing, Jason said hi and complimented his monochromatic mane, leaving Finney with a face like thunder. Aside from him, the Weavers Trust Gala was livelier than most formal events. Victor, in a golden tux jacket and matching Air Jordans, stepped away from the DJ booth as an Afrobeat track began. He sauntered to the centre of the dancefloor, clearing a way for himself, and began busting moves. A crowd assembled around him, cheering him on. A few seconds later, Charlie emerged from the crowd, moseying towards Victor in the middle, shooing him back to give him space. Victor laughed and invited him forwards, as Charlie burst into an even more exuberant dance than him. The crowd went wild. As Charlie wrapped up his set in an arms-folded pose, Victor went to raise his hand like a triumphant fighter but playfully batted it back down and started round two.

Away from the dancefloor, Amber, Cas and Steve watched on, all smiles, as they greeted each other. Amber, in a shimmering royal blue evening dress, hugged the tuxedoed Steve tightly.

'It's been too long, Steve. How are you?' she said before kissing his cheek.

'Ah, you know, same old same old.'

'Are you managing to stay a little saner than this one?' she said, laying her hands on Cas's arm.

'I don't think Steve has been sane since the nineties,' said Cas.

The trio chuckled.

Amber pointed to the dance battle. 'If you need to blow off some steam, a bit of that'd loosen you both up.'

'Only thing that'd loosen is my limbs clean off my body,' said Steve. 'What'll loosen *me* up is a treble. Can I get you anything while I'm there?'

'Can you get us a bottle of Bodegas Hermanos and two glasses please?' asked Cas, who started to pull out some cash only for Steve to bat it away.

'It's a free bar.'

'I don't think you get this on a McGlynn free bar,' said Cas, trying again to pass Steve the cash.

Steve slapped it aside. 'Just buy me some Spanish classes so I can pronounce it.'

Steve headed off to the bar. Cas put his palm on the small of Amber's back and gave her a lingering kiss on the cheek.

'*Mi amor.* I am sorry for how I was the last few weeks.'

'Months,' she replied softly.

He nodded. 'Yes, months. Too long. It's not been good here and I bring that home to you. *Lo siento.*'

She studied his face for a moment then wrapped her arms around him. 'Thank you. I know how hard things have been here. I want this for you, and I want us to be good too. Just don't push me away. Talk to me.'

'I know, I know. There's so much going on I don't know how to say sometimes.'

Amber nodded and laid her palm on his face. 'I know. When the words won't come, just be with me.' They kissed. 'Maybe when Victor's playlist has finished we can dance?' asked Cas.

'*Perfecto.*' She rested her head on his shoulder. 'And perhaps a private one later too.' Cas grinned and kissed her again.

A loud tap on the microphone signalled the music to stop.

'Ladies and gentle men. Put your hands together for this evening where we celebrate all things charitable!'

As the crowd clapped, a sickening panic rose in Cas. His gaze darted around the room until he looked up to the balcony overlooking the crowd.

There stood the microphone-toting Gunnar. 'You really are a generous lot.'

As he fell flaccid, Cas's hold on Amber loosened. The crowd stirred as others registered the speaker.

'You put your hands in your pockets for good causes. You give the sportingly impoverished your beautiful game. You allow my team and many others plenty of goals to keep things interesting. You even let me in here tonight. It's heartwarmingly charitable, truly.'

The power to Gunnar's microphone cut. He mockingly tapped the microphone then shouted up, 'Ha. Maybe not entirely charitable after all! You know what, maybe it's not charity *at all.* Maybe you're just too weak to stop others taking what's yours.'

Steve shouted up from the crowd. 'Get out, Magnusson!'

'Ah, Mr Frank!' He pointed down at Steve with his dead mike then pointed it bolt upright. 'At least somebody here has a spine.'

Steve jogged towards an exit, followed by Charlie and Victor. Finney struggled to his feet and hobbled way behind.

'You know what, Weavers? It's not your fault. A team can only be as strong as its leader.

You've seen what your players can do with strong management. Your agents have my number. Cassie is a gentle man . . . so gentle he lets others take what I'd never let them take.'

Cas froze, barely even breathing.

'He let us take one of your own at a crucial time. He let other teams back in the race just because he's desperate to prove his football is so good you needn't do a bit of dirty work. He couldn't even keep me out of this event on his own turf. What chance do you really think his leadership gives you? Is he even here?' He put his hand above his eyes, squinted and scoured the audience until he found Cas. 'There he is! Letting me speak without so much as a peep. Amber, darling . . . it's been a while . . . how'd you stay with him all this time after tasting a real . . .?'

A door behind Gunnar flew open and he was shoved stumbling by Steve. Victor and Charlie burst through the flapping doors and squared up to Gunnar.

Amber looked to her husband, who looked like a little boy lost, eyes riveted on the scuffle above.

'Yes Steve! You should lead here, not that little maggot.' He forced his way past Charlie and Victor to the balcony and shouted at Cas, 'You'd best hope they're still ready to make up for your lack of fight in a few weeks.' He gleefully dropped the mike off the balcony before Charlie, Victor, Steve and a few others jostled him out of an exit. Finney arrived through the doors just as they disappeared and slammed his crutch down.

Cas finally took his eyes off the balcony. Amber was gone. He desperately scanned the room for her and hurried out, leaving the party in disarray.

After ten minutes of frenzied searching, Cas found Amber sobbing by their car. He tried to hug her but she pulled away. His heart heavy, he opened her door. She climbed in. The only sound between them during the journey home was her sniffling. He could barely bring himself to look her way.

Hundreds of times he went to say something. Every single one of them, he failed. As she climbed into bed and tucked herself in, he almost catatonically unbuttoned his shirt. She turned away, still beside herself, and turned off the lamp, her sobs filling the darkness.

Cas woke to his phone alarm, reaching down beside the bed to turn it off. He still had not replaced the bedside table. The brush and colour of carpet still marked where it once was. His phone showed a text from McGlynn.

Meet me at the stadium, 11am.

He rolled back over. Amber's side was empty. Shifting out of bed, he noticed her closet was half-empty.

Cas skidded into the dining area. Amber sat at the table inspecting a burned-out candle, packed bags by her side. Her eyes turned to Cas, searing him for a long moment.

'Are you going to say something?'

He squirmed and broke eye contact.

'You have to *say something!* That man . . . in front of everyone . . . and you said nothing. Say something or I go.'

He trembled uncontrollably and brought a hand to his mouth. She stood, grabbed her shoulder bag and wheelie suitcase and headed straight at Cas. He averted his eyes but she grabbed his jaw and pulled his face round.

'Why didn't you defend me? SAY SOMETHING!'

Tears streamed down her face. She slammed his chest with her shoulder bag. He remained tight-lipped and his eyes flitted away from meeting hers. She shoved his face away and pushed past him towards the front door, sobbing all the way.

As she opened it, Cas broke his silence. 'Because he was saying the truth.'

Amber stopped dead in her tracks, eventually turning to face him. 'You think I . . .?'

'I know. A few years ago, just before I stopped playing. He was here. In our bed. With you. I saw how you looked at him when you met him.'

'How can you say that?! I've done nothing but love you even though you've not been right with me for years. And this is why? You think I did something with that smarmy twat?!'

'With the *strapping man*. I know you did.'

'Tell me, *Señor Genius*. How do you know?'

*

Sat up in bed, Cas took *The Art of War* out of his bedside drawer and opened it at the bookmark. He looked perplexedly at it – the bookmark was nearer the start than he had read to. A passage was underlined:

<u>Attack him where he is not prepared, appear where you are not expected.</u>

*

'The morning after my last Warriors charity party, I open the book in my bedside drawer and it had some new underlinings in it that I didn't do. I thought it's you but I forget to ask. A few days later, after we lost my last game, he told me.'

*

Cas sat and slumped his head into his hands. He felt the bench to his right give. A moment later, he was jolted out of his personal darkness as something soft hit his hand, immediately followed by a jingle. A towel rested against his right hand and a set of Range Rover keys had dropped to the floor below. A large pair of feet wearing Copas stood by them. He scooped the keys up and, without looking to his right, set them back on the towel. Then he swivelled to his left and unlaced one of his boots. Beside him, the shirtless Gunnar picked up his towel and started scrubbing his hair dry, disgust etched deep into his face.

A yell came from a player having his knee examined by a physio on one of the treatment tables. As the player lambasted the physio, Gunnar leaned in towards Cas and whispered, 'You been reading your book in your little bedside table these last few days? Did you see the new part I underlined for you? Your book wasn't the only thing I was inside while I was there, *honey*.'

Cas's insides plummeted. His eyes bulged. Breathing halted. He turned to Gunnar, who sneered back his way. He broke eye contact and turned away, mind and guts churning.

'You call yourself a man, turning your back on me . . .on us . . . and pretending nothing's happened? Say something, you little prick.' He rose to his feet, towering over Cas, who was now turned away, frantically stuffing his clothes into his holdall.

*

Amber's tears had ceased. 'And you believed him?! He came here that night utterly wasted. He was an absolute state. I saw he'd driven here and said he should get a taxi home but he asked if he could sleep it off here. I said no problem, he could have a guest room. When I went up to check on him, he was in *our* room on *our* bed. I tried to shift him and he grabbed me and kissed me, the fucking creep. I told him to fuck off and that was that.'

Amber locked in on Cas, whose face wheeled through a kaleidoscope of shock, horror and humiliation. She quietened. 'For all this time . . . I thought it was the losing that took it out of you. The retiring. Is this why you retired so young?'

'But nothing happened?'

'Of course nothing fucking happened. I am your WIFE.'

A glimmer of a smile appeared through Cas's tears. 'You were true to me.'

'Of course I was but you weren't to me. You thought I shagged your best friend and you said nothing for *years*! You thought that of me all this time. You've done nothing but push me away.'

'Sorry! I thought . . . but you're my wife. I love you. I'd never leave you . . .'

'But you'd punish me with your silence and your moodiness, smashing shit up without a word of explanation. You believed your friend over me.'

'I'm so, so sorry. He's not my friend. He's a *psicópata*. He tried to come between us.'

'He tried but he failed. You did this. You didn't have the balls to talk to me all this time just like you didn't say anything to him last night. You've barely touched me for years.

We don't have a family because of this, because of you! What sort of man are you?!' Boiling with contempt, she turned her back and left.

By the time he had snapped out of his stupor and ran to the door, she had driven off.

He shut the door and leaned his head against it. As he turned, he noticed the engagement photo from Parc Güell was crooked again. He snatched it off the wall, cocked his arm back but stopped himself from launching it. After a few deep breaths, he placed it back on the wall straight. In its reflection, his face strengthened.

CHAPTER 21

The gunmetal clock read 11:05 as the bleary-eyed Cas trudged in and sat down. Across the oversized desk, McGlynn twirled round in a larger version of Cas's office chair.

'I don't like to be kept waiting.'

'I apologise. Some things came—'

'I don't want your excuses. Excuses are for losers.' He leaned forward. 'Last night . . . was a fucking circus. You let him come here and disrespect us in our home in front of everyone. We had some very important guests here last night. You'd better pray that nobody videoed it.'

Cas started to reply but McGlynn swatted away his attempt.

'Ah ah. Have I asked for your reply yet? The last few months have been a shambles. We were clear and now it's going to the last day if we're lucky. There are concerns about your team selection and tactics. I've heard you look lost when you're giving team talks. I don't think you're fit to lead this team anymore and all that'll prove me wrong is a league win. We have a solid number two who can step in if needs be.'

'May I speak, Andy?'

'Mr McGlynn.'

'Andy, first, I didn't let him in but I take responsibility for not trying to stop him. Second, the last few months have been poor. My adaptation was bad after losing Bryan and Ian. I could have been much better talking with the team. I know this has brought us here. I want to win as much as everyone else. I see things more clear now. I will make it better.'

'Your words are meaningless without that title.'

'Have I asked for your reply yet?'

McGlynn's jaw fell open. 'What did you just say to me?'

'Even when we were top and clear, you speak to me like shit. I guess you're free to speak with me as you please but I'll speak openly too. I'm here for the players, the fans, the club. I'm not here to take shit from you. I know where I stand, now don't waste my time with these threats. I have games to win.' Cas rose, turned his back on McGlynn and headed for the door.

'How dare you come into my office and speak to me like that.'

Cas turned back. 'How dare you speak to anybody how you do.'

'You'd best hope you bring that fucking title home or I'll happily whip that throne out from underneath you.'

'Have as many thrones you want. They don't make the respect.' He slammed the door, leaving McGlynn fuming at his desk. As he headed along the corridor, he pulled out his phone.

Dmitriy sat on the edge of his sofa, flicking through phone photos of himself with Andriy. His joyful expressions in them could not be further from the sorrow etched onto his face now. The doorbell rang and he scampered to answer it. 'What're you doing here?'

'Nice to see you too!' replied Andriy. 'Can I come in?'

Dmitriy scanned around past Andriy as he let him in.

'You expecting her?'

'No, just waiting for delivery.'

Andriy headed for the living room, where he sat on the sofa and set his laptop on the coffee table.

'I have some business to go over with you. Oh, while I remember, the gate's broken again.' He started the laptop. Dmitriy, hanging back in the doorway, gazed wistfully at the back of Andriy for a while then headed over and laid a hand on his shoulder. Andriy's face softened to a smile. He kept looking at the laptop but put a hand on top of Dmitriy's. The house landline began ringing from another room. 'Ha. Well, I'll be damned.' Andriy chortled to himself.

Dmitriy squeezed his hand before letting it go and trotting out to the kitchen. He picked up the receiver and stayed silent.

'What? Not even a hello now?' asked the distorted voice. 'How rude. Maybe your well-spoken friend can teach you some manners.'

'What do you want now?'

'Have you bought it?'

'Yes. It's coming today.'

'Very well. I want to see an announcement by the end of Sunday.'

Embroiled in the call, Dmitriy did not notice a gentle knock at the front door.

'You've been very good so far. Need I remind you of the consequences if you misbehave now?'

'No.'

'Excellent. We're nearly there. I'm glad I'll be leaving you washed of your sins with some real happiness in your life. I'll be in touch. Ta taa.' The call ended.

Dmitriy walked back through to find Andriy at the front door talking with two burly suited men wearing earpieces. One carried an electronic proof-of-delivery device, the other a package the size of a Rubik's cube. Dmitriy rushed over.

'Mr Lebedev, sign here please,' said the man as he passed Dmitriy the console to sign. The other man then handed him the package.

'Thank you very much, sir. Have a great day.'

Dmitriy nodded gratefully and closed the door.

'My word. Those boys were like Amazon Prime Rib! What did you get?'

'Just a watch for me.'

'Getting some actual jewellery to firm up the cover story – smart.' He examined the package. 'That's a little small for a watch, isn't it?'

Dmitriy swapped the package into his other hand. Andriy playfully reached across him and grabbed his arm, only for Dmitriy to yank it free. 'Leave it!' he snapped in Russian.

Shocked by his forcefulness, Andriy let go. An idea dawned on him. 'Please tell me that's not a ring.'

Dmitriy froze. He tried to hold himself together, but a tear escaped down his cheek.

'What are you doing?! All we have in this world is each other!'

Dmitriy eventually pushed some words out. 'This is best for both of us.'

'No! This is pure selfishness. Don't act like half a man in my name and *don't* make this even worse than it is. I'll find us a way out!'

'There is no way out.'

'You've never even tried to think of a way out of this for both of us so how the hell would you know?!' Andriy made for the door, almost tearing it clean off its hinges as he left.

Dmitriy slumped forward, dropping the package to the floor and propping himself up with his hands against his thighs. A wash of green, he sucked in a few deep breaths before standing back up. All he could focus on was the tiny package on the floor. He booted it along the hall.

Outside, Andriy stomped towards his car as he read a new text.

FEOFAN

They have made their first error. I will find them soon.

A small plastic bag containing a book and Cas's wallet, from which a large receipt poked out, sat on the table. Cas picked up a black coffee from beside them and took a sip. He pushed another black coffee across the table. Steve had just walked into the store and was making his way past the bookshelves towards the quiet cafe. Eventually he arrived and sat, leaning back, arms folded. He nodded to the coffee.

'Cheers. What you picked up?' he said as he nodded to the bag and the receipt.

'Just some things I should have picked up a long time ago. Maybe soon I have lots of time for books.'

'What do you mean?'

'I saw McGlynn this morning. He said we win the league or I go. He didn't like the last few months and he didn't like last night. I'm not *fit to lead* anymore. He wants a real man in charge. Somebody who can lead the dressing room; who speaks when the things are going wrong. Like you, yes?' He eyed Steve for a long moment.

'I'm sorry, guv. I had to say something to him. You've not been alright for ages and I don't want the team to suffer any more for it. It's your own graft you're undoing. I wasn't trying to take your spot, I swear.'

Cas turned his cup on its saucer as he kept his eyes on Steve.

'I didn't want to go behind your back, but you weren't listening.'

Cas stopped turning the cup and sighed.

'You did the right thing. You try many times. I'm sorry. Sorry I didn't listen, sorry I made us in this position. I wasn't ready to hear. I am now. Tell me everything . . .'

Steve was taken aback. Cas was dead serious. He nodded then slid his chair forwards, sat up and leaned in.

A near-empty bottle of *Khrabryy* rose and fell, perched on top of a weight stack. Finney agonised through some triceps cable pushdowns, screaming in effort to get another rep out but failing. He let go of the bar, causing the weight stack to smash down and the bottle to fall off and roll a few yards away.

'Fuck sake.'

He hobbled over to the bottle and reached for it, shifting forward onto his braced leg and wincing. After struggling for a while, he gave up, plonked himself down to sit on one of the two yoga mats and took a swig.

'What fucking good are you?' he muttered, scowling at his injured leg. He gulped the bottle empty and rolled it in a long arc towards the open doorway. The sound of footsteps grew closer outside the room.

'Back to bed, Little Princess! Don't make me try to chase you with my gammy leg.'

The sole of a foot gently stopped the rolling bottle in the doorway then walked past it.

'I doubt you'd catch me with two good legs,' said Cas.

Startled, Finney sobered up instantly and laboured to stand. 'Gaffer. What are you doing here?'

Cas put his arm around him and helped him up.

'Lending a hand. You look like you need one. This Little Princess needs one also.'

Finney let out a single depressed chuckle. 'I can't even help my fucking self. Look at me. I can barely sit myself down for a shit. I looked after myself properly all these years and what fucking good's it done me? I might've cost us the league; and even if you win it now, I'm not even really a part of that. I might never play again. I'm useless.'

Cas looked at him sympathetically before his face changed. 'You think you're that special?'

'What?'

'You cost us the league but if we win it's nothing to do with you? You can't have it both ways, Ian. Which way is it? Did you help us or not?'

Still somewhat sozzled, Finney wrestled with Cas's logic.

'I know your future is uncertain but we need you now, Ian.'

'Look at me. I'm done. I have nowt for you. I have nowt for anyone. She fucking knew it. The club shouldn't even be paying me while I'm this fucking useless.'

Cas waited for a moment after Ian's meltdown. 'You know what, Ian? You're right.'

Finney's brow furrowed.

'You are useless to us when you ignore us and you want to be alone at the bottom of a drip or a bottle. I can't imagine how much this hurts for you but you'll lose more if you stay like this, showing your daughter her father like this. She needs more from you and so do we.' He paused for a moment. 'We still need you to power us forward off the pitch, at the training, in the dressing room. We need you, especially the young guys. They need your calm, your experience, the guidance from one of them, not management. These next few weeks we need everything from everyone. Come and play your part. Come and earn your money. Help us lift that trophy and feel like a real captain!'

Finney ruffled the front of his hair, unsettled, as Cas walked off.

As Cas reached the doorway, he rolled the bottle back towards Finney. 'She didn't go because of this. She went because something wasn't right between you and nobody talked about it . . . just like mine did.' He locked eyes with his broken captain. 'The bottle or the cup. You're old enough to choose the right one.'

CHAPTER 22

The players chatted amongst themselves as they gathered in front of the staff, ready to train. Cas and Steve arrived at the cluster of coaches. A dead silence fell as Cas walked to the front and surveyed his players.

'To play in harmony, we must trust. I damaged your trust in me. Not saying something the other night. Being strange for the past few months. Not working us defensively enough when we needed to. The truth is I let something get under my skin. I try to hide from it but it affected me. It affected us all.'

Dmitriy dropped his head.

'I know it's barely in our grasp but we can still take it, guys. I am here now. No doubt. No head in the sand. I know what we need to do to win these games, to get our football back but this time, stronger. For these last three games, will you give me back your trust?'

The players looked at their unwavering boss, at each other.

'Sign me up, boss man!' said Victor.

'Me too,' said Dmitriy with a nod.

Charlie turned to his teammates. 'Oway, fellas! Let's fucking do this!'

As the players roared, Cas gratefully smiled at the front.

'Excellent. We change here. Steve, take them into the defensive work.'

Charlie grinned at Victor in happy disbelief. 'Bet you've forgotten the way back into our half haven't you, kidda?'

'Raasclaat! I'll take that bet.'

Back near the training complex, the engine of a ride-on lawnmower misfired. The wannabe-driver tried the key again. This time it started. After trundling halfway to the training pitch, its horn honked, drawing everyone's attention. Driving was the freshly groomed Finney gleefully tooting the horn. The players whey-heyed as he rolled up to them.

'Rumour is you needed The Machine back, kiddywinks?'

Cas proudly nodded towards him, drawing a wink back.

A few of the players bro-shook Finney. As Victor did, he nodded towards the beginnings of Finney's re-emerging fleck. 'Back to your roots, big man?'

'Aye. Should have never gone away from them. What we getting stuck into today then?'

'Defending, big man. Someone's gotta do your job for you while you're chillin', fam.'

'Best learn from the master then, innit?

The guys laughed and, with Finney trundling along next to them, walked over to the training zone, ready.

His clammy skin glistening in the light of the TV, Lawler yanked the duvet around on his uber-king-sized bed and pushed some of the plentiful pillows and cushions aside, giving himself some air. 'Come this side, darling.'

Polly wandered over, rubbing her eyes. 'I can't sleep, Daddy.'

'It's alright, munchkin. Come up for a minute. Daddy'll hug it better.' He edged towards the middle as she climbed up onto his side and sat up next to him.

'I want Mummy,' she said as he wrapped his arm around her.

'I know you do but where'd she say she was going?'

'To Marbs with Nanny.'

'And when'll she be back?'

'In a few days.'

'And what's she bringing you?'

'A surprise.'

'That's right. Cos you've been a good girl.' He stroked her hair.

'Is that your team, Daddy?' she said, referring to the team in white clapping their fans on the football highlights show.

'It was. I have a new team now. We wear black.'

She nodded and rested more heavily against him, relaxing as he caressed her.

'Daddy, why can't that man walk properly?' Finney was on-screen, hobbling towards his teammates in his knee brace.

Lawler's jaw tightened. 'He hurt himself playing.'

'Aww. Will he get better?' Her voice began to trail off as her eyes grew heavy.

'Yes, munchkin.'

'Please don't get hurt, daddy.'

After a few moments, he realised he had yet to answer her. 'I won't, don't worry. I'm gonna keep playing and I'm gonna bring you a medal soon. You can put it with your gymnastics medals. How's that sound?'

'Good. Be careful though. You can't swing me round if you get hurt.'

She made her arm a pillow on his lap and quietened. A couple of minutes later, she was fast asleep. He scooped her up, took her back to her own bedroom, kissed her forehead and tucked her in. On his way out, he cleared a little space in the middle of her trophy shelf.

As he wandered back into his room and climbed into his bed, two naked, voluptuous women had emerged from under the covers and cushions on the other side.

'She's *adorable*,' said the closest woman, a bottle redhead with cherry lips. She had dropped him off at the Weavers' training ground the day before his transfer. He glowed with pride.

'Shall we leave you to it? In case she comes back?' said the other, a lithe black woman with frizzy space buns, as Lawler reached for the remote.

'Plenty of time still on the clock, girls,' he said before kissing the neck of the closer woman, who arched and gently moaned.

'Can we put something else on in the background?' asked the other woman.

Lawler hit rewind on the remote, skipped back to the start of the Weavers game, then pressed play and tossed the remote.

'Just get yourself over here and be good girls.'

Cas nestled in his chair with his tablet and notepad, glancing over at the empty sofa as he switched the TV on to the football highlights show.

'Next up tonight we go to No Man's Land to see if the Warriors could respond to the Weavers' return to form and reclaim top spot with a win against the midtable Blacksmiths,' said the anchor.

Unable to fully concentrate, Cas paused the show, pulled his phone out and dialled Amber. He anxiously rode out the rings until her answerphone kicked in, then hung up and opened his message thread with her. Everything on the screen was from him. He started typing a new message, but a few letters in deleted it and put the phone aside. Remote in hand, his finger sat on the play button. He looked out of the patio doors onto the garden, where some large cardboard boxes laid. As he breathed in, he looked to one of his shoulders, which rose a few millimetres. He set the remote aside with the phone, closed his eyes and deliberately breathed deeply for a few cycles. *Phuuuuuu.* He exhaled forcefully and shook himself loose before standing and heading for the patio doors.

The horde of fans jostled for position at the front of the barriers by the red carpet. As the next limo door opened, a current of exaltation surged through them. Emily, dressed to kill, slid out of the car followed by the suavely suited Dmitriy. Hand-in-hand, they guided each other through the blinding barrage of flashes as fans clambered to get their attention. She lay a large rouge kiss on his cheek before taking a selfie with some fans. Dead-eyed but smiling ear-to-ear, Dmitriy signed some autographs.

The couple eventually reached the cinema entrance where the majority of the press were gathered. As Emily nipped away for one last fan selfie, Dmitriy swallowed hard and shook his hands out before reaching into his pocket.

As Emily turned, Dmitriy took a knee and held out an extravagant engagement ring to her. The couple were flooded by a tidal wave of flashes and gasps. Emily's jaw dropped.

'Emily . . . I know it's not long but will you . . .'

She skipped towards him, ecstatic and tearful. 'Of course!!!'

Trembling with the adrenaline of it all, he struggled to slip the ring onto her finger; so she lent an enthusiastic helping hand, then pulled him up and laid a luscious kiss on him for the world to see. The crowd exploded with applause as the couple twinkled in a constellation of camera flashes. Emily turned them to pose for the press and to lap up the adulation, eagerly kissing and hugging him as he went along for the ride.

The next half hour whirred by him. The flashes. The requests. The hysterical screams. The same questions over and over. Her smile of unadulterated joy. When the lights went down in the cinema, there was finally quiet and stillness, outside of Dmitriy's head at least. Inside it, the chaos churned on and on, louder and louder.

A few minutes into the film, he turned to his new fiancée. 'Two minutes,' he whispered. She kissed his hand as he stood before sliding out of the row.

He flung the gents' door open. All the stalls were empty. He darted into the nearest and jerked the handle locked. Seconds later, the toilets echoed with the sound of violent retching.

Dmitriy traipsed out of the dressing room stalls over to the sink. As he splashed some cold water on his face and wiped his mouth, Victor rolled up beside him.

'You look butters, fam.'

Dmitriy propped himself up on the sink, barely glancing at Victor in the mirror.

'Were you being sick in there, bro?' whispered Victor.

Dmitriy shook his head.

'You can't be playing sick, fam. Got me a golden boot to win so don't be passing me that e-bro-la.'

'I'm OK. Just give me minute.'

'A'ight man. Pull your shit together. We got an evening of smashing ahead of us between these fools and dem fine-ass tings waitin' home for us.' He offered a fist bump but Dmitriy was still splashing water on his face, so Victor bumped it on his shoulder. 'Guess I'm pickin' up the slack then.' He crossed one foot in front of the other, spun towards the main dressing room area with a huge grin plastered across his face and swaggered forth. 'Feed me, fellas. Easy's smashing tonight!'

CHAPTER 23

The TV showed Victor celebrating with his back to the crowd, running a thumb along the name on the back of his shirt. The fans were going wild. He spun around to them, arms triumphantly open as they playfully bowed down to him. The TV powered off.

'My brudda,' he said to the player with the remote, 'don't hate the player. Man can't help havin' the golden touch.'

The remote-holder glowered at him and gestured to him to show his cards.

Victor reached over his mound of chips and flipped his cards. 'All hail, peasants.'

The players groaned and cursed as he leaned in and scooped another mountain of chips towards himself.

The remote-holder slid the remote into the centre of the table. 'I'm done.'

Most of the group shuffled around and nodded.

'All you chi chi men out?'

They all sat back in their chairs apart from Jack who gathered the cards together and shuffled. 'Yes! Prances with Wolves still reppin'!'

Jack tilted his hat down and slung the cards out. The retired players zoned in. The players checked their hands. Victor had the ace of hearts and the ace of clubs.

'What you sayin', Brokeback?'

Jack pushed a fat stack of chips forward.

'Fiddy Gs! Oh my days! Cowboy's banking on smashin' tonight but the best you're gonna do is faithful lefty there,' he said, gesturing to Jack's free hand. Victor pushed an equal stack forwards. 'Call.'

The community cards were laid out in the table's centre – six of hearts, eight of clubs, ace of diamonds. Victor did a little dance under the table, keeping his upper body still before signalling he was waiting for Jack, who muttered, 'Nope. Heads up. Your move.'

'My bad.' He pushed a huge pile of chips forward. 'One hundred Gs, Westworm.'

'Fuck you, you mouthy little prick.' He pushed an equal pile forwards.

Victor smirked and raised an eyebrow to Charlie. Jack turned the next card – the five of spades.

Victor surveyed his chips and pushed a larger pile in. 'One-fiddy. Best get out before the king taxes yo' ass.'

Jack thought for a moment then called, pushing an equal pile in. 'I reckon you're more of an emperor with no clothes.'

'And he wonders why I call him Brokeback. C'mon . . . last one.'

Jack turned the last card – a two of diamonds.

Victor surveyed Jack's remaining chips. 'Looking a little short there, peasant. Let's put you all in. No homo.'

'You come in here acting like some baller royalty,' said Jack. 'What's the betting when it comes down to it, you're just a pussy pretender?' Jack pushed his remaining chips in.

All eyes were on Victor, who lowered his head before turning his hand.

'Easy as one . . . two . . . three of a kind, peasant!' he said, lifting his broadly grinning face.

Jack dumped his chin into his chest and slammed his hands against the table.

Victor snickered, did a big slow clap, then stood and reached in for the chips. 'You've got balls, Brokeback, but you were always walking away with a fistful of nada. This shit is in my blood. EasyMoney by name!'

The guy pulled his jacket on then heaved a weighty holdall out from underneath the table.

'What you got in there, Grizzly? A brick for every whack hand you played?'

Jack smirked at him. 'Yeh, bricks for something, you prick.' He opened the bag and pulled out a brick of cash – £10,000 in twenties. The bag was stuffed with bricks of twenties and fifties.

'Whoa! Got enough to build yourself a little house there, bruv,' said Victor, eyes lit up.

'Who needs a little house when you've got a palace already?' asked Jack.

'And here I've been treating you like a peasant. Apologies, fellow king,' said Victor in a faux-regal accent. 'Would my fellow squire care for one more hand of thou finest game in all of the land?'

'You can fuck right off, you jammy cunt. Pulling cards out of your arse every hand there. I can't compete with that sort of luck.'

'A'ight, man. I get it. How about dat then?' Victor said, pointing at the American pool table.

Jack looked over at it and tilted his head to the side.

'No luck there, man. Just skillz.'

'How much for?'

'What you got in the bag, bruv?'

'About three hundred.'

'Spartan shit. I can do three large. What you sayin'?'

Jack stroked his beard as he decided. 'Go on then. Can we make it quick?'

'Quick as you want, my brudda.'

'Let's do best of three then,' said Jack as he picked up the two flashy cues from the table and gave Victor his pick.

'Easy choice, man,' he said as he took the cue with the golden handle.

A few guys who had not left gathered around as Charlie unracked the balls for the cowboy to break. Crack. As the balls broke and scattered around the table, the three-ball crept into a pocket, Victor nudged Charlie and whispered, 'Not bad but no real baller tekkerz, fam.'

Jack made the fairly routine pot of the one-ball and the two before making a long four, cueing over the top of a ball right by the white. His bridging was awkward and his cueing did not look particularly controlled. He stood up from his shot and turned to Victor with a massive smile across his bearded face, not saying anything for a long moment.

'What you sayin', blud? You look like your hemorrhoids just got sucked back in.'

'I'm just feeling it, man,' said Jack, eyes wide and smile wider. 'What do you say we make this *really* interesting?' He threw Victor a set of keys.

'Man, the snack bowl's over there and I ain't playing that shit with yo' hairy balls.'

'Between that house and the car, plus the cash, I'm saying five mil. What are you sayin', *blud*?'

'What am *I* sayin'? Nigga, please!' Incredulous, he stepped forward. Charlie grabbed his arm.

'C'mon, mate,' he whispered, 'they're fucking batshit crazy stakes.'

'I eat steaks for breakfast, fam. Rare.' He shook off Charlie's hand and stepped forwards. 'I'm sayin' show me the motherfucking money!' Victor tossed the keys into the holdall.

Jack gave him a sarcastic thumbs up and returned to the table where he had a straight shot on the five. He set up for the shot, began cueing and turned his gaze to Victor.

'No, show *me* the money,' he said as he hit a no-look shot. He immediately winced as he heard two noises in quick succession. One was a clunk in his cue. The other was the five bouncing off the cushion.

Victor howled hysterically, slapping Charlie.

The cowboy paused on the table, red-faced. 'Fucking bastard cue!'

Victor wiped the tears from his eyes and tried to pull himself together. 'Oh my days! That's what you get for trying to floss on the King, Woody.'

As Jack stepped away, Victor sauntered over the table and chalked his cue. 'And blud, you can't blame the accessories,' he said, gesturing to his cue. 'Look at this. Sick. Don't blame the game, blame the player.' He dispatched the five, perfectly placing the white for the six. 'It's like me giving you my boots – the pengest . . .' He slotted the six and positioned for the seven. '. . . and you bitching at them when you not slottin' like me.' He smashed the seven down and spun back off a cushion for the eight. 'To some people, this shit's a magic wand . . . ' He rifled down the eight, the ball careering round the cushions and landing nicely on the nine. '...and to others, it's just something to shove up yo' detty bootyhole.' Victor finessed the nine in.

Jack's face fell.

'One-nil, Grizzly.' Victor picked up the white ball and threw it to the guy. 'Best kiss that goodbye cos that's the last time you're touching it tonight. Rack a brother up, Charles.'

Charlie started to gather some of the balls from the pockets. The cowboy, hatted head bowed and hands wedged in pockets, unknowingly stood in his way to one of them. Apologetically, Charlie asked, 'Sorry mate, can I just . . .'

The guy reluctantly stepped away from the table.

Charlie racked the balls, lifted the diamond and moved back. Victor smashed the break open, downing the one, the two and the five. The six and seven sat in front of one another an inch from a corner pocket.

'Told you I'd make it quick.'

The guy looked up through the ceiling as Victor moved round to take his shot on the three.

'No point praying, bruv . . .' he said as he unnecessarily banked the almost-straight three across into the more difficult opposite pocket. As the white rebounded, it knocked the eight to within millimetres of the nine. He moved swiftly to take on the four. '. . . just book an Ibis . . .' With a behind-the-back shot, he sank it. He changed to cue left-handed for the easy six and seven. '. . . and a taxi too, blud . . .' He dispatched them, positioning the white on the right side of the eight ball to play a fairly easy match-winning cannon shot onto the nine. He sauntered around the table, positioned himself and began sliding his cue back and forwards, grooving his whole upper body before stopping dead and turning to look at the guy as he played the shot. '. . . cos Easy don't miss.' *Clunk*. Victor's eyes widened.

The cue rattled as it hit the white, miscueing it off-course a few degrees. The chain reaction was a nine that bounced wide of its intended pocket. Victor did not even have to look to know.

'You hear that, man?!' he asked, showing the cue to Jack and Charlie.

'All I hear is an excuse you can shove up *your* arse. Don't hate the game, boy.' The cowboy took to the table and made quick work of the final two balls. 'One-one. You wanna hold the white while you can?'

'I think I'll be holding it soon enough, blud,' said Victor, smirking.

As Jack gathered and racked the balls for the finale, Victor wobbled his golden cue to test it, looking to Charlie for sympathy. Charlie shook his head and rolled his eyes.

Jack settled to break and swapped his cue to his left hand. His bridge was stronger and his cueing smoother. Victor and Charlie glanced at one another. Boom. The balls burst apart from each other, two of them dropping into pockets.

'What's this? You southpaw now, bruv?'

'I am whatever I want to be.' He shifted around the table and sank two balls in quick succession. Victor's groove was gone. Every muscle tightened except for the ones that kept his eyes on the ball. The cowboy potted another shot with aplomb, spinning the cue ball off with oodles of side to get an odd, long position on his next ball, the six.

'Unlucky, Brokeback,' said Victor.

'No luck here. Only skillz, peasant.' The guy wandered around the table and positioned himself. Victor and Charlie realised the shot he was going to attempt. Charlie raised his hands in front of his mouth as if in prayer. Jack knocked the shot long, hitting the six away from its nearest pocket, cracking it against a ball six inches away – the nine. The yellow-striped ball rolled into the corner pocket. Two-one.

Victor dropped his cue. Charlie, his jaw. Jack lifted his cue like it was Excalibur. 'One king to rule them all,' he proclaimed with a satisfied, sinister grin. He lowered the cue and pointed it at Victor, staring at him as he tapped its end against the table. As he started to slowly prowl around the table, still tapping his cue as he went, all the non-Weavers headed for the exit. He arrived at Victor and put his hand out. 'Cash or cheque?'

'Yo Chaz, leave us to it. I'll catch you outside.' Charlie looked Jack up and down then at Victor, who nodded. Charlie reluctantly left. Jack eyeballed him all the way out, still tapping his cue tip against the table, until the door closed and Victor broke the silence.

'Look, man, I'm good for it. Just gimme a few weeks . . . maybe a month . . . two tops.'

'What do you think this is? We don't do fucking payment plans here.'

'C'mon, man. The chips are all yours. You know who I am. I'm good for the rest.'

'You fucking footballers! When will you get it through your thick skulls that you can't do what you want?!' He held his hand back out. 'Keys.'

'I can't, man. Car's a lease, house is rented.'

Jack shook his head and sighed. He softened his whole demeanour. He took his hat off, revealing he was bald on top and smiled. 'I know you'll be good for it.' He settled his cue on the table and extended his hand for a handshake, scratching just above his cowboy boot with his other.

Victor relaxed and shook his hand. 'I am, man. I am. Just gimme a few we . . .' Jack held a ten-inch hunting knife to Victor's belly that he had drawn from his boot. Victor's hand wilted.

'My money tonight or we're talking severe interest. What's it to be, boy?'

'I . . . I can't . . . it'd take me weeks . . .'

'Severe interest it is then.' He stroked the tip of the blade against Victor's T-shirt as Victor gritted his teeth. 'Give me your phone, unlocked.'

Victor got his phone out, hands trembling, fumbled it unlocked and passed it over. Jack dialled a number into it, pressed call and after a few seconds, the phone in his pocket began ringing. He passed Victor's phone back. 'This weekend, you play but you don't score. Get it, golden boy?'

Victor nodded frantically.

'Good boy. Make sure you deliver or else even God Almighty won't be able to protect you from what I'll do to you.' He reholstered his knife, straightened his jacket and moseyed over to collect the cash that had been put down for chips. Victor rushed for the door.

'I'll be in touch, boy,' Jack called after him.

Admiring the stack of chips on the table, he flipped over the cards from his hand that he hadn't shown – a seven and a nine of diamonds. These made his the winning hand of that game. He walked back over to the pool table, picking the golden cue off the floor on his way and unscrewed its rubber butt. Out slid a small rubber cylinder. He extracted the same from the other cue, took his phone out and opened an app. A tap of a few buttons on the screen caused the cylinders to vibrate. As he took them over to his money bag, he kissed them both before sliding them into a side compartment. His hand emerged holding an old flip-phone clipped into a frame laced with electronic components. He flipped open the phone, dialled and waited.

'Who said that romance is dead? What you did . . . it brought a tear to my eye, Dmitriy.'

Dmitriy sat at the other end of the line listening to the distorted voice, looking out at the lake and the waning crescent in the sky.

'My deepest congratulations. You'll thank me for this one day. A clean life you can live out in the open. Before we're done, there's just one last thing.'

Dmitriy sighed from the very depths of himself. 'What?'

'These have been testing times for you. You deserve a break. I want you to rest your weary bones and sit out the game this weekend. Start your summer a little early. Maybe you'll be sick or have a niggle. Take some R and R this weekend and our dealings are done.'

Dmitriy's body went limp. 'Please . . . this is all I have left.'

'Now now, don't be melodramatic. There's always next season. I'm giving you an easy life. You're welcome to a much harder one, you and Andriy, if you want?'

'Fuck you!'

'I think you were looking for *thank you*. You're welcome. It's been my pleasure guiding you back towards pure living. A few days of rest and you'll be re-energised, ready for your better future. Farewell.'

CHAPTER 24

The squad watched intently as Cas broke off from his conversation with the medical staff and headed their way. He dusted his hands off and clapped.

'Good morning, guys. Last big session today. You can see we are a man down today, maybe for the weekend also. With him or without, we need to give this everything we have. Let's go.'

From the crisp warm-up, to the zippy possession drills, to the high-octane pressing and passing in the games, the session was electric. Steve urged their intensity on, his words carried on a tidal wave of his own fervour. Hawk-eyed and silver-tongued, Cas dissected the tasks at hand and lifted his players to create solutions. Everyone was on form. Apart from Victor. His golden touch, for the first time that season, was more like lead. Nothing was going in. The guys gave him a ribbing. He laughed along with them, kind of. But the whole purred ferociously. Resoundingly. Cas nodded to Steve. They were ready.

Sat with his elbows against his knees and his head against his clasped hands, Victor fidgeted his weight from cheek to cheek on the bare wooden pew, empty but for him.

'Am I my brother's keeper?' came the reverent voice from the front of the hall.

'I hope not, fam,' said Victor as he opened his eyes and looked towards the lectern. 'You were shit in nets.'

'Victor,' said Chuka as he walked over, gesturing with his hands to their surroundings – a modest hall filled with pews and decorated with crosses, murals and Nigerian flags. 'Please.'

Victor grinned cheekily as his brother came down the aisle and along past the pew in front of him. The two pound-hugged and sat down. Chuka was almost the double of Victor physically, just a few years older. His stiffer frame was garbed in an azure suit finished with a marigold tie and pocket square. After having a gander at his brother's numerous gold chains, he grabbed Victor's black cap by its peak and took it off as they sat. Victor nursed his cap-hair, shaking his head.

'If I didn't know any better, little brother, I'd have thought you were praying just then.'

'Haha. Don't get me started on if you'd known any better, fam.' Victor laughed as he ran his finger along the cover of a nearby Bible. 'Was just waitin' for you, is all.'

'What can I do for you, brother?'

'Nothin', man. Just been a while. Thought I'd come see how you are, if you can walk on water yet.'

A flash of irritation passed across Chuka's face. He took a composing breath. 'I'm good, thank you. Every day is a blessing. Just doing what I can to help others realise the same. What's happening with you?'

'Ah, you know fam. The usual. Just droppin' bodies and makin' paper.'

'I've seen. It's been quite the season for you.'

'Yeh, man. Reppin' the Easy name. Someone has to.'

'We're all very proud of you. I know Mum and Dad would love to tell you in person.'

'I know, man. It's been a minute. I'mma get round to it though.'

'I'm sure you will,' Chuka said, unconvinced. A moment of awkward silence passed between them. 'Tomorrow's the big one, right?'

'The biggest, fam.'

'I can tell. You seem a little on edge. Not your normal chill self. May the Divine light shine down on you, brother.'

Victor chuckled incredulously. 'I think I'm a'ight, fam. The only man in here that coulda helped me actually exists.'

'This is my path, brother. Football is yours.'

'It still *could* be yours, fam! Get a decent pre-season under your belt and I'll get someone to take a look at you,' he pleaded.

Chuka shook his head, pained. 'I'm His servant now, Victor.'

'Fuck that, Chuks. We ain't servants. We're *kings!*'

'And he is King of Kings. I pray that one day you realise you aren't the centre of this Universe, little brother.'

Victor sucked his teeth, snatched his cap and stood. 'You're a waste, bruv.' He headed down the aisle towards the doors at the back.

Chuka called after him earnestly. 'May He give you what you need tomorrow, Victor.'

Victor turned back to face his brother, rattled.

'What if you've fucked up, fam? What if you've fucked the biggest opportunity of your life and it might hurt the people around you and they don't even know it?'

Chuka considered his brother's words for a moment. 'Then God forgive me.'

Victor bowed his head, tugged his cap on and swept through the double doors.

Dmitriy leaned against the doorway, his eyes teared up as the line continued to ring. The call connected.

'Hello, you've reached Andriy. Feel free to leave a message and I'll return your call at my earliest convenience.' As the line beeped, he ended the call, sniffled and wiped his eyes and nose. A text message landed.

EMILY

You have no idea how happy you've made me.
I'm going to make you the happiest man alive x
<3

Disconsolate, he locked the phone and fastened the Velcro on his weighted vest. He stepped back into the hallway and picked his scarlet winter jacket off the hook, admiring the feel and colour of it for a moment before slipping an arm in. Shuffling forwards as he slipped the other in, he pulled the front door closed behind him and took a moment before turning.

The May evening was mild and clear. No moon sat in the dusk sky over the lake and its solitary swan. As Dmitriy traipsed in the lake's direction, he zipped up his jacket halfway. A minute later, he arrived on the bridge.

Never had so few steps taken so much out of him. His limbs weighed heavy, his breath laboured. But there it was. The babble beneath his feet.

He raised eyes to the star-dotted sky and then lowered them to the glassy expanse ahead. The swan was gone. His breathing suddenly accelerated into hyperventilation, so he turned away, bowed his head and clenched his eyes shut. Just him and the sound of the water. His breathing began to level out.

'Chop chop,' he muttered to himself before pulling the zip of his jacket right up to his throat. He opened his eyes, turned, walked to the edge of the bridge and placed his hands on its cold, stony barrier.

'Dmitriy.'

With the fright of his life, Dmitriy jumped back and turned to see Cas walking onto the bridge.

'Sorry to scare you. The gate was half-open and the buzzer didn't work. I just came to see how are you.'

'I'm fine, boss,' Dmitriy bumbled.

'Ah, you're feeling some better?' said Cas, stopping a few metres away.

'Oh . . . no. Just better with the fresh air.'

'Aren't you too warm in that?' Cas pointed at Dmitriy's jacket.

'No. I'm hot and cold. Up and down, you know?'

'Yes. You look pale still.' He paused. 'You think maybe you're better for Saturday?'

Dmitriy reluctantly shook his head.

Cas nodded disappointedly. 'Let's hope you're wrong. I want to talk anyway.'

'What about?'

'What's been happening with you these past months?'

'What you mean?' He looked at Cas and realised the boss was buying none of it. 'Some things outside the team.'

'You want to talk about it?'

Dmitriy shook his head and looked down into the water.

'I'm always here for you if you want to speak or you need any help.'

Dmitriy nodded and rested his hands back on the stone.

'I saw it in the news but didn't speak with you about it yet,' Cas said, pointing towards Dmitriy's engagement band. 'Congratulations!'

'Thanks,' said Dmitriy, lifting his left hand to scratch his head.

'When will you marry?'

'I don't know.'

'You know it took me and my wife years to marry after I propose?'

Dmitriy shook his head.

'Her father is a hard man. She never took any boyfriends home to him. His grandfather died in Spain fighting for the resistance against the fascists before World War Two. He hates the Spanish also. She wouldn't tell him we were together . . . definitely wouldn't let me tell him. He had a very bad heart. She was scared the stress would kill him. All the years we were together, she was always scared he would find out and drop dead. You know why she end up telling him?'

Dmitriy shook his head again, more interested now.

'He got very sick. He was in hospital, she thought he would die and for some reason, she suddenly tell him. He cried. It was the only time she ever saw him cry. He apologised if he was the reason she never had a boyfriend. He wished he'd seen her happy like that. He wanted the grandchildren too. I don't know how she did it but she told him, there in the hospital, hooked up to the machines, that she was seeing a Spaniard she wanted to marry.'

'How did he react after that?'

'Well, he didn't drop dead. He's still alive, still saying he hates Spaniards but he's OK with the one his Amber loves. And with my family too. One by one, his heart opens.'

'I don't know how she tell him.'

'Neither do I. She never thought she could do it . . . then she did it. There was never going to be a good time but I guess it was the one chance of things being right. Or maybe it felt like it didn't matter anymore. I hope your love is more simple.' He paused and looked out at the lake. 'I should leave you rest. If you feel better for the weekend, we could really do with you so let me know.'

Dmitriy nodded sluggishly.

'I would shake your hand but . . .'

'You can't get sick. I know. *Dobroy nochi*, boss.'

'*Buenas noches.*' He began to turn away and stopped to marvel at the scenery. 'Is beautiful out here. The water, moving and still at the same time. So nice.'

Dmitriy forced a smile out across to Cas.

'Look,' said Cas, eyes wide, mouth hanging open, pointing out to the lake. 'So beautiful.'

He walked off leaving Dmitriy observing a pair of swans.

Thud. A full trophy case and Warriors memorabilia covered the walls. Gunnar, in a sweat-drenched martial arts gi, pulled a wrestling dummy to standing and viciously suplexed it again to the matted floor. He climbed back to his feet, undid his belt and gi jacket to get some air and walked over to grab a drink. As he swigged away, an old Nokia ringtone sounded. He reached down into a nearby training bag, pulled out a brick of a phone and answered it.

'To what do I owe the pleasure?'

'They're gone . . . the pictures . . . the videos. I don't know how but they're gone . . . the back-ups, the lot!' said the exasperated Jack.

'I know how. You fucking lost them! What the fuck am I paying you for?!'

'I took every precaution. I dunno what happened.'

'You weren't careful enough is what. This wasn't just a few syringes to take care of, Ted!'

'No real names!'

'Fuck off. *Jack* . . . *Ted* . . . it doesn't matter what fucking name I use if the line's safe, does it?'

No answer came.

Gunnar pressed him. 'It is safe, isn't it?!'

'It is, yes,' replied Ted with the tone of a man holding his tail tucked between his legs.

Gunnar restrained himself, scrunching his gi belt as he thought. 'Can we still press him?'

'I mean . . . we've got no leverage. There's a chance he might not know depending on how it all vanished, but I doubt it. I guess we could still let word out.'

'What's his thing?'

'You said you didn't want to know.'

'That was before you fucked this up,' said Gunnar. 'I need to know now to decide what to do. What . . . is . . . his . . . thing?'

'He's a woofter. Banging his fucking agent.'

'Lebedev?!'

'Lebedev and his agent. In no uncertain terms. From Russia with fucking bum-love. We could still let the rumours fly online, unsettle him before the game.'

Gunnar weighed up the options. 'You still have the other ball in play?'

'I do. He'll not be potting anything.'

'That'll be enough then. Leave the Russian. He might not know, and he's been useless for months anyway. See if you can salvage any copies we can still use down the line.'

'OK.'

Gunnar hung up and tossed the phone back into the bag. Brow furrowed, he tugged his gi jacket back closed, yanked his belt fastened and marched back over to the dummy.

CHAPTER 25

One double espresso ready, Andriy tamped down the coffee for a second cup. As he attached the filter to the machine, the doorbell rang. 'It's open. Come in.' A few moments later, Feofan entered Andriy's black granite-topped kitchen and put a holdall on the table. 'Perfect timing! How would you like it? Milky? Irish to celebrate?' He showed Feofan a bottle of *Khrabryy*. 'Irish with a Russian twist?'

'None for me, thank you. I can't stop. I fly this afternoon.'

'Understandable. Bet you can't wait to get back to the motherland.'

Feofan opened the holdall and pulled out a few melted, battered hard drives. 'It's all gone, from these, from the cloud, from his phone, from email accounts, from everywhere. You can rest assured they have nothing of substance against you.'

'Who was it?'

'Unless you're planning some sort of professional retribution, it's best you don't know. Nothing good will come of you personally going after them. The fact that everything they had is gone without a trace should be enough to scare them off entirely.'

Andriy nodded. 'Sounds wise. You have no idea how grateful I am for your assistance.' He picked up a large brown envelope from behind the coffee machine and passed it to Feofan. 'Here's what I owe you plus a little something extra. I can't thank you enough.'

Feofan nodded matter-of-factly and fastened the envelope in his bag. Andriy stepped forward and heartily offered his hand to shake. 'It's been an absolute pleasure.'

Feofan took his hand, turned its palm to the ceiling and spat on it. Astounded, Andriy froze just long enough for Feofan to yank him forward. Before he knew what was happening, he had been punched in the gut and kicked in the back of a knee, buckling him to the floor.

'Fuck you and your pleasure! The only ones worse than blackmailers are you fucking abominations,' said Feofan as he booted Andriy in the ribs a few times.

Andriy tried to cover up and squirm away.

'You put *me* in danger, having to keep this from your father, you fucking deviant.' He barraged Andriy with blows then, in utter disdain, spat on him again before taking his bag and leaving. Andriy lay face down, motionless, red trickling onto the cold, black floor.

All the players and staff huddled on and around the common room sofas and chairs, hooked on the words of Cas, ahead of them.

'Thank you so much. You're ready. Rest well tonight, guys.'

A chorus of applause filled the room as the team got up, embraced and said their goodbyes, each one shaking Cas's and Steve's hands before they left.

After Cas's last farewell, he pulled out his phone and checked his texts. Still no reply from Dmitriy.

The cursor blinked away as Dmitriy stared through the screen.

Still not well

He had started composing the text, buried under a duvet on his sofa, when a call from an unknown caller came in. He cringed, barely breathing for a moment as the ring went through him. Eventually, he accepted the call. 'What?'

His scowl softened. 'Yes, that's me. What's wrong?'

Dmitriy hurried through the doorway and halted. Ahead of him in a hospital bed laid Andriy; eyes closed, one cheek and the opposite eye badly bruised a deep burgundy, his expression riddled with pain. With Dmitriy's eyes fixed on Andriy's shallow breathing, he reached around behind him for an age before finding the door handle. He gently closed the door and tiptoed over to the bedside, surveying the damage.

'Are you just going to stand there and admire the view?' groaned Andriy as he peeled an eye open.

Dmitriy edged forward, restraining his urge to reach out and to show his upset. 'How are you?'

'Ah, you know, a little sore. Just not in a good way.'

'Who did this?'

'What are you – FSB?' Andriy chuckled, squeezing his eyes shut at his self-inflicted wave of pain. Dmitriy stayed stoic. 'The man I flew over here to clean up our mess. On the plus side, I got the airmiles.'

'You got someone?!'

'I did.'

'Why did he . . .?'

'Well, it turned out he was a consummate professional. He found everything he was looking for but the problem was he looked at it. Turns out he doesn't like our type much. Abominations, apparently.' Another wave of pain gave him pause. 'But as I said, he's a professional and deleted everything. You have nothing to worry about anymore.'

Relief washed over Dmitriy. He closed his eyes for a moment and basked in its warmth, taking the fullest outbreath he had in months. As he opened his eyes, he saw Andriy clasping his side with his eyes squeezed shut. 'I'm so sorry. This happen to you because of me.'

'Nope. If I remember correctly, you were against this. I wanted us back as we were. I wanted to protect you. I just hadn't banked on having to protect myself in the process.'

Dmitriy checked over his shoulder to the closed door and took Andriy's hand, positioning himself to hide the view of anybody who might walk in. 'Look at you.'

'It's nothing that won't mend. You're safe now. We're safe now.' He clasped Dmitriy's hand tighter, feeling something.

'Let me have a look.'

Dmitriy reluctantly raised his hand, showing his gold engagement band. 'She buy me it. I have to . . .'

'It's very elegant.' He smiled wistfully. 'She seems a delightful girl.'

'She is.' Dmitriy sighed. 'I don't know what to do.'

'Look . . . I've loved you since you helped me haul my bags upstairs in that bloody boarding house. Four storeys with all that. You basically saved my life and I've still not learned to travel light. I'll always love you. I understand that in this game, we can never be, not openly. Now, you have a lovely wife-to-be. She can give you things I can't. A life in the open. I'll still manage you. I'll see you all the time. If you want, I can still give you what she can't.'

Dmitriy rubbed his thumb against his engagement band. 'You can't. Not for me. You have a life too.'

'If the roles were reversed, you'd do it for me.'

Dmitriy gulped at the thought.

'And yes, I have a life and the centre of it is you. I will always take care of you.'

'I don't deserve you,' Dmitriy said, fighting the tears back. Without a check over his shoulder, he leaned forwards and kissed Andriy's forehead. '*Ya lyublyu tebya vsey dushoy.*'

Andriy smiled and nodded towards Dmitriy's ring. 'Then tomorrow, bring me some gold too.'

The night had fallen outside. Cas looked out of his bedroom window, down past the remnants of the charred patch of grass and across the garden to a finished wooden playhouse. Most of its front had been painted in vibrant colours to resemble the mosaics from Parc Güell. He opened up a photo of it that he had taken on his phone when the light was still good, and selected the option to share it. When the application asked him to select a contact, he hovered over Amber's name for a long while before eventually scrolling to Steve.

Believe me or not, enjoyed rolling up my sleeves.
Maybe could have been a CB :P

After hitting send, Cas wandered over to his bed, catching a glimpse of a framed photo on Amber's bedside table. Him and her, all loved up, smiling in the sun. He slid onto the bed, reached into the top drawer of his new bedside table and pulled out his new copy of *The Art of War*. He opened it to his bookmark, near the end, and began his final study.

CHAPTER 26

The sun scorched down like a golden-white spotlight from the pure blue sky. Shimmering through the hot haze, the white Weavers coach rolled along a sleepy street of four-storey Regency townhouses. One turn of a corner and it entered a different world – a twisty labyrinth of filthy brick buildings, takeaways, betting shops and a sea of black and gold shirts. A plastic bottle slammed one of its tinted windows.

Warriors fans screamed obscenities and gave the coach various finger salutes. As the stadium appeared, the smoky street narrowed. Police marshalled roadside barriers, keeping the ever-growing hostile crowd at bay.

A boy in his early teens jumped a barrier, parked himself in front of the coach and began hurling abuse at it, to the amusement of many onlookers. Two officers led him away. The coach trundled on. A flash of gold flew past the driver-side window as a golden flare fell to the floor in the road ahead. The coach rode over it, in through a set of giant black iron gates, down into the underbelly of the stadium.

After the coach parked up, Cas was the first to alight. Directly ahead of him was his old parking space. Head held high, he pressed on followed by his team. A slick-looking Finney, his grey fleck back and with a knee brace but no crutch now, hobbled off-board. Charlie and a procession of others marched on. Detached behind the main group came Victor – shades, cap and headphones almost hiding him in plain sight. The support staff followed before last of all, strong in his stride, came Dmitriy.

As Cas and Steve approached the entrance, a suited security guard in some brand-new Italian leather shoes opened the door for them, looking down sheepishly as he welcomed them in.

'Was that . . .?' asked Cas.

Steve nodded. They carried onto the main players' entrance, the sign above which read ENTERING NO MAN'S LAND.

Eventually, they reached the away dressing room, which was cordoned off with hazard tape and a handwritten sign saying:

NO RUNNING WATER
Please carry on to the labelled
room at the end of the corridor.
Sorry for any inconvenience.

They walked on to find another door with a sign taped to it. The way it was written, it looked less like WEAVERS than WEANERS. Cas opened it and walked straight into a wall of heat. The room, no larger or more lavish than a Sunday league changing room, registered somewhere on the thermometer between hot yoga studio and sauna.

Steve entered, wincing immediately. 'Boil my ballbag!' He turned to Cas. 'What a bunch of cunts.'

The claustrophobic sweatbox of a dressing room, even with the fire-door jammed open, was a far cry from the Warriors' spacious, airy sanctuary. Grime and Afrobeats brought the groove in the Weavers' room; death metal ripped through the air in the Warriors'. Finney limped around, patting shoulders and bro-shaking his teammates, exchanging words of encouragement and advice; while Gunnar stood forehead-to-forehead with his team's captain, both hands clasped around his nape: barking at him and the onlooking team, rallying their bloodcurdling battle-cries.

Returning from the toilets – his studs against the tiles the only sound in the room hushed in anticipation – a hollowed-out Victor squeezed on to the bench beside Finney.

'Not looking your regular million-dollar self there, Easy,' whispered Finney. 'You alright?'

'I'm a'ight, big man.'

Cas finished his diagrams on the whiteboard and turned to the group. 'Here we are, guys. Last season, nobody gave us the chance to stay up. Now, we're a three-goal win to be the champions. I know we lost our way for a while but look at what we did the past few weeks. The truth has set us free to play again.'

Victor wiped his clammy brow.

'I've sat in their dressing room before. I know them. Trust in me when I tell you they will do everything possible to take the result today. They care about nothing except the full-time score, no matter the cost. To them, this is war. You remember last time; what they did to us when we came to play.'

Many in the room looked to Finney.

'Not today. Today, we fight too but not like them. We don't fight for blood in the name of victory. We fight for each other in the name of football. We fight for all the hard work we made together every day to perfect our game. We fight for our families to be proud. We fight for the fans who want to believe the hard work and the skill can beat the cheating and the cynicism. Today, we cannot hide. Today, we put everything we are out there!'

Dmitriy's eyes flickered down.

'Today, we fight for football!'

The players rose in a thunderous ovation.

Dmitriy led the Weavers out into the tunnel. Standing tall, they bumped and slapped each other, primed for action. From behind them echoed a chorus of yells. A parade of boot studs grew closer until the Warriors stood beside them, silent, glancing across at them like wolves watching their suppers. Lawler, in the middle of the line, stared straight ahead.

Charlie stared across at him. 'You're a shitbag, Bry.'

Lawler's head snapped round to meet Charlie's gaze as the player behind him stepped across into Charlie's face. 'The fuck d'you say?'

'Gents, calm it. Young ones here,' said the referee, who came up between both lines and pointed behind him. 'No monkey business before we've even begun.'

The Warrior stepped back, allowing the referee to continue forward with his assistants, who led a double-file line of child mascots for both teams. The officials made their way to the front of the tunnel as the kids took their places by the players. Some scrubbed the hair of their mascots or gave them high-fives, some were too in their zone to notice. As the referee signalled the teams to walk out, two of the mascots held hands across the gap.

The teams emerged into the vast, black cauldron of hostility. Almost 70,000 home fans made their presence heard.

A tiny pocket of white travelling supporters sat up in the nosebleed seats.

Lawler eventually looked down to find his daughter next to him, shamefaced he had not noticed her earlier. 'Munchkin!'

'Hiya Daddy!' She was holding hands with a Weaver mascot.

'Made a friend?'

'I did. Her daddy plays too.'

Lawler looked across at the other girl – Finney's daughter, Lulu. He peered over his shoulder to see Finney hobbling towards the away dugout then encouraged his daughter to let go of Lulu and file off to their line-up by the centre circle.

At the pitch entrance, Cas emerged and checked the Warriors dugout. No Gunnar yet. As he turned towards his dugout, Gunnar blindsided him, a smug grin on his face, one hand outstretched to shake and his other obscuring his mouth from the cameras.

'Come on, darling. Last chance before I have my hands full of silverware.'

Cas knocked Gunnar on his way straight past him, leaving him hanging. Some of the crowd noticed and stirred. Gunnar, taken aback for a split second, regained his cool and his Cheshire Cat grin.

Cas arrived at his dugout, clapping towards his players. 'C'mon, guys. Today, we show them.' He turned to Steve, who nodded solidly back at him.

'It's not just us behind them.' Steve nodded towards the directors' box. Cas lifted his gaze and spotted Amber. He tentatively smiled her way. She replied in kind. A few seats from her McGlynn shuffled in his seat to get Cas's attention, seemingly just so he could scowl at him. Cas gratefully patted Steve on the back as they turned their attention to the pitch.

On the long, unwatered pitch, everybody took their positions. Charlie jumped on the spot, charging himself up for a quick start. Victor, sweating profusely, circled his hips. Dmitriy ran back over to the bench and passed his engagement ring and a hospital wristband to the kitman. Nearby, Finney shuffled around in his seat to get his leg comfortable then yelled some encouragement towards his teammates.

Lawler banged his thighs loose, ready for battle. He glanced to the mascots' seating section where Polly was sat with Lulu.

Stood in his technical area, Gunnar looked over towards Cas, intending to get his attention but failing. He turned back to the pitch and instructed one of his players to reposition themselves. Cas focused singularly on the kick-off.

CHAPTER 27

COLIN

What a finale this promises to be! The Weavers, back on form, need a three-goal win to take the title. Anything less and the Warriors, undefeated here since Magnusson took over, are league champions. Here we go! Fire versus finesse.

PETE

And we're off. Listen to that noise!

COLIN

It's deafening here as the Warriors play the ball back to Lawler, who circulates it out wide. Look at the pressure Nixon's applying to the Warriors' right back. He feeds the ball back inside to Lawler. Lebedev is straight on him. He turns to find his centre back. Ezemonye is running him down. We've never seen a Weavers high press like this before. Look at their back line's starting position. The ball comes back to Lawler, who didn't want it there. Lebedev's bundled past him and nicked it. He feeds it forward to Ezemonye, who miscontrols and the Warriors can breathe a sigh of relief. This is quite some start, Pete!

PETE

It is! The Warriors won't have expected Velasquez's side to have come here flying out the traps with a plan B. Who knew they even had one? Let's see how Magnusson's side deals with this. Game on!

The relentless pressing continued. From back to front, the Warriors barely had a second or a metre. Dmitriy and Alex were winning the duel in the middle of the park. Nothing the Warriors played up to Ayissi was sticking. Both managers barely left the front edges of their technical areas. Gunnar pointed and barked instructions; Cas applauded every harry and urged his players to keep the pace.

COLIN

The ball comes to Lawler midway into the Weavers' half. Xavier is in his face so he turns only to find another, Nixon, snapping at his heels. He just about lays the ball off to his centre-mid companion but there's Lebedev again! He's picked his pocket. He spins and launches a diagonal pass down the channel towards Ezemonye. That blur of gold flashes past the centre back. The full back can't get goal-side of him. He's in. He sets himself. Oh! He's dragged his shot horribly wide. He's not been at the races today, has he Pete?

PETE
Not at all. Midas looks like he's lost his touch today. You can see Velasquez on the touchline there. He thought they were in front there. He'd have put his house on it.

The stadium clock read 43:31. Lawler threaded a pass through the midfield line to Ayissi, who turned under pressure and managed to get a half-blocked shot off that trickled to the Weavers 'keeper, Cope. He launched the ball forward to Victor whose touch bounced off him but fortuitously broke to Dmitriy, who took it in his stride past a few men. His team charged forwards in support. The noise from the white section built. He passed out to his right winger who made himself a yard to cross into the now-busy penalty area but then reversed the ball back towards Dmitriy. Seeing he was going to be in the way, Victor tried to get himself out of it but got his feet tangled and fell. First-time, Dmitriy drilled a shot along the deck. He knew as soon as it left his foot it was destined to go wide, but he hadn't accounted for a freakish deflection off

Victor's flailing heel, which wrong-footed the Warriors 'keeper and looped the ball up in the air into the unintended side of the net. One-nil Weavers!

The bench went wild, Cas and Steve pumping fists on the edge of the technical area. The white pocket of Weavers fans in the highest corner of the stadium roared as the players ran towards their accidental scorer, who lay belly-down on the turf, staring at the ball in the net. The players piled on him, eventually pulling him to his feet. Shell-shocked, he tried to hide his terror with a smile.

'Fucking hell. You gonna claim you meant that, you jammy bastard?' said Charlie as he slapped hands with him.

Suddenly, a ray of sunlight fell on Victor as the clouds parted. He looked up to the perfect sky. Awe washed over him. He murmured to Charlie, 'Nah man. That one ain't mine,' then lifted his arms overhead, pointing to the sky in thanks. As his teammates began jogging back for the restart, Victor, on the brink of tears, fervently pointed skywards.

A minute into stoppage time, Lawler carried the ball into the Weavers' half. He desperately scanned for a forward option but nobody was in space. Dmitriy ran out to hassle him. Forced to turn back under pressure, Dmitriy gave him a hefty bump as the half-time whistle blew. As Dmitriy turned away, Lawler shoved him in the back, causing a stumble. Dmitriy turned and eyeballed him; but, before either could do anything, players from both sides swarmed over and a full-on skirmish broke out: everyone shoving and squaring up to one another.

The referee ran over to diffuse the ruckus, pointing them apart and waving them towards the tunnel. As they passed the dugouts and Cas patted Dmitriy on the back, Gunnar spat a blob of chewing gum at Dmitriy's feet and hid his mouth with his hand.

'Sorry there. Shoulda just swallowed like a good boy.'

Dmitriy frowned, angry and disbelieving, but Cas went to launch himself at Gunnar, only to be restrained by Steve and some of his other staff, who dragged him and Dmitriy to the tunnel.

'What sort of man are you?!' yelled Cas back after Gunnar.

'A fucking winner,' said Gunnar, sneering.

The dressing room buzzed as the coaches' huddle began to disperse. As Dmitriy slurped a pouch of recovery drink dry, a ringtone sounded nearby. A Pavlovian panic seized him, causing him to almost choke on his drink. Next to him, Victor reached into his jacket, pulled out his phone – identical to Dmitriy's – and hung up. Dmitriy oozed relief.

Victor held his hand up towards the coaches. 'My bad.' As he silenced his phone and put it away, he saw three missed calls and two texts from COWBOY. His eyes flickered down for a moment before he gazed up through the ceiling, took a deep breath and let his shoulders drop.

Cas took centre stage. 'Amazing first half, guys. Amazing. We have them on the ropes. They don't have the creativity to get through us if we keep this pressure on them. When we win it, we pounce with our quality; with our football. We keep going like this, showing who we are, and we'll do this.' His last word cracked as he panned around the faces of his players. Emotion overcame him.

'I made us in this position . . . but what you have given for me this last few weeks . . . even though maybe I don't deserve it . . . I can never thank you enough.'

Dmitriy rubbed his ring finger; half listening, half elsewhere.

'I promise you, I will deserve it. I will give you the same back and more. Just forty-five minutes, guys. Let's give this everything we are. *Hala* Weavers!!!'

The team went wild as they rose, ready for the biggest half of their careers.

As they left, many of them slapped hugs on each other and the staff. Dmitriy hugged Cas tightly then looked him properly in the eye for the first time in months.

'You already deserve, boss. Now I need to deserve too.'

Cas smiled gratefully.

Dmitriy toiled with something before eventually speaking again. 'After the game, will you help me do something?'

'Of course.'

'. . . by any means necessary. That's what being a Warrior is. Show me that, show our fans that and WE WILL BE CHAMPIONS!'

The team went ballistic. Gunnar's words rang in their ears as they started to filter out of the dressing room. Last out, Lawler felt the hand on his shoulder.

'This is it, Bry. Today we make your Polly proud. Just one last push . . . one more reach.

Lawler nodded forcefully, re-energising himself.

'Lebedev is playing out of his skin. We stop him, they're done. He's yours, Bry.'

'I know, chief. I'll do better with him this half.'

Gunnar stared at him. 'I don't want him to have a half.'

Lawler's face sank.

'It's just one more, Bry. One more to be a winner forever. When it comes down to it, this is what winners do.'

Lawler agonised as he looked away.

'What sort of man are you, Bry?'

Without meeting Gunnar's gaze, Lawler nodded.

'Good man,' said Gunnar as he put an arm around Lawler's shoulder and led him out. 'Good man.'

After the players had ran out onto the pitch, Gunnar emerged out of the tunnel and turned towards his dugout. In front of him – with one arm out for a hug and the other propping himself up with a black and gold walking cane – was Krugg, fresh from a half-time pitch interview.

'Here he is, my old brother in arms!'

Gunnar plastered on a smile as Krugg struggled over to him and embraced him.

'It's good to see you, mate. Been too long,' said Krugg.

'It has been a while.'

'Best let you get to work! Hopefully catch you and the lads after.'

Gunnar patted him on the back heavily a few times as they parted.

'Good luck!' Krugg said with a massive smile before waving to the fans. As he went to walk off, he cringed with pain. After kneading below his knee, he grinned through a grimace towards Gunnar. 'And this is it in summer.'

As they went their separate ways, Gunnar approached his assistant and covered his mouth. 'Don't let that fucking cripple anywhere near the lads. I don't want them running with the lame.'

The players took their positions on the pitch ahead of kick-off. Lawler looked up to Polly. Her and Lulu were as thick as thieves. Cas stood at the front of the Weavers' technical area. For the first time during the game, he cast a glance across towards the home dugout. Gunnar's gaze awaited him.

CHAPTER 28

COLIN
Here we are, just over forty-five minutes from knowing who the Alpha League Champions will be. After an explosive end to the first half, will the Weavers be able to carry their momentum forward into a huge second half? Or will the Warriors have unsettled them enough to get a foothold back in this game? The Weavers still need at least two more goals to take the title. Can they do it or will that steely Warriors defence be able to keep them at bay in what's been a fortress for the past few months?

For the first few minutes of the second half, the Warriors struggled to string more than five passes together. They were still being suffocated by a relentless wave of white, the crest of which swished after the ball as it moved from black to black.

Lawler looked benchwards. His potential replacements were limbering up.

As the play built up from a Weavers goal kick and they probed for a Warriors weakness, shifting the ball from side to side, Lawler saw that Dmitriy had dropped deep and wide to pick up possession. As he began to move over towards him, Dmitriy demanded the ball, received it, bamboozled two Warriors and burst forwards down the sideline near the dugouts.

Lawler came steaming across, face contorted, mind churning overtime. Just as he got close enough to lunge in, he clutched his hamstring, bowed out of the challenge and fell to the floor. Dmitriy passed forwards to Victor, five yards from the edge of the area, and carried on his run. Victor buffeted a centre back away and turned inside, looking to get a shot off. A Warriors midfielder came back to challenge him and had the ball slipped through his legs. The second centre back rushed out to block as Victor set himself to shoot but the shot never came. Victor threaded a reverse ball through the space left by the centre backs to the onrushing Dmitriy, who lashed the ball first-time into the top corner. Two-nil to the travelling team. The Weavers' bench let loose. Victor, pointing to the heavens, was the first to mob Dmitriy as they ran to their fans to celebrate.

Lawler had watched the entire move from the floor. He continued nursing his leg as his teammates berated the referee for not stopping play for their injury. As the Weavers returned to their half, their physio helped Lawler to his feet. As he limped off the pitch towards the sideline, Gunnar stared at him knowingly. As the two passed, Gunnar laid his hand on the front of Lawler's shoulder. 'You're done,' he muttered before immediately turning his attention towards rousing Lawler's replacement, number thirteen. As Lawler laboured down towards the tunnel, his eyes flickered across to the

Weavers' bench. Finney peered right back into him until he was swallowed by the tunnel.

Thirty seconds after the restart, Xavier won the ball and passed it across to Dmitriy. He dropped his shoulder and swerved away from one Warrior, only for the newly introduced number thirteen to blindside him with a brutal challenge diagonally from behind. The Weavers' bench, especially Finney, were outraged. Dmitriy lay motionless, hands clasping the outside of his lower leg, as another scuffle broke out.

Cas remonstrated with the fourth official and glanced across at Gunnar, who met his look with a trace of a smirk. On the pitch, the referee showed thirteen a red card and was immediately surrounded and decried by the other blacks. Thirteen dawdled off the pitch, only to be shoved along by a few Weavers on his way. As he crossed the touchline, Gunnar patted his back and clapped his hands frantically to rally his remaining troops.

Dmitriy, still motionless, his face pressed into the turf, was being tended to by a physio as Victor arrived by his side and crouched.

'Dimmy . . . you done?'

The throbbing was excruciating. He groaned as he rolled his head to see Victor's golden boots.

'I can't be,' he puffed out, sucking in a few deep breaths as he repositioned himself. 'I promise I take gold home.' He sat himself up and exchanged a few words with the physio, who rolled down his sock and examined his battered leg. With a hand from the physio and Victor, he climbed to his feet and slowly shifted his weight onto his throbbing leg. It held.

'Aww man, you got it bad,' said Victor. 'Thinking of bringing the bling at a time like this. She's a lucky lady.'

'Who said it's a she?' Dmitriy limped into a walk and then a jog, to the applause of the away fans, as Victor puzzled over his remark.

Now ten against eleven, the managers gesticulated zealously: Cas telling his defenders to step up another few yards and Gunnar ordering his players to reorganise.

The Warriors battened down the hatches, sitting deeper and closer together, but still the Weavers were wriggling through. The Warriors' 'keeper made a few big saves from Victor and Dmitriy. Victor also struck the outside of the post and had a goal-bound effort blocked on the line. Nixon somehow managed to put the ball over from three yards out during a goal-line scramble.

The clock had ceased counting up, the game now in stoppage time. From the edge of his technical area, Cas urged his team forward. The fourth official ushered Gunnar back inside his technical area as he desperately growled orders at his tired team.

The Warriors blocked a pass on the edge of their area, but the ball broke to Dmitriy. He aimed a pass to Victor, which a Warrior beat him to, clearing it off Victor's foot and looping it high out of play for a Warriors throw near the dugouts.

The Warriors breathed a sigh of relief and stepped ten yards forward as the ball bounced off their dugout to Cas, who controlled it perfectly. Gunnar smugly waved for the ball from Cas, to pass to his player to take the throw-in. Cas chipped it perfectly into Gunnar's hands, who in turn went to throw it to his player. They had already received a ball from a ballboy so Gunnar held on to it.

The player threw long to Ayissi near the corner. He held it up there, running down the clock until another player also came to press him. Seeing a clear gap, he played the ball back infield to his teammate, who took a lackadaisical touch, not realising that Dmitriy was sprinting his way behind him. Dmitriy's momentum got him to the slack touch first. He had already taken a look. The Warriors defence had stepped up to the halfway line. First-time, he wrapped his boot around a sweeping diagonal ball. From the moment he made contact, everybody could see it would bypass the Warriors' last line. Victor was off.

The crowd rose, transfixed. Cas shot to the edge of his technical area with bated breath, watching the ball glide through the air. The seconds felt stretched out, like he was watching in slow-motion. All Victor needed was a good touch and he was clear. As Cas watched Victor take a sublime touch out of his feet, he sensed something behind and checked over his shoulder. A ball hung in mid-air. *Whack*. He had seen this hundreds of times before, just never with him in a suit. Gunnar had volleyed it. Cas's jaw dropped.

The ball cut low and fast through the air. It bounced in front of Victor, putting him out of his stride, and rolled towards the on-rushing Warriors 'keeper, who made a baffled, instinctive move towards it. Victor recovered his stride and slotted his ball into the net, but not before the whistle blew. He looked round to the ref. A moment of collective confusion hushed the crowd before the referee indicated play had stopped before the ball went in.

The away fans exploded vitriolically. The full Weavers bench, up in arms, shot to their feet and crowded the fourth official as he waved the referee over. Gunnar, nostrils flared and eyes wide, swaggered towards his dugout. As he passed Cas and their eyes met, his smirk, wider than usual, was warped. Even he could not believe what he had done.

The referee, who had not seen where the rogue ball came from, ran over to the fourth official. After a moment of consultation, he strode over to Gunnar and hoisted his red card high. Gunnar sneered at him then clapped to his players before making his way up into the stands. The away fans jeered his every step full-tilt, while some of the Warriors fans congratulated him on his way past them.

Some of the Weavers remonstrated with the ref, who was signalling for a free kick around thirty-five yards from goal, roughly where the match ball was meant to have been as the intruding ball first crossed the sideline. The wind had well and truly been knocked out of the sails of some of the other Weavers. The home fans' whistles screeched ever louder.

Cas just about reoriented himself and yelled to his team to concentrate and organise. Dmitriy gathered the ball and set it for the free kick. The angle was fairly straight – not good for a ball into the box – and the distance would require a wonder-strike. Everybody knew this would be the last move of the game. The Weavers poured forwards. Even the 'keeper Cope ran up to the Warriors' box. The defending team had everybody back.

The Weavers' bench were on their feet. Cas and Steve stood on the edge of their technical area. Dmitriy measured his run-up and lifted a hand, signalling to his teammates in the box. The seventy-odd thousand were almost silent. He raced towards the ball and struck it with venom and precision, bending at pace towards the farthest post.

The bodies shifted the ball's way; so many that the Warriors 'keeper dared not come for it. All it would take was a white touch. Charlie nicked one. The 'keeper somehow kept it out, but pushed it into the six-yard box in the process. Black and white bodies flurried towards it. The ball ricocheted around. A clean contact. The ball was smashed clear. The full-time whistle sounded.

The Weavers dropped, like sledgehammers had smashed their legs out from under them. Some doubled over. Others fell to their knees and on their backs as the Warriors threw their hands skywards and tore around the pitch in celebration.

A dejected Cas turned to Steve, who shook his head in disbelief. The two briefly hugged and shook hands with the rest of the support staff. Cas wandered on to the pitch, where he congratulated and commiserated his distraught players.

Gunnar ran down from the stands to celebrate with his staff and players, as the vast majority of the home fans rapturously sang for their team and their manager. Yet, scattered amongst the Warriors supporters, some small clusters only clapped along mutely.

Cas led his team and staff over to applaud their fans, who cheered them back at the tops of their lungs. Finney hobbled amongst them, encouraging them to hold their heads high. Amidst the home-team celebrations, they eventually headed for the tunnel, gutted but proud. As they entered, Cas peeled off the group and back onto the pitch. He flanked Gunnar and tapped his shoulder. As Gunnar turned, his smile weakened.

'Some of them can't even look at you,' said Cas, nodding towards the crowd. 'Now all the football sees some of the coward you really are.'

Cas turned and marched away. Gunnar struggled to find a retort before he gave up and returned to his celebrations, soured for a moment. Cas clapped again to his fans then looked towards the directors' box. McGlynn's seat was free. Amber was on her feet, clapping. Cas put his hand on his heart then headed into the tunnel.

Along the tunnel next to the makeshift away dressing room door waited McGlynn. As Cas proceeded, sharing handshakes and words with staff and media as he went, McGlynn glared all the while until he reached him.

'My office, ten a.m.,' he murmured, aware of the people nearby. Without any sign of whether he had heard the message or not, Cas walked straight past him into the dressing room. A few minutes later when he came back out with Dmitriy and Victor to do post-match interviews, McGlynn was gone.

Victor handed Dmitriy the man-of-the-match trophy and pound-hugged him. 'Sick, Dimmy. Sick.'

Dmitriy smiled as best anybody could after the loss and the cameraman indicated they were done. The two started towards the dressing room.

'Easy – I'll see you in there,' Dmitriy said as he signalled towards Cas. Victor nodded, pounding fists with him before he carried on away. Dmitriy stepped towards his boss, who was waiting to be interviewed. The two smiled bittersweetly at each other.

Cas leaned towards him and whispered, 'The world saw who we are, who they are. And they saw you today.' He put his arm around him. 'That's what I knew was in there,' he said, tapping on his chest.

As Dmitriy smiled gratefully, an Ezemonye 'Oh ho hooo!' echoed from around the corner. Dmitriy lowered his eyes, took a deep breath and looked back at his boss.

'After you make your interview, are you still good to help me?'

'Of course. What is it?'

Dmitriy went to answer but stopped dead. From around the corner behind Cas, with one crutch, hobbled Andriy, smiling through a grimace. Cas turned to look as

Dmitriy rushed past him to Andriy, putting a hand against his shoulder, almost propping him up.

'What you doing here? The doctors let you come?'

'They weren't going to stop me seeing this.'

Dmitriy showed him the man-of-the-match trophy. 'I'm sorry. It's not the gold. Maybe I have something better.' He took hold of Andriy's free hand, clasped it with both of his and kissed it. 'It's our time.'

Andriy's eyes widened. A nod and a tiny, excited grin followed. Keeping hold of his hand, Dmitriy lowered it to his side and opened his body position up for Cas to see.

Cas saw their hands linked and the expressions on their faces. Dmitriy nodded to him. After a moment, Cas nodded back warmly. The trio looked over to the reporter and cameraman, the latter of whom panned the camera away even though he was not filming yet. The silence hung.

'We need to talk,' said Dmitriy.

CHAPTER 29

Out of the darkness, the gold glimmered in the light of the TV as Gunnar, sat in his armchair, inspected his winner's medal. In his other hand was a glass of *Khrabryy*. Footage of him lifting the trophy played on the sports news.

'. . . as the Warriors managed to hang on for an unprecedented, controversial crowning as league champions. Now to some breaking news . . .'

A few generations of Ezemonyes sat watching the sports news, Victor and his brother side by side.

The news anchor continued '. . . that Dmitriy Lebedev of the Weavers has become the first current male footballer in a top professional league to come out as gay.'

The segment cut to Dmitriy with Cas stood by his side. 'I lived in fear for too long following these invisible rules of our sport. Now it's time for me to live by my own rules.'

In his home-gym, Finney, with Lulu sat on his lap between sets, watched along, smiling in admiration for his teammate.

'I'm the same player, maybe better now I can live not scared of people finding out.'

Charlie sat cuddled up with his wife on their sofa watching, him nodding along with a raised brow and a proud grin as Dmitriy spoke.

'People close to me have inspired me to be brave on the pitch and off.' Dmitriy rested a hand on Cas's shoulder.

Cosy in a hotel bed, Amber smiled bittersweetly as she watched on.

'Maybe one day it's easier for men like me to be accepted by this beautiful game. I just want to play the game I love and be free, like the other players, the fans, to live outside with who I love.'

Across the world, football fans and others were tuned in, captivated by the interview.

*

Cas came through the dressing room door. 'What are you doing down there? I worried maybe you drive home drunk already.' The leather soles of his dress shoes did not provide the best traction as he walked across the tiled floor towards Gunnar, who was slumped on the floor in front of his locker space, sozzled, staring at the ground. He sat on the floor next to his teammate, bumping shoulders with him to get his attention. 'C'mon. You can't see it but trust in me, the best is coming next for you. Let's go. You need to be sober. Is a big weekend ahead.'

Cas got up and offered Gunnar a hand up. 'Last chance. Let's take it with both hands.'

Gunnar pondered Cas's words then lifted his glassy, bloodshot eyes to look at him. After a few moments, he took the outstretched hand. Cas shifted to try to give himself the leverage to get his mountainous friend up, but Gunnar was deadweight. He eased off for a moment to try again but then was yanked down by Gunnar, who grabbed the back of his head and kissed him with the force of a man repressed for a lifetime. Stunned and still clinched by Gunnar's massive hands, Cas struggled to break free of Gunnar's iron grip and the kisses he was planting on his neck. After a few seconds of full-on tussling, Cas eventually squirmed free and both of them fell to the floor. They lay side by side, gasping. Eventually they sat, unable to look at each other.

After catching his breath, Cas broke the silence. 'You . . .? I . . . I had no i—; I'm not . . .'

Gunnar gazed down and held his face between his hands, almost hiding himself. The silence hung heavy.

Cas searched for the right words. 'I can't even imagine . . . how hard this world must be for you . . . my God. Is awful. I'll never say anything to anybody, I promise.'

Gunnar rattled with emotion but no words came. The fingers of one hand drummed hard against his temple.

'I'm your friend . . . I always will be,' said Cas.

After a moment, he put a palm down to push himself to his feet. Gunnar swept the hand away and scrambled over him, wrapping his limbs around the back of him until he had him in a jiu-jitsu chokehold. Cas floundered for what seemed like an eternity before losing consciousness.

Manic, Gunnar let Cas's limp body go and scrambled over him. He unfastened Cas's belt, tugged his trousers and briefs down then rolled him over to lie face down. Gunnar leapt to his feet, hyperventilating, tears in his eyes. Looking down on the unconscious Cas, he snarled then booted him hard between the legs.

'You fucking pity me?! There's only one little bitch here. I'll fucking show you.' He stormed out of the changing room as Cas slowly came to.

*

Dmitriy centred himself. 'What is all this without love? If I can't be me?'

The winner's medal in his lap, Gunnar silently sobbed his heart out, watching Dmitriy and Cas through his tears. Out of the shadows at the back of his pitch-black living room emerged the silhouette of his heavily pregnant wife.

THE NEXT CHAPTER

To read an exclusive extra chapter, go to

www.artonjames.com/foul/emily

If you enjoyed this book, please post a review on the book's page at www.amazon.co.uk

WITH THANKS

To my Total Football brothers Stephen Ashcroft and Jonathan Frank. The time, attention, thoughtful input, and enthusiasm you've given this at every stage have been unbelievable. I can't thank you enough.

Stephanie Vernier – thank you for everything since that awful seminar. Your encouragement, the way you have fed back to me on everything I've done, and your friendship has been invaluable.

Thank you to Adam McCulloch for giving this your time and lending me your literary sensibility. Hopefully, it gave you some entertainment usually lacking in your football viewing.

Mike Bullen – thank you for recalibrating your view of me and telling me that I'm a writer. It meant a lot. I appreciate your to-the-point feedback and backing of my work.

Shaun Hughes – I owe you a cuppa of Foundation's finest. Thanks for casting your eyes and your narrative knowledge over this.

To my editor, Richard Arcus. Thank you for your expertise and for helping me get this match-fit before it stepped onto the field of play.

To my other Total Football brothers and everyone else that has made the game beautiful for me. I hope some of you spotted loving nods to yourselves throughout the story.

Last but not least, Cally Higginbottom. You have supported me at every turn and lived with me as I (sometimes painstakingly) unfurled this universe in my mind. Then you created the perfect cover for it so that others are compelled to enter it too. Thank you. I love you.

ABOUT THE AUTHOR

Arton James is author of the football drama-thriller *FOUL*. Coming from careers in sports performance, data, and marketing, he now writes novels and screenplays that explore the depths of the psyche and morality through gripping, fast-moving narratives. He occasionally turns his dark sensibilities towards comedy.

Arton hails from the mean streets of Stockton-on-Tees and currently resides in London.

Printed in Great Britain
by Amazon